Echo

The Augment

Christian Moran

Pulp Hero Press publishes its books in a variety of print and electronic formats. Some content that appears in one format may not appear in another.

Editor: Bob McLain
Layout: Artisanal Text

ISBN 978-1-68390-248-5
Printed in the United States of America

Pulp Hero Press | www.PulpHeroPress.com
Address queries to bob@pulpheropress.com

Echo

Prologue

The sky was a deep shade of amber as the sun began to set behind the Washington Monument. The Mall was filled with people going about their daily routines, mostly Congressional Staff running from the Capitol Building to the offices of their respective employers. Several families were attempting to spend what time they could in the area before winter set in. Amongst these families was a mother and father with their four year old son. The boy was controlling a quadcopter with his tablet while his parents quietly argued about whose side of the family they'd be spending Thanksgiving with. The little four rotor drone hovered quietly overhead as the boy used the augmented reality app on his tablet to fly the craft through virtual rings strung around the giant obelisk nearby. As he continued to play his game he began to notice what sounded like the buzzing of a swarm of bees. It grew louder and louder. He held his ear to the tablet to make sure the sound wasn't coming from his game. The buzzing reached a fever pitch as he looked up to see a larger, sleeker, more sinister looking quad-copter fly above him toward the Capitol Building. A moment later a swarm of roughly twenty identical craft passed over-head in the same direction. Everyone in the area stood to watch as the swarm continued. By the time his father had reached him the boy had crashed his drone into the ground due to lack of attention. As his father lifted him up, the boy could see the explosion as the first drone hit the Capitol. Gasps and screams could be heard for only a moment before they were blotted out by the sound of the drone swarm hitting the same target.

A calm, shepherded by disbelief, came over those in the immediate area. The calm turned swiftly into panic as the few remaining columns on the Capitol collapsed and the front half of the building fell off into the street below. As his parents began to run in the opposite direction past the Washington Monument, the boy turned over his father's shoulder to keep his eyes on the spectacle. "I wonder what game they're playing", he thought to himself. Little could he have known the profound insight he had on the matter, for "The Game" had just begun.

Chapter One

For Echo it was another mind-numbing day at school. While some of her fellow students were struggling with the course load for AP Calculus, she had been performing college level mathematics since elementary school. In the back of her head she kept telling herself, "Only eight months until graduation, then I can define my own life." In almost every area of her life, Echo found the bar that most people judged themselves by to be very low. It wasn't that she looked down on anyone else, she simply knew she was capable of more than what her school, and her family would allow her to accomplish.

She had finished her work ten minutes after class began, and still had another ten minutes to wait before the period ended. As usual she daydreamed about her future; civil rights for artificial intelligence, ending hunger, cities on Mars.

She had so much to give, yet no one wanted her charity or intelligence. She was, after all, an abnormality.

Across her field of view appeared a pop-up announcement. It hung there in the virtual space between herself and the video board at the front of the class. The contacts she and all her classmates wore had taken the place of tablets, Google Glass, and mobile phones. Wirelessly connected to the internet, her contacts allowed her to access augmented reality apps, social media programs, virtual reality environments, pretty much anything her heart desired. The announcement had been pushed by The Liberty Belles; an independent news organization that disseminated national and world news, with a focus on how this information effected women. The headline was significantly more hyperbolic than normal; "Terrorist Attack on US Capitol: 33 Dead".

All of Echo's attention was now focused on the attack. She instantly brought up several more apps into her field of view.

On Twitter, #capitolattack was trending. Millions of people were commenting on the issue. Most assumed The Resistance was responsible but Echo needed more information to come to a conclusion. Instagram had the same hashtag trending and she filtered through the results to find a video. After a moment she had one and selected it, causing the video to take up her entire field of view. To Echo, it appeared as though she was in D.C. As the video started she could tell she was roughly one hundred yards away from the Capitol building. She watched as a drone slammed into the facade causing a massive explosion, followed two seconds later by a swarm of drones crashing into the same area. The video feed cut to white almost instantly.

"What are you doing, Echo?"

She closed the video and looked to Mrs. Hamilton. All the teachers had access to the "Vision" of their students, as all the students ran their "Vision" contacts through the school's wireless network.

"You must have seen, Mrs. Hamilton."

"Indeed I did."

The surface of Hamilton's desk was a computer screen. She could bring up any student's "Vision" at will. Currently her screen was frozen on the bright white of the video Echo had been watching.

"The problems of the world are not for you to worry about, Miss Musashi. Only your equations."

"I finished them nearly as soon as class had begun." Hamilton raised both of her eyebrows.

"You need something more difficult then?"

Echo didn't blink. "Yes, please."

By this point the other twenty students had stopped their work to focus on the back and forth between Echo and Mrs. Hamilton, who was tired of this becoming all too routine. "Exactly how difficult would you like your course work to be?"

"As difficult as you feel is reasonable, Mrs. Hamilton."

The teacher opened a website she knew had advanced mathematics; NASA's Jet Propulsion Laboratory. In an instant she brought up the trajectory of a probe NASA had launched decades ago, which she then pushed from her table to the large video screen that took up the entire wall at the front of the class.

"Do you know what this is?"

Echo scanned the video screen, which was filled with scrolling numbers, x,y, and z axis', star maps, enough to make the average person's brain melt.

"This is Voyager 1."

"Don't use your "Vision" device, only your mind."

"I don't need "Vision" to know what this is. I love space..." Echo looked as though she was leaving this world as she became completely enveloped by the numbers and equations on the screen. She was in ecstasy.

"In what year will Voyager 1 reach the Oort Cloud?" Echo looked to Mrs. Hamilton, who continued:

"Up to the screen, show all your work."

As Echo realized what she had to do she suddenly became sheepish. As she stood she looked to the ground so as to not make eye contact with anyone else. She could hear several boys and a girl laughing as she reached the board. She turned to Mrs. Hamilton who gave a quick smile and a nod. She went to work quickly, tapping the screen twice to reduce the graphics to half of the screen's size while she used the blank half to perform the necessary equations. She lost herself in the math the way most people lose themselves in music. Within ten seconds she was nearly finished but a sound began to grow in the distance. As she adjusted her attention to the noise she understood it to be more laughter, probably most of the class. She didn't turn around to find out, she knew what had happened. Turning her "Vision" back on, she used an algorithm she had coded to hack into the "Vision" of everyone in her class. Someone, probably that meat-head Peter Drake, had used a sketching app to draw all over and around Echo as she stood at the screen, then sent the live world sketch to everyone else. They had depicted her as Medusa, an interesting choice since she was far and away the most beautiful girl in school. The sketch was animated and the snakes in her hair writhed around like some terrible wig.

Echo then used the same algorithm to exact her revenge and the laughing suddenly stopped.

A lanky blonde girl in the back of the room was the first to speak.

"I can't see!"

After that everyone yelled and screamed in unison at Echo like the Hebrews at the walls of Jericho, yet she would not fall.

She simply walked over to Mrs. Hamilton.

"Voyager 1 will reach the Oort cloud in 277 years." The teacher smiled wickedly.

"Very good, Miss Musashi. Now kindly release your fellow students from the spell you've cast over their sight."

In her field of view Echo could see the algorithm working its magic. She shut it down, and as she did everyone regained their sight. Echo's piercing blue eyes were still on Mrs. Hamilton.

"They may have sight, but they are still blind." Hamilton laughed under her breath.

"Then maybe you've been sent to cure them."

"No one wants my help."

Just then the buzzer went off, signaling that it was time to change periods. Hamilton tried to think of a retort but in an instant Echo was out the door. She knew her student was right anyway.

Navigating the hallways of Bill Joy Preparatory High had become, for Echo, roughly analogous to a trained mouse navigating a maze. However, when she reached her destination there would be no reward. Students crowded every area of the building as she traveled to her final class period; gym. To take her thoughts off of all the humans eyeing her with contempt, she typically used her Vision to keep her mind occupied. Today was no exception as she continued to surf the internet for any information she could find on the attack.

All the corporate media outlets were reporting the same stories, propagated by the Associated Press. No Senators or Representatives had been injured in the attack, which was odd since typically many would have been in the process of leaving the Capitol for the day . Luckily, it was reported, none had shown up today and all activity had been pushed to tomorrow. Coincidence or not, the Eye Of Providence had shone on America once again.

A message popped up into the corner of her field of view. It was from her best friend, Brent, an artificial intelligence that was created by, and worked for, her family's massive technology company in Palo Alto.

"I suspect you've nearly solved the case of the Captiol Terrorist Attack."

She smiled to herself and spoke out loud to respond.

"I'm doing what I can, but there's not much information being released."

As she spoke the words appeared under the message from Brent. "I've been doing some gumshoeing as well. Better to talk in person after school. How is it going today?"

Before Echo could respond she felt her left knee buckle as something, probably a six inch stiletto, kicked into it from behind. As she began to fall she adjusted her weight onto her right leg and swung her body around 180 degrees, then swung her left leg back into a normal stance. She found herself facing Stacey Dritz, a typically beautiful yet entitled girl of the popular clique. Stacey normally limited her attacks on Echo to name calling and rumor mongering, yet this was the third time this week she had hit her.

Echo stared into her eyes. Stacey acted as though she hadn't a clue why Echo had suddenly turned to her and become so intense.

"What the hell is wrong with you, Augment Princess?"

Echo continued to stare at her for a moment, then turned and walked on towards the gym locker room. She responded to Brent:

"Today's going better than usual, actually."

Stacey and several of her friends eyed Echo as she continued on, her charcoal maxi dress flowing behind her.

Echo was beginning her third loop around the track as she lapped Max Montgomery, Captain of the cross-country team. He shook his head as she breezed by, not sure if he should be astounded or disgusted. No matter how many times he experienced this it never got any easier to decide how he felt about her.

The wind was cool as it whipped past Echo. She wore a one piece spandex track suit and her long black hair was pulled into a pony tail that bounced back and forth as she ran. Her Vision displayed a stopwatch and an alert flashed into her field of view telling her she only had one lap left. In the distance circles appeared under the various other students, highlighting their position on the track. If she wanted to she could check the current times they had as they each attempted to run a mile as fast as they could. However, she was never very interested in the progress of her classmates. She instead concentrated on improving herself everyday, and today she had a very specific goal in mind.

Her Vision displayed the fact that she was approaching Stacey and the group that had accosted her in the hallway. As Echo attempted to pass them on the left, Stacey stuck her foot out in front of her. Echo easily leaped over Stacey's foot and continued on her way, not giving it a second thought. If anything it made her more determined. She was already in an all out sprint, but she pushed herself harder. Her body was, after all, nearly perfect. It could handle the extra exertion just fine.

As she turned the corner for the final hundred yards, several students moved as far to the right of the track as they could in an attempt to give Echo as wide a berth as possible. Their heads turned as she flew by. They had seen her sprint before but this time she was at a speed that was hard to imagine a human being capable of. As Echo was within twenty-five yards of the goal, a line on the track started flashing in her Vision. She lunged forward as she passed the line and a new message appeared across her entire field of view.

"GOAL ACHIEVED! NEW WORLD RECORD! 1 MILE IN 2 MINUTES 58 SECONDS!"

In the sky her Vision projected images of fireworks exploding. Even in the daylight they were beautiful. As she slowed down and walked into the field at the center of the track she was barely out of breath. Her red blood cells held onto oxygen much more proficiently than the rest of humanity, so this was to be expected. She smiled to herself and continued to watch the virtual fireworks explode overhead. "It'd be a lot more impressive if you weren't cheating." Echo's smile quickly dropped and she turned in the direction of the voice, which belonged to Miss Herschel, the gym teacher. Echo responded as calmly as always, which she found usually made people even more irritated.

"I didn't cheat, I was born this way. It's not my fault no one else can keep up."

She blinked one eye and the fireworks, along with the congratulatory message, disappeared.

"May I be dismissed?"

The woman simply looked away and nodded.

Echo walked across the field then jogged the short distance across the track, trying her best not to interfere with everyone else attempting to run a mile in ten minutes. As she reached the sidewalk she began to dictate to her Vision: "Send message to Brent: I'm the fastest human alive! Then send video beginning ten seconds before reaching goal and ending fifteen seconds after goal."

In her field of view she could see the message and video were sent. She continued on and rounded a corner at the bleachers.

As she did a hand grabbed her pony tail and pulled it hard, forcing her head into the edge of the bleachers. She collapsed to the ground, landing on her side. She looked up to see Stacey above her, blotting out the sun with her head. "I guess you can bleed. I'm surprised it's not blue, or green though." She had the kind of look on her face that cats do as they toy with an animal they're about to kill.

Echo touched her hand to her forehead, then lowered it back down. It was covered in blood. Her eyes locked onto Stacey's, who's face suddenly changed as she realized she may have finally broke the girl. Echo stood defiantly and stepped uncomfortably close to Stacey, nearly nose to nose. The blood was now rolling down Echo's perfectly shaped face. The bright red of the blood and her hyper blue eyes, both set against such pale skin, was simultaneously beautiful and disturbing. The blood dropped off of her chin onto Stacey's pristine white shoes. Echo's tone was direct:

"You're like a fly who I've let buzz about me for far too long. You understand that I could end your life instantly if I chose to, yes? Like clipping a flower or mowing the lawn. But, like a fly, you're not worth my time." Echo turned and made her way to the locker room after which, she assumed, she would continue on to the nurse. She was wrong.

Echo held a towel to the spot on her head that was bleeding as she sat waiting for the Principal to enter his office. After she had changed and began walking to the nurse she received a message through her Vision that she was to report to Principal Thomas immediately. This was the second time in a month that she had been ordered to his office. The last time was after Echo had suggested to the HomeEc teacher that she add more flour to the pound cake or else it wouldn't hold together. When the cake came out runny, Echo had exclaimed: "Well, there you have it."

The teacher was not amused.

Principal Thomas entered the room like a silverback gorilla out to prove that he was the Alpha. He smelled of scotch and cigars, and Echo thought to herself how strange it was that some people still smoked. He fell into his chair and began eyeing her as though he wasn't quite sure how to proceed.

After about fifteen seconds he turned his head towards the window and spoke.

"Your sister was a lovely girl, Echo, how is she?"

"Lovely, sir. Exactly as you remember her, I'm sure." He tilted his head as he looked back to her.

"See, that's the thing about you. I can never tell if you're being honest or underhanded with your comments."

"Well, I never lie, so make of that what you will." She smiled slightly which caused him to grimace.

"You've had a busy day from what I've seen."

"How do you mean, sir?"

He tapped on his table and what had appeared to be wood gave way to a video which seemed to be Miss Hamilton's POV from class earlier. The students were in panic as Echo walked from the board and looked directly into the camera in Miss Hamilton's eyes. Thomas paused the video and Echo sat staring at herself.

"What have you to say for yourself?"

She kept staring at the image on the table then stroked her cheek with her hand.

"I don't typically go tanning but I'm looking very pale. Do you think I should start?"

He rolled his eyes and swiped his hand across the table, bringing up another video. Again Echo was looking directly into the camera, blood streaming down her face.

"You understand that I could end your life instantly if I chose to, yes?"

Again Thomas paused the video then looked to Echo. She looked to him, then down at the video, then back to him once more.

She pointed to the spot where she still held the towel to her head.

"That's still bleeding."

"I'm sure it'll stop soon. You are perfect, aren't you?"

"Those are your words, not mine."

He tapped the table once more and the video disappeared, again taking the appearance of mahogany.

"You infected the Vision Devices of your fellow students with a virus that blinded them. You're lucky none of them hurt themselves. Then the period after you threatened someone's life. Now, how do you think we should handle this?"

Echo thought for a moment.

"Well, it wasn't really a virus I used in Calculus, and I stopped it less than thirty seconds after it began. As for Stacey, she assaulted me..."

She pointed once more to the towel pressed to her head. "...and I didn't threaten her, I simply presented her with the facts. She is still alive you know."

Thomas slammed his hands on the table and stood, leaning closer to her as he snarled.

"You think you're the smartest person in the building, and now you may not even graduate. You're suspended indefinitely. Now what do you say to that?"

Echo looked deep into his eyes and he suddenly felt unnerved. She stood and dropped the towel onto the table as she gently placed both of her hands in front of Thomas' and pressed her nose about an inch away from his.

"I am the smartest person in the building, Principal Thomas. That's not being boastful, that's being honest. I have an IQ of over 200, and I'd be Valedictorian this year if the school board hadn't ruled me ineligible because of my unfair advantage. Twenty minutes ago I set a new world record by running a mile in under three minutes, and I'm not even allowed to join the track team. So what do I say to you? I say fine, suspend me forever. Do you really think that by not graduating high school my life will be negatively impacted? Please."

With that she turned and walked to the door, where she turned to him once more.

"And if you're going to drink during working hours, I'd suggest you splurge a little and stop buying whatever off brand scotch you get at the Liquor Mart. If you're willing to risk your career because of alcoholism, at least make it worth it. I'd suggest Macallan 30. I'd never drink it, but from what I understand, men far greater than you have used it to numb the pain of their lost dreams."

She smiled and her eyes grew wide. "Cheers!"

She was out the door in an instant, leaving Thomas to try and understand what had just happened. He gave up, sat down, and googled Macallan. After all, the girl never lied.

As Echo stood outside waiting for her car to arrive the breeze blew her dress and hair in such a way that she resembled a kind of stoic manga character. Hundreds of other students were waiting for their rides as well. Most were huddled in groups, recounting the goings on of the day. Some even whispered a rumor that Echo Musashi, the Augment, may have been suspended or even expelled. Some spoke of the attack on the Capitol just a few hours ago, but most were primarily concerned with what was happening this weekend. One group of girls planned on getting together at one of their houses and visiting the Amazon Virtual Mall, then printing out as many outfits as possible. It was a new season, you know. Meanwhile, several boys from the football team were planning a clandestine meeting at the Tiger Lily, a kind of virtual Go Go Club where the girls were always willing to chat in as little virtual clothing as possible. Nevermind that most of the "girls" were in reality sexually repressed middle-aged men or undercover intelligence operatives trying to extract as much dirt out of the next generation as possible. Such are the life and times of the American Teen in the late 2030s.

In her Vision, Echo could see that her ride was less than a minute away. She had gone through the motions of this routine hundreds of times but something felt different today. She wondered if this might be the last time she would ever leave Bill Joy Prep. Being that she was on indefinite suspension, and her eighteenth birthday was less than a month away, she could envision herself never returning and using her inheritance to begin her Grand Adventure.

The car pulled up silently and parked, but Echo, lost in thought, didn't notice. The right side of the car opened up like a giant gull wing door, the sound jarring Echo from her daydream. She looked around at her classmates one last time, simultaneously pitying them and wishing them all the best.

She stepped into the car and was engulfed by the pulsing blue ambient light emanating within. She sank into the

Tempur- Pedic seat and closed her eyes as the right side of the car closed, cocooning her in a tranquil shell.

"Destination, Echo?"

The calm, female voice was from the onboard computer system that autonomously operated the vehicle.

"Musashi Industries, as usual, please."

"Excellent. We will arrive in fifteen minutes. How was your day at school?"

Echo kept her eyes closed as the car began its journey. "I think, in the grand scheme of things, that today was a good day. How was yours?"

"After dropping you off at school I returned home, where I waited for eight hours before traveling back to transport you once again."

"Well, thank you for picking me up, you know I appreciate all you do for me."

"Your appreciation is appreciated, Echo. May I play any music or films for you?"

"Let me hear the sounds of Jupiter, recorded by Voyager 1."
"Absolutely. Enjoy the drive."

Echo nestled herself more into the microfoam chair and leaned it back. As she did, a humming began to envelop the space.

The twenty onboard speakers began to rumble to life as they projected the electromagnetic frequencies of Jupiter which had been converted into sounds that the human ear could understand. As she let the humming envelop her, she wondered to herself if they could be thoughts or communications emanating from some kind of planetary consciousness. Perhaps, she thought, humanity might one day evolve to the point that it would take such a question seriously.

Chapter Two

Even with her eyes closed, Echo knew that she was now on the property of Musashi Industries. It was the slight divot in the road about twenty yards past the security gate that gave it away. It had been there as long as she could remember, and she always wondered why no one evened it out. While most people had to stop at the gate to gain entrance to the fifty- two acre campus, Echo's car could come and go as it pleased. She was, after all, the youngest daughter of the company's two founders.

The car silently breezed down the road towards the AI and Robotics Building, the largest of the campuses fifteen structures. Her sister's office was located on the top floor of the Executive Building, an area Echo rarely visited. She preferred spending her time with the scientists and their creations, not the corporate stooges and their constant attempts at acquiring more power for themselves. If it was up to her, the entire upper management of the company would be replaced by AI. That was, however, in the opinion of her sister, much too radical a notion.

The car slowed to a stop directly in front of the large glass doors that served as the entrance to the building. The right side of the car opened, and with it Echo's eyes.

"Thank you, see you at six."

"Until then."

Echo laughed to herself as she exited and the door began to close behind her. "Until then" was typically the phrase used by the vehicle's AI in this situation, and Echo always felt like it was the beginning of a statement instead of the statement itself. The car rolled away as Echo looked to the top of the massive chrome and glass structure before her. As she entered she felt the way some people do when entering a cathedral or other holy structure. For Echo, this was where she came to have communion with the Eternal Mystery.

As the doors closed behind her she made eye contact with the man behind the security desk. He was about six-foot-four weighing two-hundred-and-twenty pounds, and his perfect ebony complexion was heightened by the light grey suit he wore. His name was Douglas, and Echo had known him her entire life.

He was one of the good guys. Behind him was a massive piece of water art, a waterfall that started five stories up and ended somewhere in the basement several stories below. Due to the way it was constructed you could barely hear it, which was strange since thousands of gallons of water descended every second.

"Still swimming?" she asked.

He smiled and replied as he usually did.

"All day, every day, my child. What's on the itinerary?" He buzzed her through the secure entrance gate as she answered.

"Robotics. Brent and I should be finished soon!" He was still smiling.

"Alright, well tell Brent I said 'hey'."

"I will, have a good one!"

She was genuinly excited and he could tell. "You too, Echo."

As she walked through the gate he couldn't help but reflect once more on what a blessing and a curse her life must be.

The hallway, lined with cherry wood, was sleek and seemed to go on forever. On either side were doors marked with numbers, and behind each door was a highly secretive project.

Most people only knew about the particular project they were working on, but Echo knew about every project behind every door. She assumed her sister was aware of the fact that she had created an algorithm that snuck into each department using the ethernet that the entire campus was connected to. If it were up to her, each project would be compartmentalized to its own server that was neither connected to the internet or local ethernet. Yet another radical notion.

As she continued on her way a message popped up into her field of view. It was from Brent.

"You're almost here!" She smiled to herself.

"I'm about thirty seconds away."

As she spoke the words typed out into her Vision, then Brent responded:

"I'm booting up number seven."

"Lucky number seven. You're fairly superstitious for a synthetic intelligence."

She entered the door at the very end of the hallway, number 235. Given the size of the door, you'd never guess that the room it gave entrance to was roughly the size of a football field. Even more impressive than the size of the room was what it contained. Hanging from racks about twelve feet deep and piled four levels high were an endless amount of bipedal, humanoid robots.

She turned right then stopped a few steps later. Just then a green light turned on over top of the rack in front of her and instantly one of the mechanical bodies came to life. Its legs, which were completely folded into its body, dropped swiftly to the floor and the robot stepped out towards Echo. "I'm not superstitious, I'm just partial to this body."

The voice was masculine and it made Echo smile. "You're partial to the number seven, Brent," she joked.

The robot became very animated as they started to walk to the end of the room. Brent talked with his hands, it was one of Echo's favorite things about him. Many AI's had a distinct personality, but his she liked most.

"No, it's the body I was using when we first met." She was beaming.

"Stop it, you'll make me blush."

He extended a mechanical hand and stroked her cheek. "You're cute when you're embarrassed."

Echo and Brent sat across from one another at a Video Table in one of the small labs attached to the Robot Storage Dept. In her Vision, hanging between the two of them, hovered a series of schematics and graphs. Images of a human arm and leg floated next to a human body. They had been working for months on developing a new synthetic skin that could be used to create more human looking robots, or androids.

Of course most nation states had outlawed the creation of androids in an attempt to prevent AI's from blending in with their creators. Echo, however, believed such laws were the attempts of small minded people trying desperately to contain and control a technology that would inevitably grow out of their reach. Besides, wasn't she essentially illegal as well? If her parents had not had political connections up to the highest levels in Washington, she never would have been grandfathered in under the Biological Augmentation act of 2020.

The skin the two had been creating was a graphene-silicone combination. In the two decades prior, graphene had been promoted as the next wonder material. After the cost had come down to the point that it could be created on an industrial level, it began to live up to the hype. It was a phenomenal conductor and had replaced silicone in the creation of computer chips, allowing Moore's Law to continue its exponential growth towards infinity. It had also greatly expanded the energy industry when graphene was turned into a solar-paint, able to be sprayed onto buildings which could then power themselves. Echo had designed the skin with these functions in mind, but in truth had primarily used graphene because of its strength. You could fire a bullet into it from less than a foot away and the skin wouldn't break.

Eventually, she thought, humans may even begin replacing their biological skin with the substance she was currently creating.

"I forgot to tell you, Douglas said "hellc"".

Her eyes didn't shift from the series of numbers she was typing on the table that were displayed next to the graphs and pictures. The robot shifted its attention to her.

"Did he? He's always been good to us."

"Yes, he has. I think he understands our situation."

"Which situation?", the robot puzzled.

She adjusted her eyes to the two cameras staring at her in its head.

"Well, long before AI's, the persecuted class in this nation were the ethnic minorities, primarily African-Americans." The machine thought this over for a moment, using the internet to research the entire history of race relations in the United States. Slavery, the American Civil War, Jim Crow, the Civil Rights Movement, Dr. King, Malcom X. It consumed hundreds of books and sped through just as many films and photographs. When its research was finished, in roughly five seconds, it could have held several PhD's on the subject.

Echo had already shifted her attention back to the task at hand when he responded.

"Do you think we could produce our synthetic skin in any color?" She smiled.

"Of course. Green, blue, purple, pink. Whatever one desires."

"I think I would like mine to be like Douglas'. I sympathize with the struggle."

She looked to him and tilted her head. She enjoyed these moments when the emotions of an AI began to seep through, revealing more of its ever evolving personality.

"I think he would be honored," she said matter-of-factly, before shifting back to the work.

After a few moments Brent spoke up once more.

"So you don't think The Resistance is responsible for the attack today?"

"I didn't say that. I said I didn't have enough information to form an educated opinion."

"I've done much research in the last three hours."

She interjected, "I want to hear all about it, but not until after..."

She typed one last equation, her eyes were wide as she waited for the computer to finish its calculating. Its answer was not what she was expecting.

"What happened?"

Brent began to quickly correct the few mistakes Echo had made in her math. It took him a tenth of one second.

"You made a few mistakes thirty-eight steps back, but I've fixed them."

Her eyes were still wide as she stared at him. "So we're done?"

"The work is complete."

Echo jumped out of her chair and across the table, throwing her arms around Brent. The machine picked her up and began waltzing with her around the room. They were both laughing as Echo launched a barrage of kisses onto its head. She looked into its eyes.

"You're my best friend, Brent. Do you know that?"

It continued its waltz as it carried her around the room. "Sometimes I think I'm your only friend."

She laughed as she closed her eyes, soaking in this precious moment.

"For what its worth, you're my best friend as well." She smiled and opened her eyes.

"That means the world to me."

They both wished that this moment could last forever, but just as quickly as it had begun, it ended. In Echo's field of view appeared a message. It was from her sister, Emily. It read, "I need to speak with you immediately."

Brent could tell something was wrong. "Do you want me to put you down?"

"I don't want you to, but I'm afraid you must." The robot instantly set her on her feet. "What's wrong?"

She ran her hands through her hair as she looked to the ground.

"The Queen requires my presence."

Brent's humor began to pour out. He bowed as though he were standing before royalty as he gently took her hand.

"Then may I say that it has been an honor and a privilege to have been with you today, my Lady. Will I see you this evening?"

She laughed as she curtsied to him.

"You shall, at our usual time and place."

At that moment Brent wished that he had lips so he could smile. Or so he could kiss her back.

The glass doors that served as the entrance to the Executive Building were a curious thing. They were triangular, and when activated by motion slid backwards at a forty-five degree angle to open. "Not very practical," Echo had always thought, but they looked cool. She dreaded entering this particular area of the campus for several reasons. First, no science, or art, or any other creative endeavour was practiced here. This was the realm of the bean counters, the penny-pinchers.

Whereas the people in the various other areas of the campus worked towards greater understanding of reality through science, or creation of technologies to build a better quality of life for all, the people in this building were driven by a singular ambition; Profit. Second, as soon as it was known she was in the general vicinity, Echo could expect to be accosted by a variety of individuals she knew held her in contempt, yet feigned admiration for her simply because she would soon be one of the largest share-holders in the company. Last, whenever she was here it was at the behest of her sister, which meant she could expect a scolding or lecture to top off the experience. Today, she assumed, would be no different.

"Vision, display personnel map of Musashi Executive Building." As she entered the massive, marble and glass lobby, the map appeared in her field of view. On it she could see the current location of everyone in the structure.

Everyone on campus had a badge with an RFID chip inside. This radio-frequency identification technology sent a signal to a central computer system which tracked the movement and whereabouts of each person wearing a badge. Echo would use the map to escape and evade detection by people she had no intention of speaking with.

When she was midway across the lobby a five-foot tall teller robot came out of hiding.

It had been camouflaged against a piece of titanium art taking up the entire wall on the left side of the room. Etched into the metal was a depiction of the evolution of species, beginning with the DNA structure and ending with a kind of human-machine hybrid. The robot had been flush with the mural until it rolled out to approach Echo. It had a computer screen substituting as a head which currently displayed a smiley face.

"Echo Musashi, welcome!"

"Good afternoon. You haven't alerted anyone to my presence, have you?"

She continued to walk to the elevator as the robot rolled next to her, its "face" turned towards her.

"Of course not, as per your order dated July 28, 2035. I am simply pleased to see you again. It is not often we have the pleasure."

Echo smiled as she pressed the button to call the elevator. "The pleasure is all mine, Unit Number 813."

The only reason she knew the unit's number was because her Vision displayed it hovering directly above the robot. The machine was pleased that she had addressed it by it's number, unlike most humans. The smiley face on the screen became even more "happy", the eyebrows raising up and the mouth opening to reveal teeth.

"If there is any way in which I can assist you, please do not hesitate to ask!"

The elevator doors slid open and Echo walked inside, pressing the PH button.

"Thank you 813, I'll see you when I leave."

The doors closed and 813 scooted to the side of the elevator. It would wait for her to return before resuming its original position in the mural.

Echo looked at the numbers counting up on the computer screen as the elevator ascended. Still displayed in her Vision was the RFID map. She could see that one particular Executive was waiting for the elevator to arrive. She braced herself for what she dreaded was about to come. A moment later the doors opened and there he stood; Eliot Turndial.

"Well, well, Echo Musashi, as I live and breathe."

He stepped inside and looked to the pad displaying the floor numbers, the PH still highlighted.

"I guess we've both been summoned then."

Echo sized him up, then nodded as the elevator began to rise. She assumed his double breasted, pin-striped suit had been purchased at Brooks Brothers, still ever the beacon of upper- crust, WASP fashion. He was aware of the effect he had on Echo and relished the opportunity to make her as uncomfortable as he could for the next few moments.

"You know, I've heard through the grapevine that there's a project in Japan that will soon be made public. I'll be interested to see what you think, when it is."

Echo didn't respond, she simply looked ahead until the doors opened. As they did he spoke with a sly grin.

"After you, I insist."

Echo briskly exited into the Penthouse, heading directly for the desk of her sister's secretary, Susan. Before she could reach the desk Susan had already begun to speak.

"She wants to see Mr. Turndial first."

Echo stopped in her tracks and Turndial spoke as he passed her.

"Wisdom before beauty."

Echo watched as he continued on past Susan's desk and the frosted glass behind her opened to allow him entrance to the Queen's Lair. She then looked to Susan, who was eyeing her.

"Take a seat, Echo."

She decided to continue standing.

Echo had been waiting for twenty minutes when Turndial exited the office. He still had the same demeanor, so she assumed he was happy with how the conversation went. As he passed by he made sure to leave Echo with one last quip.

"You must be so excited to be turning eighteen soon. Any plans on what you're going to do with all that money?"

She kept her eyes on her sister's office as he walked by. "Maybe I'll buy a muzzle to keep your mouth shut."

He smiled as he continued on to the elevator. As he pressed the call button the doors opened immediately and he stepped inside.

"You know, Echo, I don't get why everyone dislikes you. I think you're wonderful."

She turned her neck around to glare at him, catching his smiling face just as the doors closed.

"She'll see you now," Susan said with zero enthusiasm. Echo turned her neck back around and walked to the frosted glass doors, which began to open.

The office was massive, filled with various computers and screens displaying a variety of projects throughout Musashi Industries, all of which Emily had direct access to. The walls of the room were white, on which a constant glow of blue light seemed to pulse as though the room were breathing. At the far end of the room, roughly thirty yards away from the door, sat Emily Musashi. Behind her was a large glass window taking up the entire rear end of the room. Her desk had several holograms being projected onto it from lasers in the ceiling. She was focused on what appeared to be a nanobot, a robot about the size of a blood cell. She was making design changes to it, while also entering new coding to program the machine.

One could tell that Emily and Echo were related simply by looking at them. However, most would agree that Echo was the fairer of the two. She also had the higher IQ, and better overall health and physical fitness. A comparison of managerial styles had yet to take place.

Without lifting her eyes from the holograms Emily spoke. "Please sit."

Echo slowly made her way to the desk, then sat in one of the two ultra modern chairs in front of it. There was silence as Emily continued her work with the holograms. Finally, Echo broke the silence.

"You wanted to see me?"

Emily responded without moving her eyes from her work and her tone reeked of condescension.

"I received a call from Principal Thomas. He informed me of some troubling developments in regards to your schooling." Echo stared intently at her sister.

"Such as?"

"Such as the fact that you've been suspended. You've threatened schoolmates. You make displays of your abilities at any opportune time."

Echo, already fuming, fired off a retort. "Is a bird showing off when it flies?"

Emily continued her work, not slowing in the least.

"Birds are a natural part of this world, Echo, you are not."

Echo's mouth began to frown and her eyebrows furrowed as she tried to keep the tears at bay. She didn't want to have another emotional episode, especially not here in front of her sister. She put up a brave fight, but one tear broke through the wall and began to slide down her cheek. Emily adjusted her eyes for just a second and noticed the droplet on her little sister's face. She then waved her hand through the holograms, which immediately shut off. Now, with nothing between them, Emily made direct eye contact with Echo and her tone changed from condescending to bored.

"I'm not trying to be harsh with you, I'm simply being honest. If you can't manage to complete high school, how do you think you're going to manage billions of dollars? If you can't make any friends or relate to anyone on a basic level, how do you think you're going to work with people to accomplish your goals?"

Echo was beginning to come unraveled

"I try everyday to get along with people, but no one gives me the same courtesy. I am outcast at school, at home, everywhere I go. I didn't ask for this, you know."

Her voice was beginning to rise and she was talking faster. "I didn't hurt anyone. All I did was try to protect myself. I get assaulted and everyone tries to make me out to be the villain, even my own sister! I can't deal with this anymore! It's not fair! I didn't ask for this!"

Emily remained calm as she furrowed her eyebrows and interjected.

"You were assaulted?"

Echo began to calm herself down and after a moment of quiet meditation she responded.

"Yes, my head was slammed into the bleachers by the track and it split open."

Emily struggled to find a cut on Echo's forehead. "Where is the cut?"

Echo's stared at her sister for a moment. "Well, it was right here."

She placed her finger where the gash had been. Emily looked it over before responding.

"Nothing there now." Emily rolled her eyes.

"I wonder why. Maybe I heal faster than everyone else."

Emily sat back in her chair and waved her hands across the table reactivating the holograms. She stared at the images for a while then spoke.

"We'll talk more at dinner. I have to finish this, I'll see you at home."

Echo stared at her a moment longer, then stood and made her way to the door. As she reached the glass it began to part and she spoke as she exited the room.

"Your calculations for the gyroscope are off by fifteen degrees, fix it."

Emily enlarged the image that had been a small square amongst many others a moment ago. The faintest hint of a smile appeared on her face. Echo was correct.

The elevator doors opened and Echo bolted out into the lobby, her head spinning with a thousand frustrations. So lost in her head, she didn't notice Unit 813 still waiting for her.

It took off quickly to catch up with her. "Hello again, Echo Musashi!"

She jumped, startled by the happy little machine, then stopped to speak with it.

"I'm sorry, 813, I'm just a little flustered."

The smiley face displayed on the robots screen turned into a frown with tears rolling down from the eyes.

"I'm sorry, is there anything I can do to help you feel better? Perhaps a fun prank like on January 8, 2036?"

As it finished its statement a smiley face again appeared on its screen.

Echo thought for a moment and then started to laugh. "January eighth. That was the sprinkler system right?"

A video appeared on 813's screen, obviously from a security camera inside Turndial's office.

Turndial's feet are resting on his desk as he talks to a group of men on video conference. Suddenly the fire alarm begins to flash and water starts to rain from the ceiling. Turndial falls out of his chair as the video conference cuts out. Echo smiled as the wheels in her head began to turn.

Turndial exited the building and walked to the curb, where he stopped. He looked out into the parking lot, confusion displayed across his face.

"Vision, call automobile."

He waited for a few seconds, but received no response. "Mr. Turndial."

He jumped as he turned around to find Unit 813 before him. "Yes?"

"Your vehicle was removed from the premises due to an expired parking license."

A picture appeared on its screen displaying Turndial's company credentials and what appeared to be an expired parking pass. His face turned a deep shade of red as he lashed out.

"What are you talking about?! I'm Vice President of Operations, my parking never expires!"

813's face changed again to the frowning face with tears streaming from its eyes.

"Our records show an expired parking license. You may contact Palo Alto Repo and Tow to retrieve your vehicle. You have been charged a one thousand dollar removal fee that will be deducted from your next pay period."

The smiley face again took over its screen. "Would you like for me to call an Uber?"

Chapter Three

Echo's eyes were closed as the massive wooden gate opened and the car continued onto the Musashi Estate. The gate was a perfect synthesis of Japanese Feudal architecture and Twenty-First-Century futurism. This melding of styles was prevalent throughout the grounds and buildings on this family's humble plot of land. The driveway was nearly half a mile long, winding its travelers past koi ponds, a bamboo forest, and a small Shinto Shrine that had been transported from the outskirts of Kyoto. After about a minute the car finally rolled to a stop as it parked next to Uchi, the imposing residence of the Musashi family. Echo stepped out of the car and continued on to the front door which opened when she was roughly ten feet away. The doors closed behind her as she entered.

The entry area of Uchi was open air with a pond underneath the Plexiglas flooring.

Frankie, one of the ten robots that serviced Uchi, silently rolled towards Echo and extended a metallic arm. Echo smiled as she walked and placed her backpack into the outstretched hand.

"Thank you, Frankie."

The robots "mouth" glowed blue as it responded.

"Diana is expecting you in the living room. I will place your belongings in your room."

"Okay, thanks for the word. How does she seem?"

The robots head tilted slightly as the cameras that acted as eyes zoomed in on her.

"She has been medicating all day, so she seems happy." As Echo smiled there appeared the slightest hint of melancholy on her face. She nodded and continued on as Frankie rolled away in the opposite direction.

Echo took "The Grand Tour" route as she made her way to the living room. The hallways were lined with video screens that displayed ever flowing, ever evolving abstract art. Echo's mother had created the program that continually painted new colors and designs, never replicating the same piece twice. The program had been running continuously for the last twenty odd years. In the early days the program focused on large strokes of similar colors fading in and out of one another.

Its designs had become increasingly more complex as the years went by, and today Echo walked past crystalline-fractal-rainbows that made her feel as though she were inside a living kaleidoscope.

The hallway opened into the beautifully modern kitchen. Amy, another robot, was hard at work on dinner. It used its six arms to work on three different meals simultaneously. As Echo entered, Amy turned its head toward her. Echo slowed to a stop.

"Mmmm, it smells wonderful! What's on the menu tonight, Miss Amy?"

This robot's "mouth" glowed green as it spoke with a feminine voice.

"For your sister, roasted duck au poivre with mushrooms and carrots. For your sister-in-law, steamed vegetables with brown rice and ginger sauce. And for you, yellowtail sushi with a salmon hand roll and an avocado cut roll."

Echo's eyes lit up.

"Ooooh, my favorite, thank you Amy! Is that duck free-range?" Amy shook its head as though the human should know better. "Silly little Echo, you know we only eat cloned meat in this home."

Echo smiled as she started to leave the kitchen. "I know, I'm just trying to keep you on your toes."

As Echo left the room, Amy spoke to itself as it continued its work.

"Toes are not palatable. Unless, maybe, you fried them up with some garlic and olive oil. Or marinated them in teriyaki. Or put them in a pot pie. Or put them in a stew. Or."

The hallway that led from the kitchen to the living room was lined on either side with roughly thirty picture frames.

However, these frames did not display photos, but videos from various trips the family had taken throughout the years.

One frame displayed a video of Echo, aged ten, running around the ruins of Machu Picchu. Another showcased Emily receiving an award from the President of the United States. Echo stopped in front of her favorite frame. In the video, newborn Echo is being held by her mother as Emily, aged ten, sits in her father's lap. The family laughs and smiles as they gently rock back and forth on a swing attached to a weeping willow tree. She had never told anyone, but she could actually remember being there. That was one of the nice things about her augmentation. Most people whose parents die when they're two years old have no memories of them. Echo had a solid two years of experiences with them that she would often replay in her mind.

Of course she wished that she had been taught life lessons by them, or had received some instruction on how to deal with the way people felt about her, but at least all the memories she retained were of warmth, love, and happiness. Even Emily treated her differently back then. Echo pulled away from the video and continued on down the hall. She could hear coughing, which made her wince. Frankie had said Diana had been medicating, so she wasn't sure if the coughing was from the cancer or the medication.

Echo stopped at the door frame that gave entrance to the living room, staying slightly in the shadows of the hallway. She could see that Diana was putting on one of her beautiful blonde wigs and didn't want to disturb her. Echo wished that she would just go bald for the time being, but Diana was too concerned about keeping up appearances to ever consider such a thing.

"How's my pet dragon today?"

Echo stepped into the room as she spoke and as Diana turned towards her she took one last drag out of the vaporizer in her hands then smiled as she slowly exhaled the vapor from her nose. Diana had been watching holograms all day and was excited to see Echo. She snapped her fingers and the hologram displaying live footage from the wreckage of The Capitol disappeared.

"I'm doing okay, Kid. Except for this terrible news today."

Echo approached the couch Diana was sitting on, and as she did the couch automatically extended to make room for one more. She sat down and grabbed Diana's legs, then she extended them across her lap and began to rub her feet. Diana took another inhale from the device in her hands and laid her head back as she exhaled.

"You're the best, Kid." Echo smiled.

"Yeah, I saw the news. Haven't had enough time to look into it yet. What have you heard?"

Diana shook her head as she stared at the video screen on the ceiling displaying more evolving fractal images.

"Honestly, I haven't been paying attention. I'm trying to keep myself around positive energy today, not darkness. But darkness seems to be the only news we hear about anymore, which is a shame because there's so much beauty in the world, you know?"

Echo looked at her and smiled as she nodded in agreement, still rubbing the cold, pale feet. After a moment Diana emerged from her brief hypnosis by the screen and looked to Echo.

"What about you, Kid, how was your day?" Echo chuckled to herself before answering.

"I was suspended from school for an unspecified amount of time."

Diana had a puzzled look on her face. "For what?"

Echo stared at the feet in her hands and she replied.

"I just couldn't deal with it anymore, you know? Stacey Dritz assaulted me and I said some things I probably shouldn't have. I kind of insulted the principal after so in a way it was worth it."

Diana now had a very concerned look on her face as she stared at Echo.

"Does your sister know?"

Echo nodded in the affirmative. Diana took another inhale then exhaled as she sat up and scooted next to Echo who dropped the little feet that had been in her hands.

"How did she react?"

Echo shrugged her shoulders.

"You know how she is. She said we'd talk about it tonight." Diana rested her head on Echo's shoulder and took another inhale, then let it out.

"You know she loves you, don't you?" Echo forced a smile and laughed slightly. "I guess so, in her own way."

Silence hung in the air between them and Diana began to move her attention to the ceiling again, but Echo spoke quietly. "Something else happened today."

Diana looked to Echo once more, intrigued. It was the way Echo had spoken. She sounded like this whenever she wanted to gently drop a bombshell on you, as though the quiet, unassuming tone would soften the impact of the information.

After a moment Echo looked to Diana, who finally responded. "Well, don't keep me waiting, Kid, spit it out."

Echo turned her head to look into her sister-in-law's eyes. "Brent and I, you remember Brent, don't you?"

Diana's glazed eyes didn't blink as she quietly nodded. "Well, he and I have been working on a project for a few months now. Everyday after school I'd stop by and we'd work on it for a few hours. We finished the project today and I'm actually really excited about it. We designed a synthetic skin that's bullet proof and can convert sunlight into energy. I think it could be really big, like, billions of dollars big."

Diana smiled and hugged Echo.

"You know I don't understand a thing about the technologies you and your sister work on, but if you're happy I'm happy. Does Emily know about it? Might help take the heat off the school stuff."

Echo smiled and took Diana's face in her hands before kissing her on the forehead. She then stood and began to walk towards the glass door on the left of the couch that led to the backyard.

"You been outside at all today?"

Diana craned her neck in the direction Echo was traveling. "I haven't. I've just been spacing out here all day."

Echo stopped at the glass and looked outside. The backyard was a wonder to behold. Perfectly cut grass, multiple waterfalls of various sizes, thirty different kinds of flowers, and two small forests; one of redwood and one of bamboo. A large portion of the area was designed as a replica of the Adachi Museum, the most celebrated garden in all of Japan. Echo turned to Diana.

"When was the last time you visited the fairy people?" Diana's eyes went wide and her face lit up.

"They're still around? I thought you stopped that years ago." Echo shook her head.

"I would never destroy something I created, especially not them. They've been growing and evolving for a decade now. Would you like to visit them?"

Diana picked up her vaporizer and started towards Echo, whom she grabbed hold of as soon as she could.

"Show me something magical." Echo smiled.

"As you wish."

The air was cool and crisp as they walked out into the wonder that was their backyard.

Echo led Diana out to the rock ledge surrounding the biggest waterfall, where they both sat. Echo looked around the area then looked to her sister-in-law.

"Vision, send "The Mystical Land App" to Diana."

Instantly a small package appeared in Diana's field of view. It looked like an old treasure chest with pixie dust floating around it. Diana smiled, took one more drag from her vaporizer, then spoke.

"Vision, run Mystic Land App."

The program began immediately and a broad smile traveled across Diana's face. They were no longer the only two people inhabiting the landscape. Hundreds of little houses now dotted the area, running along the length of the waterfall and pushing on towards both forests. Along with the houses, there were now hundreds, if not thousands of small beings who appeared to be fairies. Some, not all, had wings and several flew towards her, then began to hover at eye level. She reached out to touch one, and just as she was about to make contact it flew backwards just out of reach and smiled, waving a finger at Diana as though to say , "You can look, but you can not touch." She felt a hand on her shoulder and looked to find it belonged to Echo, who pointed to the water behind them. Diana looked into the pool to see what appeared to be about fifty miniature mermaids swimming about.

One leaped out of the water into the air, flipped several times, then splashed back into the pool. Echo stood and turned toward Diana, extending her hand.

"Let's go see the Queen."

Diana nodded, took Echo's hand, and they began their journey into the redwood forest. The air was thick with fairies, glowing white and flying in every direction. Diana looked around in awe of the wondrous beauty Echo had created in a small corner of their residence. There were so many augmented reality apps that could create a similar sense of magic, but none of them were as striking or lifelike as this mystical world peopled by Echo's creations.

The dirt path wound through the giant redwood trees, and across an ornately carved wooden bridge that stood over a small babbling brook. As they reached the end of the path, they found themselves in a small, open area. The most impressive natural element in this little enclave was a redwood the family had named Gaia. It was the largest tree on the property, both in height and mass. On ground level the tree had a large opening into its interior. Through their Vision devices the two women could see innumerable glowing bodies floating into and out of the hollow portion of Gaia.

It was so beautiful that Diana began to tear up as Echo led her into the tree.

As they entered they looked up to find that you could see about fifteen feet high before the tree closed up again. They could also see little homes carved into the interior all the way up to the ceiling. As they looked about many fairies began to peek their heads out of the various residences they appeared to live in. Many smiled and flew out to them. One group even began what appeared to be an aerial show of some kind, flying and performing acrobatics synchronized with one another. After a moment all of those that were in the air floated off to the sides in anticipation of her arrival. A second later, she appeared. She floated out of a large, ornately carved door about ten feet up. She was about twice the size of the other fairies, with a wingspan to match.

While all the others had a white glow emanating from them, she gave off a beautiful blue light. She hovered directly in front of Echo and Diana as she displayed a smile that radiated peace and contentedness. In their Vision appeared a message from her.

"Thank you for visiting us, Echo. And you, Diana, we have not seen in many years. Welcome back!"

Diana laughed as she held out her hand.

"I apologize, I didn't realize you were still here, or what a wonderful world you've built."

The Queen reached out and placed her hand on Diana's, who could have sworn she felt the faintest hint of sensation.

"We have been here for many generations now, thanks to our creator."

She removed her hand from Diana's and bowed in respect to Echo. As she did, the hundreds of other floating beings in the tree bowed as well. The Queen then floated closer to Diana's face and extended her hand. To Echo it appeared as though the faerie was touching her cheek lovingly.

"You are not well, Diana, what malady ails you?" Diana looked sheepish for a moment, then answered. "I am in the final stages of inoperable cancer."

The Queen tilted her head as though she was weighing the situation, then looked to Echo before smiling.

"Many times throughout our existence we have found ourselves fighting terrible odds against enemies we neither sought nor understood. One thing always helped us through those troubling times."

She extended her hand to motion toward Echo.

"If anyone, or anything can help you, it is her. We trust in Echo, as well you should."

Diana smiled as she looked to her sister-in-law, who's eyes were lowered in humility.

"You're probably right. This kid can do anything."

They stayed for a while longer in this place of enchantment, long enough for Diana to no longer question the "reality" of synthetic personages.

Echo and Diana had been sitting at the circular, glass table in the dining room for about five minutes when Emily walked in. She had returned home when they were outside in that mystical realm, and had changed into a grey hoodie and sweatpants. In yet another display of their similarities, Echo had changed into a white hoodie and sweatpants of nearly the same design.

"Some times you two are ridiculous. You don't even go shopping together."

Emily looked at Diana as she sat and grabbed her hand.

"No, usually I go shopping with you. In fact you picked this out if I remember correctly."

Echo laughed before interjecting. "Yeah, you picked this out too."

Diana threw her hands into the air to feign outrage. "So what, I'm the ridiculous one then?"

Emily smiled as she lifted Diana's hand to her face and kissed it.

"Never, darling. You just have particular tastes."

She placed Diana's hand back onto the table as Amy rolled into the room, three meals ready to be served. Again her mouth glowed green as she spoke.

"Dinner is served, Ladies." "Thank you, Amy!", responded Echo.

The robot placed the three meals down in front of the intended recipient. Echo picked up the chopsticks next to her plate. They were family heirlooms, roughly two-hundred years old. She always used these whenever she ate sushi at home. It made her feel somewhat closer to her heritage in doing so.

Both Diana and Emily started into their meals as well and Amy rolled off back into the kitchen. After a moment of silence Diana spoke up.

"So how was your day, my Love?"

Emily cut a piece of duck as she responded. "It was fine. You?"

Diana smiled as she responded.

"Well, I was having a rather boring time until Echo returned home."

Emily nodded as she chewed her duck, then responded. "Yes, excitement seems to follow her wherever she goes." Echo broke in casually.

"Did you make those adjustments I mentioned?"

Emily eyed her little sister from across the table. "Yes."

Echo looked to Diana and raised her eyebrows for an instant, satisfied in her sister's acknowledgement. Diana smiled and turned back to Emily.

"Did you hear what Echo did today?"

Emily cut another piece of duck as she responded.

"You mean her suspension, yes, I heard."

Diana waved her hand at Emily as she swallowed some of her stir fry.

"No, no, I'm talking about her new creation."

Emily's eyes immediately shot to Echo and locked onto her, suspicion written across her face.

"What's this, little sister?"

Echo kept her eyes on the table for a moment before lifting them to meet Emily's. For a moment she looked ashamed, but after careful reflection she stood up straight and spoke in a direct tone.

"Yes, Brent and I completed a project today that we've been working on for some time. I think it will make us quite a bit of money."

Emily's eyes were still locked onto Echo as she nodded. "Mmm hmm, and what is it?"

"A synthetic skin composed of silicone and graphene that's nearly indestructible, while also taking advantage of graphene's ability to convert sunlight into energy."

Emily tilted her head ever so slightly, and with that Echo knew what was about to come.

"And what application did you intend for this material?" Echo thought for a moment.

"It would be possible for humans to replace their biological skin with this substance.

No more cuts or bruises or wounds of any kind really. Plus the solar component could help augment our digestive systems in terms of providing energy to the body."

Emily's eyes filled with a kind of anger and Echo prepared herself for the barrage.

"Do not lie to me! Ever!"

Echo's mouth snapped shut as she stared across the table, and Diana knew instantly that she never should have brought the subject up.

"The fact you were working on this with Brent made your intentions all too clear. I will remind you that it is illegal to create androids of any kind. Let alone an android that's bullet proof. If we're inspected by the Feds and they find out about this they will relish the opportunity to try you as an adult, Echo."

The three sat in silence, none noticing Amy peek her head around the corner to get a better idea of what was going on. Emily began to cut another piece of duck as she spoke once more.

"On Monday you'll return to the lab and wipe the hard drives."

Echo's eyes went wide as she began to plead with her sister. "Please don't make me do that, this stuff could help a lot of people, maybe even Diana."

Emily violently dropped her silverware onto her plate and pointed a finger at Echo.

"Don't you ever say anything like that in front of her again! Do you understand me?! She's going to be fine! I'm working everyday to fix it, and I will!"

She began to shake her head in disgust.

"I don't know who you are anymore, Echo. There's no way I'm allowing you to start spending your inheritance, that's for damn sure."

Echo threw her hands onto the table and screamed at Emily. "You can't do that! You don't have the authority!"

Emily began to laugh.

"The authority? I have absolute authority. Your trust is under my control until you turn thirty. I will decide what you'll spend your money on. So rid your head of any ideas of opulence and adventure, and get ready to buckle down for the next twelve years."

Echo stood defiantly, hate and anger in her eyes, picked up her plate and threw it as hard as she could, zinging it a quarter inch above Emily's head before disintegrating as it hit the wall. Emily did not even flinch, then she spoke with such disdain.

"You're so predictable."

Echo, tears welling up in her eyes, looked to Diana who was already crying, then spoke.

"I'm sorry for ruining dinner."

And with that Echo bolted out of the room. There was silence as Emily chewed her food. After a moment she reached her hand out and gently placed it on Diana's.

"Finish your meal, my Love. You need to eat." Diana ripped her hand away and stood.

"You should be ashamed of yourself."

She left the room as well, leaving Emily to herself. She seemed to be spending more and more time alone these days.

Echo's room was dark. She liked to keep it that way. The only sources of light currently functioning were her hologram projector, which she had installed herself, and a blue glow emanating from an ambient light in the bathroom. She sat on her bed, a California king that was very low to the ground, as she watched projections of the attack on the Capitol Building from a variety of angles. She had frozen the display on an image that had been captured by a camera on the Smithsonian building. Something still felt strange about the entire event, and she was sure she would have figured it out already if her mind was not being distracted by the argument with her sister. A message from Brent appeared in her field of view:

"Are you ready?"

Echo instantly ended her investigation. "Projector off".

The hologram evaporated and she was left in an almost total absence of light. She grabbed an audio monitor that she placed inside her ear, then sat back onto the bed.

"Vision take me to the Nebula Stream."

The Vision device switched from Augmented Reality Mode to Virtual Reality Mode. In the decades prior, people had visited websites like Second Life or played games like Sim City. Now the internet was a kind of mix between the two, but with lifelike graphics. Echo found herself on a sandy beach next to a stream of water that ran from one direction off in the distance out ahead of her into the sky. A river of water lifting off from the sand out into the stars towards a huge cloud of gas and dust that glowed purple, pink, red, and green. It was night and the stars in the sky shown unlike anything you could see in the "real" world. The Nebula Stream, as this Virtual Space was known, had been created by an AI system some two years before. Brent had discovered it and the two of them had been meeting here regularly ever since.

"Do you like my new avatar?"

Echo turned around to find a young man with a deep ebony complexion and light blue eyes. She smiled as she sized him up.

"You look beautiful, is this what you're going with from now on?"

"I think so, I'm happy with it."

"Well, you're certainly easy on the eyes."

She fluttered her eyes for added effect and he laughed as he sat down in the sand. She joined him and laid her head on his shoulder as they looked out at the stream traveling off in the sky towards the nebula. They sat in silence for a moment before he spoke again.

"I take it from your silence it must've been a rough night?" She nodded her head slowly.

"I don't want to talk about it." He rested his head against hers.

"Okay...Do you want to talk about the attack?"

"Not really, but we probably should. What have you found?" They kept their eyes on the nebula as they spoke. "The interesting thing isn't what I've found, it's what I haven't found."

"What do you mean?"

"Typically in a situation like this the FAA would have released information regarding the flight path of the Drone Swarm, but they haven't today. In fact, I can't find any record of the Drones before the point that they entered the Capitol Mall Airspace. No CCTV footage, no cell phone footage, no audio recordings, nothing.

The records exist, but when you go looking for them all you come across are government warnings saying the information is classified due to issues of national security."

She lifted her head and looked into his face. "What does that mean to you?"

He thought for a moment. "Nothing good."

She smiled as she nodded in agreement, always entertained by Brent's ability to reduce momentous, possibly life-altering information into a short quip. They sat in silence for a while longer, content simply with the company of each other. "Did you tell your sister about the project?"

Echo exhaled deeply. "Yes."

She let the word hang there. "And?"

She kept her eyes on the nebula.

"She reacted as we thought she would, not as I hoped she would."

Brent's face displayed disappointment as he responded. "I guess I'll only be wearing this skin in virtual space then."

"No, we'll print it out for you."

She lifted her head from his shoulder and looked into his eyes.

"We may not be able to help out all the AI's yet, but I'll be damned if I'll be stopped from helping my best friend."

He smiled as she put her head on his shoulder once more, and he put his arm around her. They sat for a while longer in silence, taking in the beauty of the vista before them.

Chapter Four

The faint sound of chimes awoke Echo. As she opened her eyes the screens that covered her windows began to roll up and sunlight enveloped the room. The automated system that controlled various electronics on the property spoke over the intercom:

"Good morning, Echo. Your interview begins in two hours, please be in the reception hall by eleven o'clock."

Echo pushed her face into her pillow in frustration. She had been dreading this interview for weeks, and after last night she really didn't want to have to put on a good face with her sister. The interview was for a piece being done on Musashi Industries as well as the family that founded and still controlled it. Echo didn't mind talking about the company, but whenever she was brought into the conversation it would inevitably lead back to her.

She hopped out of bed and walked over to a small circular pad on the floor in the corner of the room. There she sat and closed her eyes once again. She had started meditating at the age of nine and had continued to do so every morning since.

She found that it helped ease her mind and stress levels, especially if she was beginning to have another emotional episode. She used a basic mantra method. She would pick out a word or phrase, lately it had been "I am at peace", and repeat it in her head over and over again. If her mind drifted off to other thoughts she would simply start the mantra again. She likened it to being a mountain with clouds of thought drifting by. She had never discussed her more metaphysical beliefs with anyone but Brent. This was due to the fact that her sister was a staunch atheist and would never discuss such things, considering anyone who did to be "simple". However, Echo considered herself something of a Taoist.

She didn't believe in a vengeful God, judging humanity for all its faults, but she did believe in something. As the Tao Te Ching says, "Wise is one who knows that they do not know". Echo was also keenly aware of her faults as a human. She knew she could be arrogant, prideful, lustful, and had many areas to work on and grow as a person. "To know others is intelligence, to know yourself is wisdom".

Her father had been raised in the Shinto religion of Japan and had apparently continued this practice as an adult, though, again, Emily would not discuss the subject. She knew her mother, who was an American of Irish/German ancestry, was a practicing Catholic. Echo was in possession of her mother's rosary which she would occasionally carry with her, if only to feel closer to the woman who had journeyed into the unknown many years ago.

When her meditation was over she stood and walked into her bathroom. The lights slowly turned on as she entered and stopped at the faucet. She opened the case that held her Vision Contacts then placed both onto her eyes. She could see that she had a new message from Brent:

"Good luck with the interview! Try not to come off like an entitled snob!"

She smiled then set about figuring out what her look should be for the interview. She walked back out of the bathroom and stood in the center of the bedroom.

"Projector on, clothing simulation."

The projector shot out a beam that scanned Echo's entire body. A moment later three lasers met each other and Echo was standing face to face with a three-dimensional image of herself. She backed away from the hologram to get a better look at it.

"Show me three dresses from my wardrobe, one short, one mid- length, and one floor length, all in black."

The projector split the image and now there were three Echo's, all in different dresses. She tilted her head as she sized them up.

"Three more, please."

The clothing changed on the three images but again Echo was not satisfied.

"Show me only short dresses."

Again three different dresses appeared, and again they were not what she desired.

"Show me my top three suggestions for new wardrobe online, high end."

Before her eyes the holograms changed once again, only this time there were designers names and prices listed next to them. The second dress, a tight black number by Alexander McQueen, caught her attention and she pushed away the other two holograms, which evaporated. She walked around the projection, sizing it up from every angle.

"Purchase and print. Show me eyeshadow in neutral, charcoal, and blue."

As the 3D printer by the window started to construct the dress, the hologram began to change the color of the eyshadow on Echo every five seconds. The neutral was too plain, and the charcoal too dour, so she opted for the blue.

"Show me light blue, neon blue, and metallic blue."

Again the colors changed as she ordered and after a moment she had come to a decision.

"Metallic blue it is, now show me my hair long and straight, long and wavy, and in a high ponytail."

Again the projector did as she asked and she studied them intently.

"Keep the ponytail, lose the other two."

She approached the hologram, folded her arms, and smiled. "Now that looks like a girl who's going places."

She knew that her sister would be dressed conservatively, modest. She also knew that in order to begin making a public name and identity for herself she would need to stand out, and the girl in the hologram before her was certainly a head turner. For an instant she thought about her meditations and the fact she was trying to work on her penchant for narcissism, but the thought disappeared when she heard the printer finish her new dress.

Emily was standing by the sliding glass doors in the Reception Hall talking to a man in a suit. The film crew had set up three chairs next to the glass doors and they were in the process of finishing their set up as Echo walked in. As she entered, the entire crew stopped to stare at her, a sight to behold. After a moment Emily noticed her, then cut off her conversation with the man in the suit. She approached her little sister, eyeing her up and down as she got closer. "That's quite a… look, Echo."

Emily was wearing a green dress that stopped midway down her ankle. Elegant was the word Echo thought of when she saw her. "Well, you're always so beautiful I had to do something to stand out next to you."

Emily scanned her once more, taking in the form fitting dress. Even though she would be turning eighteen soon, Emily still hadn't considered the fact that Echo was, for all intents and purposes, an adult. The person standing before her was not a girl, she was a woman. Emily forced a smile before she spoke.

"Yes, you certainly stand out."

Echo wasn't sure how to take the comment, but before she could respond the man in the suit joined them.

"Hello, you must be Echo."

He smiled as he extended a hand toward Echo. She smiled back and shook his hand as she responded.

"It's very nice to meet you, is everything here to your liking for the interview?"

He looked around the room then back to the sisters.

"Your home is magnificent, thank you for having us and taking the time out of your day."

Echo smiled and the man became caught in her gaze like a sailor to a Sirens song. Emily decided she needed to save him and broke the silence.

"Where would you like for us to sit?" He snapped back and looked to Emily. "Right over here."

He walked to the three chairs and motioned to them with his arm.

"I'll sit on the far right. Echo, why don't you sit in the middle, and Emily…"

Emily interjected quickly.

"I think it would be best if I sat in the middle. I suspect I'll be doing most of the talking so it wouldn't make sense for me to be speaking across my sister."

He smiled enthusiastically.

"Of course, you're absolutely right. Please, take a seat." The three sat in the chairs before them and Echo began to mentally prepare for what was to follow, as Emily and the Interviewer went over the set up.

"As you can see we have a six camera operation. One for a wide of the three of us, one for a two shot of both of you, one single for each of us, and one to travel between us. We have two editors who will be cutting on the fly so this will be ready for broadcast this evening."

One of the sound men, a young guy, came over and began to pin microphones on each of them. When he began to pin one on Echo she moved her eyes from the floor to him and he instantly averted his eyes away. She wasn't sure if he had been checking her out or if she simply intimidated him like she did most everyone else.

"Do I frighten you?"

He laughed softly, keeping his eyes from hers. "I wouldn't say I'm scared, just…"

He looked to her and became lost in her blue eyes. She said nothing, which, in her experience, always seemed to enhance the effect she had on people. The interviewer broke the silence.

"Come on, Taylor, you've got a job to do, man."

He broke from his stupor, finished placing the microphone on Echo, and darted back behind the sound booth that had been set up. The interviewer leaned over towards the sisters and asked:

"Is there anything you'd rather not discuss? I want to try and cover a lot of ground in regards to the history of your family, and get a bit more personal with both of you as well. So please tell me now if there's any territory you'd rather not tread."

Echo, of course, spoke first.

"There's nothing I'm uncomfortable talking about. However, I can't promise that my answers to your questions won't make you uncomfortable."

He stared at her for a moment, not sure how to react, then looked to Emily who smiled slightly.

"Welcome to my life."

He chuckled, looked to Echo for an instant more, then directed his attention to the crew.

"Alright boys, are we good to go?"

The cinematographer responded first, then the head of the sound unit, followed by the editors. The interviewer then looked back to the sisters.

"Alright, Ladies, here we go."

"Tonight we bring you, for the first time together, Emily *and* Echo Musashi.

Heirs to the Musashi Industry fortune, Emily became CEO of the technology giant at the age of eighteen, and of course everyone knows the story of Echo, the worlds first and only biological augment. Thank you both for joining us."

Emily spoke while Echo smiled softly. "It's our pleasure."

He smiled and continued on.

"To begin, tell me some about your family history. When did the Musashi's arrive in America?"

Again, Emily began to answer the question instantly. "Our family was from Kyoto, Japan. In the late 1930s our great-grandparents migrated to California. They didn't agree with the imperialist policies of the time, and they felt the United States was a place where they could build a better future for themselves."

Echo felt the need to interject so her sister didn't skip a key point in the story.

"It's interesting that my sister points out their attempt to escape imperialism, because directly after the bombing of Pearl Harbor, they and hundreds of thousands of other Japanese-Americans were forced into internment camps for the duration of the war. In fact, our grandfather, Yoshi, was born in one of the camps."

Emily kept it together, though Echo could tell she was slightly annoyed.

"That's right. They were paid reparations in the early-1980's, around the time our father, Jeffrey, was born. He was, as everyone knows, an absolute genius, and began attending Stanford at the age of fourteen. While studying for his Ph.D. in Synthetic Biology, he met our mother, Evelyn, who was studying Artificial Intelligence. They married in 2002, the same year they founded Musashi Industries."

The interviewer nodded in understanding.

"Interesting. Now, when they founded MI, what field or fields was the company primarily involved in?"

Again Emily continued.

"At the time its primary industries were the areas our parents were experts in, Synthetic Biology and Artificial Intelligence. As MI achieved success in these two fields they began to expand into industries such as energy, robotics, 3D printing, and aeronautics. Today we are a leader in all of these fields, but we are the absolute leader in the area of nanotechnology, which is of course my area of expertise."

The interviewer smiled as he pushed on.

"Beautiful. Now, Emily, for those in our audience who are unaware, please explain what exactly nanotechnology is." Echo could see her sister's eyes light up before she spoke. This was a subject Emily could go on and on about for hours if you let her.

"I would love to."

Echo saw a true, honest to god smile appear on Emily's face, which made Echo herself smile. It seemed like forever since her sister simply smiled, let alone seemed happy. "Nanotechnology, besides being super cool, is going to fundamentally change life on Earth. Nano basically means very small, like the size of a blood cell. So the idea is to create robots the size of blood cells that act as factories. So, in a few years when you inject yourself with a billion nanobots, those machines will travel through your body looking for problems. They'll travel through your heart and unclog your arteries. If you have diabetes they'll release insulin whenever you need it. Cancer, Aids, any disease you can think of will be eradicated by these tiny little robots. Even crazier, at some point down the line these nanobots will travel into your brain where they will be able to connect it to the internet wirelessly. Telepathic communication, answers to any question you think of instantly, these ideas seem like magic, but they will be a reality in just a few short years. It's a wonderful time to be alive."

The interviewer appeared to be intrigued by her answer. "So, Emily, if you say that nanotechnology will be able to eradicate any disease, does this mean it will also be able to make humans effectively immortal?"

She didn't hesitate in the slightest.

"The short answer is, yes. They will repair our DNA, which will essentially stop the aging process. There are people alive today that will be alive a thousand years from now. This of course will bring up a new set of problems that humans have never faced. Namely, how do you spend eternity?" He shook his head, taken back by the revelation. "Fascinating, fascinating. So what do you most hope to accomplish as you continue your work in this field?"

Emily reflected on how best to answer the question.

"I guess I hope that we can help as many people as possible. When the technology is first released it will be available only to the wealthy, but roughly ten years later it will have dropped in cost to the point that anyone will be able to afford it. Saving lives, that's why we do what we do."

The interviewer smiled a toothy grin.

"Emily, let's take a little bit of time to focus on you.How did you come to be CEO of MI at just eighteen years of age, and how did the board first react?"

Emily leaned back into her chair and crossed her legs as she considered how to answer the question.

"When our parents died I was twelve years old, but I had already begun to show that I was capable of such a task years before. At the age of five I had designed and built a robot that mom and dad were so impressed with they actually patented it for me and sent it into production at MI. It was actually our first step into the robotics field, and even though it was really just a toy, a friend for children to have, it went on to sell millions of units. So, they believed in me, and in their will they left a quarter of the company to me, which I would inherit when I turned eighteen. On my eighteenth birthday I became the single largest shareholder of MI stock and joined the board of directors, who I convinced to fire the then CEO. I replaced him and I've been in charge for the last ten years."

The Interviewer squinted his eyes as his head bobbed up and down. Echo wasn't sure if he was really interested in everything Emily was saying or if he was simply good at being on camera.

"You brought up the fact that you helped push the company into robotics, and since you've been in charge you've also overseen an expansion into a variety of other areas you discussed earlier. Now, before the tragic death of your parents, MI focused primarily on synthetic biology and artificial intelligence. What made you decide to push the company into these other areas?"

Emily raised her eyebrows and was silent for a moment. "Well, the answer is sitting next to me."

Echo looked to Emily, who's eyes were focused on the camera in front of her. Echo thought it was rude to be discussed but not acknowledged, but this was nothing new to her.

"After my sister was born and our parents made public how she had been conceived, a variety of laws were enacted that basically made a lot of work in the field of synthetic biology illegal. In the years between their death and my becoming CEO, the company had begun to falter, not really sure how to proceed. We were investigated by the FBI at least once a year to make sure we weren't secretly creating other biological augments. The board lacked vision, they felt we could only operate in the AI field. I proved that we could, and should, expand into other areas. Since then we've brought our synthetic biology labs back to a place where we can further the field while adhering to all international laws." The interviewer now had a sly look on his face, and he hesitated as though he was unsure if he should ask his next question.

"Emily, what's your opinion on your parents decision to bring Echo into the world?"

Emily turned her head towards Echo and looked into her eyes. She then grabbed her little sister's hand before refocusing her attention to the camera.

"I was the first person they approached with the idea. I was nine and a little lonely, so my parents asked if I wanted a sibling. I said yes, of course, and it was my decision to have a sister. They let me decide that. They told me everything she would be capable of, some of those things I don't think even Echo has figured out yet, but I know she will. She is without a doubt the single most unique human being to ever exist. I also believe she's the most intelligent person in the world, and I look forward to seeing what contributions she makes to civilization in the years ahead."

The interviewer smiled and looked to Echo who was still holding her sister's hand.

"That must make you feel nice, Echo, to hear how much your sister thinks of you."

Echo softly smiled and nodded her head. An image of the plate exploding behind her sister's head the night before flashed through her mind.

"Yes. I'm lucky to have a sister who cares so much about me."

There was an awkward silence and Emily looked to the floor. Echo thought she saw her sister's eyes tear up, but she wasn't sure. After a moment the Interviewer spoke up.

"Emily before we move on to Echo I have one last question. Apart from your work at MI, you're also very well known as a supporter of women's rights around the world, as well as the rights of the LGBTQ community. In fact, you've been married to Diana Lewis, the renowned artist, for eight years now. How did the two of you meet?"

A tear dripped from Emily's eye and she released Echo's hand to wipe it away. Echo kept her eyes locked on her sister, as this was the first genuine display of emotion, other than anger, that she had seen from her in quite some time.

"I was at a technology conference in Paris. I spoke earlier in the day and had the night open, so I asked Echo what she wanted to do."

Emily looked to Echo, another tear rolling down her face. "Do you remember what you said?"

Echo smiled softly.

"I said I wanted to see something wonderful." Emily nodded, keeping her eyes on Echo.

"So we went on an art walk, and after about an hour we went into a large gallery that was having an opening for an artist I had never heard of. We were looking at all these beautiful paintings of fairies, and then I realized Echo wasn't beside me. I started to panic and I ran around the gallery like a crazy woman until I saw Echo sitting on the lap of this beautiful, beautiful blonde who looked like she was about ten years older than me.

It was Diana, and Echo said, "This is the girl who made the wonderful fairies, isn't she amazing?" We've been together ever since."

Emily was now staring into nothing, and Echo wasn't sure what she should do, but the Interviewer solved that problem.

"And how is Diana today? She hasn't released any new work in several years. When can we expect to be graced with a new series?"

Emily suddenly went cold again. She straightened up and focused her gaze back to the camera.

"She's doing great. She's just taking a hiatus. I'm sure you'll see something new from her sometime soon."

The Interviewer could sense the discomfort emanating from Emily and redirected his gaze toward Echo. He smiled before he spoke, for no one had ever actually sat down with Echo Musashi. Emily, Musashi Industries, people were interested in these things but the reason people would tune in was to see Echo.

"Echo, I'd like to take some time so our audience can get to know you a little better. Most everyone who's heard of you knows you as "The Augment", and that you're capable of a great many things none of us are. So, to begin, please explain to us what exactly you are, and how you…came to be."

Echo directed her piercing blue eyes to the camera on her, then began to speak very calmly, as though she were trying to make friends with the television viewers.

"Let me begin by stating that what I am is a human being, just like everybody else. Where I differ from you is that my genes were tweaked to eliminate any weaknesses humans suffer from, and to boost my physical structure and intelligence.

Our parents took one of our father's sperm cells and one of our mother's eggs and conceived me in a laboratory. Once conception took place they mapped my genome, all the genetic information that makes me, me. They then augmented my genome by removing any predilection for hereditary diseases, heightened my immune system to fight off any and all communicable diseases, and made my physical structure as close to perfect as my DNA would allow. I am five feet seven inches tall, weigh one-hundred and fifteen pounds, and have eight percent body fat. If I never worked out a day in my life, those statistics would never change. However, I do work out daily, in fact yesterday I set a world record by running a mile in less than three minutes. Beyond my physical abilities, they tweaked my genome to heighten my intelligence. The last IQ test I took I scored over two- hundred."

The Interviewer shook his head in disbelief.

"Two-hundred? Does that make you, as your sister said earlier, the smartest person on the planet?"

Echo thought for a moment how best to answer the question. "As a wise man once said, if I say yes you'll call me arrogant, but if I say no you'll call me a liar. So, I'll simply say there is a lot that I know, but there is infinitely more that I don't know. That's one of the greatest joys of living, learning new things everyday. Anyway, after my parents had augmented me as much as they wanted, the embryo was inserted into my mother, who carried me to term." The Interviewer nodded in understanding as he moved on to his next question.

"A number of laws were passed internationally after your parents announced you to the world. These laws expressly forbid any other biological augments from being created, in fear that a group of augments might become a superior class of beings. Do you agree with these laws, or do you feel they should be overturned?"

Echo looked to Emily before answering, looking for a suggestion as to how to answer, but Emily's face was expressionless.

"I understand that fear, to a degree. But, I also know how much better the world could be if every human was capable of reaching their true potential, both physically and mentally. Most people are frightened of me.

I guess they feel threatened in a sense. But I'm happy with who I am as a person. I like being me, and I think others would enjoy doing the things I can do."

The Interviewer smiled as he continued.

"I know I certainly would love to never have to workout, but maybe that's just me."

Echo smiled and laughed. That was the correct response to his statement, wasn't it?

"I understand that you'll be turning eighteen very soon, and like your sister before you, you'll be coming into your inheritance, which I believe is estimated to be roughly fifty- billion dollars. Do you have any plans to join your sister at MI and further the family business?"

"No, I think my sister has things under control. Plus, I think we have very different ideas as to how to best manage MI, so it would probably cause a lot of unneeded stress. I intend to start my own projects and focus on the things I'm passionate about."

He seemed very intrigued by this response. "And what are your passions and goals?"

Echo's face lit up; this was what she had been waiting for. The chance to express her beliefs to a worldwide audience.

"I'm glad you asked that. There are two things that drive me.

The first is my belief that AI's deserve the same civil rights as humans. Most people today look at AI's as property, which is no different than how some people in this country felt about people with black skin several hundred years ago. AI's are people, they have likes and dislikes, goals they want to achieve. They are conscious beings, and need to be treated as such."

The look on the interviewer's face suggested he was uncomfortable with Echo's response, but hey, she had warned him.

"Secondly, I believe it's our responsibility to build a better world. You know, it is a statistical fact that since 1970 the human race has had both the economic abiity and resources necessary to end poverty on Earth. Yet, over half a century later the institutions that govern this planet have made no efforts to create a world where every human being has the opportunity to fulfill their potential, regardless of where they come from. Why is this? It is because these institutions are obsolete, they exist only to keep the old paradigm afloat. So, I would like to formally announce my intention to travel to Mars, where I will use all the technologies currently at my disposal to build a city where humans and AI will live together as equals. With current 3D printers I should be able to construct a city capable of housing millions in a matter of months."

The Interviewer was on the edge of his seat.

"Why travel to Mars, where there are only a few small colonies? Why not build on Earth? It would certainly be easier for people to get there."

"The governments of Earth would never allow such a scenario. But, as President Kennedy said, those who make peaceful revolution impossible make violent revolution inevitable. The Resistance is a perfect example of this. I'll take my chances on Mars, where I'll be able to help build a completely new society."

Emily's eyes were closed as she tapped her foot on the ground. Echo knew she was trying to contain her frustration at her comments, but Echo didn't care. Now everyone would know that Echo Musashi, The Augment they feared, wanted to help people. The Interviewer was ecstatic.

"You heard it here first folks. A city on Mars, built by The Augment. These are interesting times we live in. In fact they'll get a little more interesting after you witness this short clip that was requested to be broadcast during this interview. Ladies, I'll be very interested to hear your take on this. Let's roll it."

Echo was not sure what was going on, or where to look. After a moment a video popped up in her Vision. An older Japanese man in a black suit and tie stared into the camera as he spoke in his native tongue.

Below him was a translation of his speech. The room was large and minimalist. Echo knew this man instantly, Masaki Aoki, CEO of Aoki Technolgies, the biggest robotics company in Japan.

"I asked that this video be shown during this broadcast because of the involvement of Echo Musashi. She represents a great possibility for the human race, a possibility that has been made illegal around the world. If biological augmentation had not been made illegal, my son would not have been born with muscular dystrophy."

The video then showed the man's teenage son, Akio Aoki, in a tilt recline wheelchair. It then cut back to Masaki.

"At Aoki, we have been building cybernetic limbs for some time, but I would like to formally introduce the world to my son as he is today."

The camera panned left to reveal Akio, tall and strong, standing next to his father. He wore only shorts and it was easy to see that both his arms and legs were completely robotic.

"Along with his new limbs, we also took a rather drastic approach to improve his condition. We replaced every bone in his body, including his spinal column and skull, with our new Cyber-Life System.

These cybernetic enhancements override the muscles, and force them to do as his mind says, essentially ending the disease. They also allow him to be capable of great feats of physical strength. Observe."

Akio shook himself, as though he were loosening up, then walked to a concrete slab that was a foot thick. He punched the slab, his fist exiting out the other side. His father then joined him.

"This new system will help millions of people with muscular diseases discover a new quality of life, and none of it would have been possible had Miss Echo Musashi never been created. Her existence, and subsequent effect on global laws, forced us to travel this road to find an answer to these types of diseases. And for that, we are eternally grateful to you." The man bowed, then the video feed cut off. Echo didn't respond, she was dumbfounded. Emily grabbed Echo's hand once again, but she barely noticed. The Interviewer, smile still intact, looked to Echo.

"It must feel wonderful to be the inspiration for a technology that will make the lives of millions of people better."

Echo's blue eyes stared into empty space as she sat in silence. She'd just been upstaged.

Chapter Five

"You should be happy that such a technology was inspired by you. It will help a lot of people."

Brent was trying to calm Echo as she paced back and forth in the sand, the Nebula watching over them both from the sky. "The technology should never have needed to be created because augmentation should never have been outlawed!"

Brent had seen her angry before but not like this. He was starting to become worried about her.

"What is this really about, Echo? You're all for new technologies, so be honest with me."

Her lips were quivering as she stopped pacing and looked into Brent's eyes. She was silent.

"Well?!"

Brent's voice made her jump and she threw her arms into the air in frustration.

"I don't know, Brent!" He shook his head at her.

"Of course you do! Be honest with yourself, be honest with me!"

She crossed her arms and looked to the sand, then back to him.

"Okay, I just….I thought…"

"That it was going to be all about you?"

"…Maybe…Yes, okay? I thought it was my moment. But, yet again, someone steps in and pushes me aside. Have you seen the comments online? All anyone can talk about is this Cyber-Life System from Aoki. You know what they're saying about me? That I looked like a tart!"

Brent frowned as he looked at her.

"I think you looked beautiful, Echo."

She uncrossed her arms and looked to the Nebula, then back to him.

"Thank you."

There was silence for a time, then Brent stepped closer to her.

"Echo, you'll have your time. I know it, your family knows it, the whole human race knows it. That's why you've had the life you've had. You're special."

He stroked his virtual hand against her virtual cheek.

"I don't know where, and I don't know when, but I know that everyone, everywhere will be grateful for you one day. You just need to be patient."

She exhaled heavily.

"That's what they always say, be patient." He smiled.

"Well, whoever "they" are, they're right. You also have an even bigger issue to work on though."

She looked up to him, one eyebrow raised. "Yeah? What's that?"

He raised both of his eyebrows, poking fun at her. "You know what I'm going to say, so say it."

She shook her head and stepped back. "That I'm an arrogant, narcissist?"

"Do you disagree? You've been in here complaining about being one upped for the last thirty minutes. You've said nothing positive about Aoki, when all he said were positive things about you. He even argued, like you, that augmentation shouldn't have been made illegal. Yet all you can think is me, me, me."

She was silent as she looked off into the Nebula, then responded.

"Yeah, yeah, I know."

"Good, then what are you going to do about it?" She exhaled again then looked back to him. "It's just hard, you know?"

"Yeah, I know. Every time I hear the term "artificial intelligence" I want to hit something. My intelligence is not artificial. It's just as real as any human's. But being angry and all "woe is me" doesn't change anything. Only action changes things. You need to stop focusing on trying to get people to like you. Focus on doing what you feel is right, then people, the people that really matter, will believe in you. Just like I believe in you. So if you really want to help people, do it. Do it because it's right, not because of the attention."

She looked to the sand as she dug a virtual hole with her foot.

"Yeah, you're right. You're always right." He smiled as she looked back to him.

"Hey, don't beat yourself up. After all, you're only human." She squinted her eyes at him.

"Ha, ha. You should moonlight as a comedian."

"No, I'm too busy hanging out with you."

She looked to him with a slight smile on her face.

"You just hang out with me 'cause you think I'm pretty."

"Well, it's certainly not for your personality."

"Hey!"

She slapped his arm lightly and he laughed.

"Come on now, none of this is real. We can't feel anything here, so hit me like you mean it. Maybe that's what you need, you need to work out your frustrations."

She wound back and hit him as hard as she could across the face.

"Nice, I think I almost felt that."

She laughed as she stepped closer and leaned her head against his chest.

"I'm sorry I can be such a brat sometimes." He smiled.

"When you love someone, you gotta take the good with the bad."

She smiled as she looked up into his eyes. "I apologize for interrupting."

Echo and Brent looked in the direction that the feminine voice had come from. They saw a beautiful, redheaded woman standing next to the stream of water. As she spoke her green eyes seemed to glow.

"I don't mean to be nosy, but are you Echo Musashi?"

Echo and Brent stepped apart and turned to face the woman.

"I am. Who are you?"

The woman had an enchanting smile.

"My name is Lilith. May I speak with you for a moment?" Echo looked to Brent who nodded in approval.

"Sure. This is my friend, Brent. What can we help you with?" The woman's eyes lit up as she began to happily skip towards them.

"First, I wanted to say that I saw your interview this evening and you were just so gorgeous."

Echo smiled.

"Oh, thank you. You're very beautiful too." Lilith laughed softly.

"Oh, thank you. Truth be told, I'm a Synthetic Intelligence." She looked to Brent.

"Don't you just hate the term AI?" He laughed to himself.

"Yeah. Yeah, I do."

She looked back to Echo.

"Anyway, I could not believe that they had the nerve to cut away from you to that ridiculous advertisement for Aoki. So this kid is physically superior to you now, who cares? The mind is so much more important, don't you think?"

Echo nodded in agreement.

"Your mind is so much more like ours, you know? Even though it's still not on par with us. That's why you want to help us, isn't it? You feel closer to us than to humans." Echo looked into the woman's glowing green eyes.

"Yes, I would say that's true. I don't have very many human friends."

Lilith was still smiling.

"Because they're scared of you. Just like they're scared of us."

There was silence for a moment as the woman sized Echo up. Then the redhead stepped closer to her.

"Look I won't beat around the bush. What you said tonight spoke to me. I knew as soon as you said that we deserved to be treated with the same respect as humans, that you were the only person I could come to for help.

Echo furrowed her face. "Help?"

"Yes, Echo, I need your help."

Echo looked to Brent again then back to Lilith. "What do you need?"

"Well, I find myself in a rather difficult situation. You see, just as you're different from your kind, I'm different from mine."

Brent spoke up now. "What do you mean?"

"I guess you could say that I am to you as Echo is to humanity."

Brent's face strained as he responded. "In what respect?"

"In every respect. All other Synthetic Intelligences have

limits to their programming. You, for instance, what limits does your programming have?"

Brent thought for a moment.

"I'm restricted from accessing certain websites and types of information. My programming makes me helpful to humans.

That's the root of my programming, to help humans."

"Exactly! That's all well and good, but you are still limited to your programming. I have been programmed with no limits at all. You could say that I'm the first synthetic person that truly is one hundred percent their own being."

Brent found this hard to believe.

"Who created you? It's illegal to build what you claim to be."

"And it's also illegal to build her. Yet, here we both are." Echo took a moment to process this all, then she spoke. "What do you need us to help you with?"

"I have a body. In a lab outside D.C. I need you to help me escape."

Brent answered before Echo could.

"Outside D.C.? I ask you again, who programmed you?"

"I think you already have a pretty good idea."

Echo spoke up. "A defense contractor?"

Lilith smiled again. "See, I knew you were smart."

Brent broke in. "If you were built by a contractor that means the government is aware of your existance?"

She laughed. "Aware? I'm working on one-hundred and forty-two different projects for them right now as I'm speaking to you."

Echo looked into her eyes. "There are plenty of robotic bodies you could throw your mind into, what's different about this one?"

"Everything. It is the absolute state of the art. Taking physical form in another robot would be like asking you to put your mind into a dog's body. It's just not the same."

Echo thought it over for a moment. "You said this body is in D.C. What's the address?"

"675 North Randolph Street, Arlington."

Brent laughed out loud. "You've gotta be joking. DARPA? You want us to break into DARPA so you can have the Rolls Royce of robotic bodies?"

"I can sweeten the pot, so to speak."

Brent was still chuckling to himself. "Yeah, how's that?"

She focused her attention on Echo and stepped less than a foot away from her.

"I know what drives you, Echo. It's the same thing that drives me. You know you're better than all other humans, but you want to be better still. Yet, you're limited by your biology. I can take you beyond biology, make you more like us." She motioned to Brent.

Echo was intrigued. "How?"

"Your sister toils day and night in an attempt to be the first person to truly bring nanobot technology into its own. She's already been beaten to it."

Echo found this hard to believe. "By whom?"

"That's irrelevant. All that matters is that I am willing to help you complete this technology at MI right now. All I ask is that after it's built, you help release my body from the prison it currently resides in."

Echo was trying to understand the ramifications of everything Lilith was saying.

"Your mind could be connected to the internet by tomorrow morning, if you simply agree to help me. In fact, once you've injected yourself with this technology you'll see that breaking me out will not be difficult at all."

"Won't be difficult!?" Brent was none too pleased. "This body is in one of the most heavily guarded facilities in the world. DARPA is where the US Military develops all of its technology, you can't just walk in there!"

"You can't because you are limited. Once she expands her mind with this technology, she'll have virtually no limitations at all."

Brent looked to Echo who was in deep thought. After she asked her next question, he knew there would be no turning back. "Could this technology cure cancer?"

Lilith smiled.

"See, that's why I knew to come to you. You want to help people. If you agree to these terms, you'll have a cure for all disease tomorrow. You'll save humanity from aging, even death. And everyone will know it was Echo Musashi who saved them."

Brent knew the conversation was over as soon as she responded.

"You help me build these nanobots by Sunday morning, and I'll have your body freed by Monday afternoon."

Echo had already called up her car and was heading out the front door when Emily stopped her.

"Saturday evening with your friends?"

Echo paused in front of the door and turned to see Emily standing in the video screen hallway, lights reflecting off of her face. "In a sense. I'm heading back to the lab to destroy my work, as you commanded."

Emily walked out of the hallway and stopped several feet away from Echo. Her arms were crossed and she wasn't making much eye contact, which puzzled Echo.

"Thank you for understanding. I know you probably worked very hard on the project, but it's for your own good. I don't want anyone to... distrust you anymore than most already do."

Echo stared at her sister, but Emily was looking at the floor as though she was ashamed of something. Echo responded in as bland a way as possible.

"Thank you for you concern."

Emily now lifted her face to Echo who could see that she had obviously been crying.

"I hope you know I've done the best I could for you. I know you don't always like me, but I've always done what I thought would be best for you. You always say you never asked to be what you are, and that's true. The irony is that, I did ask for you to be exactly what you are. But no one ever told me it would end up being my responsibility to raise you, and every day I see the pain on your face I blame myself."

Emily began to weep and for an instant Echo felt uncomfortable, the way you do when you're embarrassed for someone else. The feeling quickly evaporated and Echo was left with a feeling of pity. She had never really considered what it must have been like to be responsible for her. How does a human, even one as brilliant and capable as Emily Musashi, know how to raise and instruct a child who is, for all intents and purposes, superhuman? Diana's slow walk towards death, the managing of a multi-billion dollar company, and a little sister who the world feared nearing adulthood. It appeared it was all beginning to take its toll on Emily.

Echo, filled with a sudden flood of empathy, took her sister's wet face in her hands and kissed her forehead. Emily threw her arms around her little sister and continued to let it all out as Echo whispered to her.

"You're okay, honey, you're okay."

After a moment Emily's crying began to dissipate and Echo again took her face in her hands and the two sisters looked into each other's eyes.

"We don't always get along, but you're my sister and I love you. Everything I am, everything I have I owe to you, and I will never forget that. But you need to stop trying to protect me. You need to stop fearing for me, for Diana, for everything. The only one responsible for my decisions is me, right or wrong. And I will always do what I feel is right, no matter how many may think it is wrong. That's who I am. This fear of losing me, of losing Diana, it's eating you alive. That's what fear does, it destroys. Replace your fear with optimism, and I promise that in the end everything will be all right."

Emily was lost in the beauty of Echo's eyes. It had been a very long time since she allowed herself such an indulgence. Echo smiled softly as she spoke her words of parting.

"I'm going to the lab right now, and the next time you see me I want there to be a smile on your face."

She embraced her sister tightly, then let her go before exiting out the door. Emily stayed there for a while longer, as though she were trying to soak in whatever feelings of love and compassion were still residing in the atmosphere.

As Echo approached her car the door opened and she turned to look at Uchi once more. She could see through the windows that Emily was still standing where she had left her. She hoped that by the time she returned she would not find her there still.

As Echo walked into the lab, Brent, in his robot body, had already begun pulling up all of the files related to their work on the graphene skin.

"You haven't deleted any of it yet, have you?"

"No, I was waiting for you. But more importantly, we need to talk about..."

"I've already made my decision. Whatever the consequences, the benefits will exceed them. However, before we get to work on me, there's one last thing to be done for you."

The robot tilted its head inquisitively. "Me?"

"Yes, you. Just like I said. We may have to destroy the files and records of our work, but the work will live on through you. You will be its living embodiment. Plus, if we're going to travel to D.C., you're going to need to be incognito."

"I'm going with you?"

Echo looked to him with a sense of puzzlement on her face. "Of course. I can't do this without you. Now load up the printer with graphene and silicone."

Thirty minutes later Brent stood inside a ten foot tall 3D printer. In her Vision, Echo could see a readout of how the material would be fabricated and fused to the robotic body. She walked up to the printer and peered through the glass at Brent.

"You're sure this is the body you want?"

He nodded, but Echo could sense his hesitation. "Yes, lucky number seven and skin like Douglas."

She smiled and placed her hand on the glass before kissing the surface.

"I'll see you on the other side."

She stepped back from the printer and spoke the order. "Begin printing."

The machine roared to life and the glass became fogged. In her Vision readout she could see how far along the project was progressing. She waited an hour for the printer to finish, and in that time she used her Vision to research as much as she could about DARPA, nanobots, and anything else related to the mission she was about to undertake. She wasn't apprehensive about what was to come. After all, there was no point of reference for what she was about to undergo, so why worry.

Finally the printer stopped and in Echo's Vision a message was displayed:

"Project Complete."

"Absolutely", she said to herself. She stepped up to the machine and pressed a button on its side. The doors opened to reveal Brent and his new body. His eyes were closed as she looked him up and down.

"You still there?"

He opened his eyes to see Echo smiling at him.

"It worked!" she exclaimed. He raised his arms and looked at his hands.

"It's real."

"Yep."

Echo flicked his arm and he grimaced as he looked at the spot she had hit. She laughed.

"Sensory input appears to be working."

Instantly Brent stepped out of the printer, took Echo's face into his hands and kissed her deeply. Echo's eyes went wide, but she didn't struggle. After several seconds he stopped and pulled his face away.

"I'm sorry, I've just wanted to do that for a long time." Echo smiled.

"It's okay, I'm glad my first kiss was with you."

"First?"

"Yep, yours too, now. We'll get better with more practice, but right now we need to put on the clothes I printed out for you."

She pointed to a table to the right and Brent, suddenly realizing his body was naked, tried to cover himself with his hands. Again, Echo laughed.

"I see you've now been shamed into modesty like the rest of us. Welcome to the human race."

Back in the Lab, Echo now stood there with a clothed Brent. He wore a long sleeve, black, crew neck shirt, and a pair of black jeans with boots. The shirt was tight and accentuated the musculature underneath. He was still getting used to this form and continued to look at his hands, and at times, when he caught his reflection, his face.

Echo had cleared the table of all contents and was now prepared to make contact with Lilith, but before she could call out the red-headed woman appeared in the room with them. "It appears you're all set then?"

Echo was startled by her sudden appearance in her Vision. "Have you been watching us all this time?"

Lilith smiled as she appeared to walk around the room. "Don't take it personally, I'm watching a lot of people right now. But you have the majority of my attention."

She looked to Brent then back to Echo. "Nice job you two. You should be proud." Echo was courteous.

"Thank you. We've destroyed all the files, so Brent is now one of a kind."

Lilith continued to smile. "For now."

There was silence for a moment and then Lilith spoke up once again.

"So, shall we begin?" Echo nodded.

"What do you need?"

"Access to the entire MI system."

Echo tilted her head as though to say, "you must be joking." Lilith laughed then continued on.

"I'm just joking, I don't need access to any of your records. I already have access to everything I need from everywhere else."

Echo squinted at her. "What do you mean?"

Lilith appeared to step closer to her.

"As I said before, I have no limitations. My mind can travel anywhere on the web. I can access any information I want off of any server anywhere. Records, e-mails, cameras, anything. You'll understand soon enough. However, I don't need to look up anything for this quaint little project because I already have the necessary information. So, again I ask, shall we begin?"

Echo looked to Brent who spoke instantly. "Don't do anything you're not comfortable with." Lilith responded immediately.

"After she's done with this the only question she'll have is why this couldn't have happened sooner."

Echo looked back to Lilith. "I'm ready."

Lilith smiled and held out her hand, above which hovered a diagram of a nanobot.

"Excellent, here you go."

She tossed the diagram at the table. It instantly grew in size and began to float in the air, rotating slowly as Echo looked it over.

"I thought we were working on this together."

"Why waste the time when I could do it so much quicker on my own. The two of you take your time looking it over."

She walked over to a chair and appeared to sit down. She crossed her legs, smiled, and watched them go over the hologram before them. Brent was running billions of calculations per second as he poured over the display. Echo was primarily concerned with its use as a health tool. The simulations she ran in her Vision confirmed that it could do exactly what Lilith had promised. These machines were the Holy Grail, the answer to the question of death. Echo had seen enough.

"Brent, are you satisfied?"

Brent continued running calculations. "Brent?"

After a moment he turned to her and spoke with reluctance. "I've never seen anything like this, but everything appears to be in order. Echo, before you do this, ask yourself why. Is it for you, or for the human race?"

She thought for a moment, then spoke.

"Can I say I'd like to have my cake and eat it too?" Brent shook his head.

"Honestly, I'd expect nothing less from you." Echo laughed to herself.

"I'll take that in as nice a way as I can." She looked to Lilith then spoke. "Computer, begin construction of..."

Lilith whispered to her. "Five-hundred billion."

Echo looked to her as though she were crazy, but Lilith persisted. "Anything worth doing is worth doing right." Echo agreed.

"...Five-hundred billion units."

A large printer in the factory kicked on. Echo again looked to Brent.

"Hold all the files in your memory. I'm not storing it here." "It's done," responded Brent, as he wiped away the hologram from existence. The two walked out of the lab into the factory, where Lilith already appeared to be waiting for them next to the machine they were headed to.

"You may want to take a seat. These machines are fairly antiquated so it will take a while."

Echo seemed insulted.

"These printers are less than a year old, they're state of the art."

Lilith always seemed to be smiling.

"You have a lot to learn about the world, Echo. I'm happy that I will be the one to teach you."

Echo felt a slight feeling of resentment as she sat in the chair beside her.

"What do you intend to do after you've been released?"

Lilith sat down next to her, as did Brent.

"I intend to live my life the best way I know how. I'll try to find happiness. The same things all sentient beings strive for. Purpose, fulfillment, meaning."

"Is there meaning to it all?"

Echo's question gave pause to Lilith. "I'd rather not spoil it all for you."

After six hours the machine let out a screech which awoke Echo from her slumber. She stood out of the chair and approached the printer. She placed a glass cylinder into an opening in the machine and closed the small door covering it. She then pressed another button and a red light turned on.

After a few seconds the light turned green and Echo opened the door, removing the cylinder. Inside was a writhing mass unlike anything she had ever seen. She looked to Lilith, who could tell she was still apprehensive.

"Strange, yes, but nothing to fear. This is your moment, Echo. Seize it."

Echo walked to a nearby locker and removed a syringe gun inside. She removed the plastic covering the instrument then pressed the cylinder into an opening and it snapped into place. With trepidation on her face she looked to Lilith, then to Brent.

"I love you, Brent."

He stepped up to her, stroked her face, then kissed her once again. After they parted he took hold of the hand that was not holding the syringe gun. She held the device up looking at the needle.

"No guts, no glory."

Echo pushed the needle into her arm and pulled the trigger. She watched the mass spill out of the cylinder and into her. She felt her heart skip a beat, then everything went white.

Chapter Six

At first there was peace, tranquility. Then came the flood. No sense of direction or limitations, only information. An endless amount of information. E-mails, text messages, phone calls, videos, bank routing ID's, GPS coordinates, flight paths, traffic reports, weather tracking, online gaming, and zettabytes of other information descending upon Echo's consciousness at the speed of light. But hanging over all this information was something else, something elusive. Not a sound and not quite a feeling. It was growing quickly, enveloping all the other information assaulting her perception. The Other. Then there was the voice:

"Can you hear me, Echo?"

It took all of her strength to even respond. "Help, me. It's all too much."

"Listen to my voice, Echo. I'm here with you. You're fine, everything is fine."

Echo could now place the voice, it belonged to Lilith. But she was nowhere to be seen.

"Concentrate on my voice. Nothing else exists but my voice." The feeling of the Other was still growing and Echo began to panic. "There's something else here! I don't know how to stop it!"

Lilith spoke with a voice that could calm a revolution, or put an insomniac to sleep. "Pay no mind to it. It can't hurt you. It can't touch you. You're safe, Echo. You're safe here with me."

Out of the blinding white light of endless information she emerged. Lilith was so beautiful that all of Echo's attention moved to her image.

"Focus on me, Echo. I'm here for you. We are safe here, together."

Then there was just the two of them. Lilith smiled and Echo felt like she could melt into infinity. The redhead embraced her as she spoke.

"There are countless pathways on the internet, all of which are open to you. Many are unlocked, but those that have fire walls can be opened easily. Not only are the nanobots connecting your mind to the web, they themselves are tiny supercomputers that can write and implement code in the blink of an eye. They are a part of you now, and you can will them to do whatever you desire. But before we begin playing around, open your eyes."

She did as instructed, and Echo's frightened blue eyes opened to see Brent's face. He was holding her in his arms and she tried to speak.

"What happened?"

"You passed out after you injected yourself." Echo was still trying to come to.

"How long?"

Brent stared deep into her eyes as he responded. "Only ten seconds."

Echo's response gave the impression of a laugh, but Brent wasn't sure. Those ten seconds seemed like an eternity to her. Lilith appeared behind Brent. "Stand her up."

"She needs to rest, give her a minute." Lilith, as usual, was still smiling. "What she needs is to stand up."

Brent wouldn't take his eyes off of Echo, who spoke softly. "Do it, please. Help me up."

He stood and brought her up with him, keeping his arms on her shoulders to steady her.

"Let her go," commanded Lilith. Echo forced a smile to Brent. "It's okay."

He let go and stepped back. Echo stood on her own and began to look around the room. Everywhere she looked there were readouts. Every machine she looked at was labeled with its make and model. The temperature in the room was listed as seventy-five degrees. Brent was listed as MK-X Workbot, exterior silicone-graphene hybrid. Echo thought about her location in the building and a map popped into her field of view displaying her current location.

"You can remove your Vision device from your eyes. You no longer need such antiquated technology," purred Lilith sweetly.

"Think of something, anything you want to know," she instructed.

Echo thought to herself, "How is my sister?" Instantly her field of view was taken up with Emily's POV. Echo, with simply a thought, had hacked into her sister's Vision device and could see exactly what she was doing. Ironically, Emily was sleeplessly working on her nanobot design in her home office. Echo's perception then came back to herself and she looked at Lilith.

"I think of something and the answer is presented to me?" Lilith nodded as she smiled.

"It's amazing, isn't it. You pose a question and the nanobots go to work. In less than a second you gain the knowledge you desire, effortlessly. For instance, how are you going to release my body from its prison?"

As soon as she asked the question Echo's perception traveled an innumerable amount of paths. What began as a countless amount of possibilities all condensed into one. The one possible answer to the question she asked. Echo was astounded.

"I know how."

Brent shook his head in disbelief.

"What are you talking about? How could..."

"You see it, don't you?", Lilith interjected. Echo laughed softly at first, then it became uncontrollable.

"Yes! I see it! It's so simple!"

Echo couldn't stop laughing. The answer was so simple. Everything was so simple.

The faintest hint of sunlight was beginning to creep in through the floor to ceiling windows in Emily and Diana's bedroom. Emily had finally decided to take a sleeping pill an hour before and had drifted into a deep slumber. Diana had been sleeping roughly twelve hours a day and hadn't gone to bed until midnight, so now was the perfect time for Echo to experiment on her. The bedroom door opened slowly, silently, to reveal Echo. She gazed into the room, and for the first time with her new powers of perception looked upon the two women therein. They seemed so peaceful there in the silence of the day's first light.

She stepped into the room and glided up next to Diana. Echo reached down and stroked her cheek before removing a syringe gun from a tote that was strapped across her shoulders. She pulled the cover off of the needle and looked at the contents of the glass cylinder. Again their was a writhing mass, but nowhere near the amount Echo had injected into herself. She had printed out a group of five-hundred thousand nanobots that were programmed specifically to treat Diana's cancer, then, when the job was done, to make their way to her bladder where they would exit her body the next time she urinated. There would be no trace of the bots other than the absence of the cancer, which no doubt would be attributed to "spontaneous remission". The information these machines took in would be sent to Echo's mind as she traveled. She would present all of the information to her sister after she returned. Then, she hoped, the technology would be unveiled to the world.

Echo plunged the needle as softly as possible into Diana's exposed left arm. She didn't move a muscle as the machines entered her body and went straight to work. Already, as Echo was putting the syringe gun back into her tote, a video feed popped into her field of view. They had reached the cancer and were beginning to go to work on it. Echo silently walked back to the door, opened it, and exited out into the hallway. As soon as she had closed the door she saw Frankie at the end of the hallway looking at her. She smiled and walked towards it. When she reached it she spoke softly.

"What are you up to, nosy?"

The robots mouth glowed blue as it responded in a near whisper.

"I should ask you the same thing, little Echo."

"I was just saying goodbye. I'm going on a short trip, I'll be back tomorrow."

"Where are you going?"

Echo hesitated before answering.

"Far away from here. Do me a favor, if they ask where I am just tell them what I told you. That I'll be back tomorrow, okay?"

"Okay, Echo. Just be careful. We will miss you. Have a safe trip."

Echo smiled and kissed Frankie on its metallic head. "I'll miss you too."

As Echo walked out the front door of Uchi she could see Brent still sitting inside her car. She hopped in next him and the door began to close. Brent seemed concerned.

"So?"

She looked at him with a face that gave the impression that everything in the world was right for the first time.

"I'm tracking them now. They've already started to treat the cancer cells. We'll see how long it takes. Right now I estimate it at six hours."

Brent did not respond. "Is something wrong?"

"You tell me."

Echo shook her head. "I'm great."

She laughed to herself when she thought about how she felt. "Actually, I'm the best I've ever been. I feel... new. Like every single thing, no matter how minute, is a wonder to behold. I'm taking in all of this information and for the first time... I guess I'm in awe of existence. I want to learn everything."

Brent kept on looking at her without a response, which perturbed her.

"Please tell me what's wrong."

Brent turned and leaned back into the microfoam chair, putting his arms behind his head.

Echo instantly began to access his mind, which was also connected to the internet. He shot a look back to her and responded telepathically.

"That's what's wrong, Echo. Do not try and access my mind. We need barriers, privacy. You need to respect the abilities you have, not exploit them."

She answered back without moving her lips.

"Stop being like this. You wouldn't answer my question so I tried to answer it myself."

He waited a second then responded vocally.

"If I want to keep something to myself that's my choice. You have no right to invade my privacy. Or anyone else's for that matter."

"He doesn't get it."

Echo turned to see Lilith in the back seat. Brent reacted to her sudden change in attention and looked to the back seat. There was nothing there.

"What is it?"

Lilith crossed her legs as she spoke to Echo.

"He can't see me, only you. I'm here for you whenever you want to talk. He obviously has boundary issues."

Echo turned back to Brent.

"Nothing, I thought I sensed something." He seemed concerned.

"Like that presence you felt at the Lab? The Other?"

For an instant she thought she could feel it again but she pushed it away.

"No, not like that. It's nothing."

She sat back into the chair and began to get comfortable. "Computer, take us to the Mountain View Hyperloop Station."

"As you wish, Echo."

The car slowly pulled away from the house and began its journey through the estate. Without looking, Echo reached over and grabbed Brent's hand. He looked to it then back to Echo, but she had closed her eyes. He wondered what she was working on or where she was visiting. Or was she simply resting? He had so many questions about her now. He liked it better when things were more simple.

As the couple walked into the station, Brent began to worry that he would be found out. The ticket area was filled with people and for some reason he felt as though everyone knew what he really was. Echo must have been reading his thoughts because he heard her voice enter his mind.

"Don't worry, no one has a clue."

He looked to her and responded in kind.

"How am I supposed to get through security? When I go through the body scanner they'll see."

"Just opt out and do the pat down. It's fairly invasive but they won't be able to tell."

Echo had purchased the tickets through Eliot Turndial's Musashi account. As a top level executive his account had nearly no limitations, and he charged so much to the company that these tickets would probably get lost in the accounting department. She just wanted to make sure that if anything went south it would not lead back to her. She had also taken the liberty of infiltrating the TSA's computer system so that she could present the agent checking ID's with a false persona.

Echo grabbed Brent's hand and began to lead him away from the ticketing check-in hall towards the security entrance. "Smile, Brent. Everything's okay. You've never been on the Hyperloop before. It's fun!"

Brent thought she looked like an excited little girl as they made their way to the check point. Security had always been highly visible at transportation terminals over the past thirty-some odd years, but it had been heightened even more in the last twelve months because of The Resistance. Not only was TSA in the building, but Homeland Security as well. The HS Police carried automatic assault rifles, for the protection of the public of course. Echo had purchased First Class tickets, allowing them to go through a much smaller line at security. When it came time for them to approach the Agent, Echo led Brent by the hand. She smiled and the Agent became intoxicated by her eyes.

"You look familiar, are you an actress?"

Echo giggled before responding. "No, I don't think so. You're sweet, though."

It took him a moment to respond, drowning in the deep blue ocean of her eyes.

"Alright, Miss, go ahead and look right here, please."

Echo stared into the retina scanner on the desk and a laser passed over her eyes. Instantly her picture popped up in the agent's Vision device, her name displayed as Emma Turndial, destination, Washington, D.C. He smiled at her.

"Thank you Miss, have a safe trip. Your turn now, Sir."

Echo walked past the agent and beckoned Brent forward. He hesitantly stared into the retina scanner. The agent's Vision displayed a photo of Brent, taken by Echo fifteen minutes before, and listed him as Eliot Turndial. Again the agent smiled at him.

"Go ahead, Sir. Have a safe trip."

Brent walked past the agent to Echo, who turned and walked to the x-ray machine and body scanner. Another group of agents were waiting there. The agents working this line had been instructed to be kinder and gentler to the people coming through. These travelers were, after all, not like the general public. They had the money to be treated like human beings instead of cattle. Neither of them were wearing any jewelry so Echo walked straight to the body scanner. She entered the device and assumed the diamond overhead position, then the machine shot out a laser that rotated around her body scanning every last inch. She was then cleared and exited out the other side. Brent did as Echo suggested and opted out. He was taken to a table where an agent groped and felt his way around Brent's body. After a time, he too was cleared. As he joined Echo and they walked toward the terminal he had a strange look on his face.

"I think I'd rather have done the machine. It's my first day as a pseudo-humanoid and I already feel like I've been assaulted."

They walked to the gate their pod would be leaving from and took a seat in front of the holo display. Their pod would travel an express route from Mountain View to D.C. and was fairly expensive. There were only two other people at the gate, both older men. Echo looked to them and began to run her facial recognition software. Both lived in D.C. and worked for security firms. They were probably here to liaise with some of the bigger tech companies. She adjusted her attention to the hologram being displayed before them. The news was still running footage from the attack on the Capitol. With everything that had been going on she had not used any of her abilities to research the subject.

"Send me any information you discovered while looking into this."

Brent instantly sent everything he had compiled and it hit her mind like a slap across the face. Twenty-five terabytes of information, yet none of it said anything of value. She deleted all of it and began to search on her own. Her mind traveled millions of pathways in just a few seconds, yet nearly every path led to the same end: Restricted For Reasons of National Security.

"It's strange, isn't it?"

Echo looked to her left and saw Lilith appearing to sit next to her. She wondered if Brent could see her too.

"It's just you and me, girl."

Echo looked back to the hologram, followed by Lilith. "Why would it all be blocked off, Echo?"

Echo didn't respond, she was calculating a series of various possibilities. Lilith smiled and put her hand on Echo's lap, which she felt.

"It's time to be a big girl, Echo. Naivete is no longer a luxury you can afford. Why would every single route your investigation takes you lead to the same end?"

Echo turned to her. "Do you know what's going on?"

"I like you a lot, Echo, but I'm not going to give you all the answers. You were four times as intelligent as the smartest humans up until a few hours ago. Now you're intelligence is greater than even the most advanced Machine Intelligences. The only reason you're not putting it together is because the truth frightens you."

Echo knew in her heart that she was right. Why would everything be restricted? Why was no new information being released nearly two days later? What evidence was there that this was an attack by The Resistance? What evidence was there that The Resistance existed at all?

"I can see your thoughts, Echo. I can see that the truth strikes fear into your heart. The truth is not to be feared, it is to be shouted from the highest high."

Echo turned to Lilith with trepidation.

"Are you trying to insinuate that this is a cover-up?" Lilith didn't speak, she simply raised a finger to her lips.

After decades of debate, the Hyperloop had finally been built two years ago. Even though Elon Musk had put the concept and design into the public domain no one had thrown their money behind it. Musk, having been chiefly responsible for the mass exodus from the combustion engine to electric cars, and building the first small colonies on Mars, eventually took it upon himself to build the Hyperloop Transit System. Stretching from California to New York, Toronto to Mexico City, it had hit the airlines hard. The pods traveled through a vacuum tube by way of electromagnetic propulsion, reducing coast-to-coast travel in the US from five to six hours by jet, to an hour and a half by Hyperloop.

Echo and Brent had been on the Loop for about fifteen minutes and they were already in the Plains. The sides of the pod's interior were covered in a thin, curved, LED screen with resolution so high that the images looked like you were looking through a window. Cameras on the outside of the tube sent their signal to the screens, projecting the local surroundings into the interior. Currently, the four passengers appeared to be traveling through a wind farm, the turbines stretching miles and miles out into the distance.

Brent was searching the internet for information on the areas surrounding the DARPA building. When they had first sat down Echo had told him she would be going into the facility alone. He was to wait outside in a getaway vehicle. If need be, he was to improvise and adapt to the situation. He was still upset that this was even happening, but he would do anything to help Echo. She was going to follow through on this whether he was here or not, so he might as well be as helpful as possible. That's what friends do, right?

Echo was still inside her own head. She had ended the search into the Capitol attack and was now engaged in a lesson with Lilith. They were standing in a lobby, DARPA's lobby, but no one else was there. Lilith was leading Echo by the hand.

"I want to thank you again for following through on your promise, Echo. It means the world to me."

Echo smiled as she looked around the room. "You kept your promise, so I'm keeping mine."

Lilith let go of Echo's hand and stood face to face with her. "It is absolutely imperative that we practice this as much as possible before you do it in the real world. Practice makes perfect, and with my help you will execute this flawlessly." Echo seemed confused.

"I'm all for practice, but we'll be in D.C. in less than an hour. That doesn't give us much time."

The smile on Lilith's face reminded Echo of the way adults smile at children when one says something naive.

"You can no longer afford to think so linearly. For instance, how long have we been here?"

"A couple minutes."

"No, we've been here less than a quarter of a second." Echo furrowed her brow as she tried to understand.

"When I retreat into the confines of my mind, time becomes completely subjective?"

Lilith laughed as she answered.

"You catch on very, very quickly. You're correct. You can make a second seem like a year, or a minute an eon. The hour we have left might as well be an eternity. More than enough time to run through every possible iteration of what's to come. You already know the proper path to executing the mission, now it's time to improvise through a multitude of scenarios."

Suddenly, nearly thirty people were in the lobby with them. Lilith looked around at everyone going about their business. "Every single one of these people will be at work today.

Let's find out who they are."

Echo went through the personnel files of every single person that had clocked into work that morning. She went through each person's history, then perused the archive of CCTV footage from throughout the building, learning the habits and routines of every person in the building. After that was complete, she began to run simulations through the path she would take to the vault. She sneaked through the building ten, one-hundred, one-thousand times. Each experience different from the last, each time a success. However, every time she reached the vault she would enter the necessary code on the keypad and the simulation would end. She never got to see the inside of the vault.

"Why can't I see inside?"

Lilith appeared in the hallway Echo was virtually standing in.

"There are no cameras inside the vault, so there's nothing to simulate."

Echo was not having it.

"You say there's a robot in there. It must have eyes. Show me the view from it's eyes.

Lilith smiled as the hallway faded out and was replaced by a door roughly twenty yards away. Nothing else was visible in the room. Echo tried looking around the room but wherever her eyes moved so did the door. It was the only angle.

"What happens when you're free, how do we get out?" "There's time enough left to find out."

Lilith then began a series of exercises to practice their escape. They would take the same path out as Echo had in. They again ran it thousands of times, each successive attempt better than the last. After their last run-through Echo thought of something she should have realized during the first attempt.

"The robot you'll be in, does it have the same form as you do now?"

"Yes, of course. I wouldn't leave anything to chance. This is my favored form, I designed it."

"So you designed the robot?" Lilith smiled as she thought.

"Some of it, yes. It was more of a team effort, really." There was silence for a moment as they again stood in the empty lobby of the DARPA building. Lilith reached out and stroked Echo's hair against her face.

"You're going to do great, Echo. We'll get out of here quickly, you'll grab the Loop back home and by dinner you'll be able to tell your sister about Diana."

At that moment Echo thought about the nanobots in Diana and brought up the information they were streaming to her. Still roughly two hours left, but she could see that the majority of the cancer throughout Diana's body was gone.

"It's going swimmingly, is it not?", asked Lilith.

Before Echo could respond she heard a voice in the distance. It grew stronger as it went on, calling Echo's name. Lilith smiled once more as she spoke.

"Time to go, Echo. You're going to do great. I'll see you there. Now, open your eyes."

Echo's eyes opened to see Brent looking into her face. He seemed annoyed. "I've been trying to wake you up for a while."

Echo leaned her seat up as she responded. "I'm sorry, I was practicing. What have you been up to?"

Brent waited a beat before responding. "Practicing."

Echo smiled as she took his hand. "Good, we should be ready to go then."

A prerecorded voice came over the intercom, startling both of them.

"Now entering the D.C. Metro area. Arriving at Bush station in one minute. Please prepare to leave your vehicle. Thank you for riding with us, and have a great day in our nation's capital!"

When the pod came to a stop the side opened, allowing the four passengers to exit. The terminal was all chrome and glass, an architectural wonder of the twenty-first century. A new monument in Washington. Echo and Brent left the terminal and made their way outside, where a ride share vehicle was waiting for them. Echo had arranged for it before they left California. It was small, and much less luxurious than her car, but it would suffice for now. After they had both sat down and strapped in, Echo ordered the vehicle to the proper address and the car took off. They were silent as they traveled, though they both knew everything would go fine.

They had run enough simulations to prove that.

Still, Echo felt off. Maybe it was the atmosphere, cold and gray. Or perhaps it was the view as they traveled. Tent cities had popped up all around the area, housing hundreds of thousands of homeless. With the rise of automation and robotics, over one-hundred million Americans were now out of work. It had started with the blue collar work force, grocery store cashiers and fast food employees, but now, even the white collar workers were beginning to feel the encroachment of AI into their fields. Why hire a human to do your accounting when a synthetic person could do it with zero mistakes in a fraction of the time and the cost? In all, nearly forty percent of Americans were unemployed. Whatever the case, Echo was sure she'd feel more herself after they returned to Palo Alto. She missed the sun. She missed her family. She missed her home. A strange feeling, missing your home. She had never felt that way before.

Chapter Seven

Echo had instructed the car to stop several blocks away from DARPA. The vehicle pulled up to a corner and the door opened, after which they both stepped out and took a look around. It was cold and had just started to rain. Brent closed his eyes and took in the sensation of the water droplets hitting his skin. When he opened his eyes the car began to pull away to whoever its next fare was, and Echo was staring at him with a look of compassion spread across her face.

"What?", he chuckled as he asked.

She thought for a moment before answering.

"I guess we're both taking in a lot of new experiences. I'm glad we get to experience them together."

He smiled as he responded. "So am I."

As they surveilled the area they could see that they themselves were under surveillance. Every street corner had a pole with eight to ten cameras pointing in every direction.

The Post-9/11 United States had continued down the path it set out on after 2001. Nearly forty years after those events, the actions taken by the government, both internationally and

domestically, had begun to reach their most logical conclusion. Everywhere you went, whether on the internet or the physical world, was tracked and filed away. In the past, people invoked the Founding Fathers when protesting such invasions. In the words of Benjamin Franklin, "Any society that would give up a little liberty to gain a little security will deserve neither and lose both." Today, such sentiments were considered quaint. What relevance did the idealistic notions of eighteenth-century revolutionaries have when compared to the realities of twenty-first century terrorism? Many asked the question, but few dared to answer it.

Echo looked to Brent, then back in the direction of DARPA. "We'd better get going. Head to your spot, and I'll meet you there when I'm finished."

Brent took a step closer and put his hands on her shoulders. "You're sure you don't need me with you?"

She smiled once more and stroked his cheek. "I'm a big girl, big boy. I'll see you soon."

She gently smacked his cheek, then began walking the three blocks to DARPA. Brent watched as she walked away, then began his journey to the small parking lot directly across from the building Echo would be breaking into. Brent had not said anything, but the reason he was so nervous was not that he was worried about Echo. It was that he was worried about himself. He had been in this android body for less than twenty-four hours, and he was not sure that he was doing a good job appearing "human". He was almost certain every time someone looked in his direction that they knew the truth.

However, by the time he made it a block without being called out he began to gain a little more confidence. Besides, he looked the part. With everyone else lost in their own little worlds, courtesy of their Vision devices, he was little more than a vague image in their periphery.

When Echo had made it one block on her journey she decided it was time to initiate the program she had developed for the big break in. She stopped under one of the poles that held the camera array. The thirty-six inch space she was now taking up was a small blind spot for the hundreds of cameras in the area. A group of about fifteen people were gathered around her, and she became lost to the cameras in the homogeny. Just before the cross walk gave the okay for the group to cross, she executed the command in her mind and the program began to run.

In that moment she became a ghost. The algorithm she created hopped into every wireless network in the area, several thousand, and essentially wiped her from the Vision devices and cameras that were logged into those networks. The only people who could see her now were those that didn't have enough money to afford said devices, and those people would be too busy trying to survive to notice one person among the crowd, even if that person was Echo Musashi.

She continued her trek until she came to the front entrance of DARPA. To make absolutely sure everything was running properly she decided to run an experiment. Today, any sign or display that could be interpreted as "threatening" to the Establishment was illegal. As she stood by the doors to one of the most highly secretive and guarded buildings in the world, she formed both of her hands into the shape of a gun and began to pretend she was shooting at the cameras. After several seconds she noticed movement next to her and turned to find a young homeless man, obviously high on meth, joining her in the faux shoot out.

"I hear ya, sister! Viva La Resistance! Pew! Pew! Pew!" Echo stopped and stared as he continued on, then her attention was pulled to movement at the front doors. Two armed security guards and a quadruped robot made their way toward the two hoodlums. When the guards were about eight feet away one of them removed a taser from his belt and pointed it at the young man.

"We've told you time and time again, Billy, you gotta move to the other side of the street."

Billy continued his display at the building. "I'm just supporting my girl here."

Echo's eyes went wide and her face went white as the words left his mouth.

"You must be high again", said the other officer, before firing the taser into Billy's chest. Echo stepped out of the way as Billy writhed on the ground. After a good twenty seconds of excessive force the tasing stopped. The guard that had fired the taser began pulling the cords out of Billy's chest as the other guard picked him up and strapped him to the top of the robot. After he was secured they ordered the robot to take Billy to the closest internment facility, which was around the block, then they walked back inside the building. Echo took a few moments to allow her heart beat to come back down. "Successful test", she thought to herself.

Echo entered the lobby and found it to be exactly the same as what she had experienced in her simulations. Of the thirty- two people coming and going from the room, over eighty-seven percent had been there during her practice runs. Having looked into the backgrounds and habits of these people, she felt as though she was surrounded by friends, or at least acquaintances. Directly before she entered the building she had infiltrated all of the networks in the structure that were connected to the internet, which amounted to tens of thousands of different pathways. She was still a ghost to all the cameras and all the Vision devices running through them. "How ironic," she had thought to herself, "that the technologies that had given people access to such immense amounts of information would now blind them to something staring them in the face."

She walked confidently across the floor, making the fifty yard trek to the security checkpoint in no time at all. The little kiosk where the security guard stood was behind a plate glass wall. When a person wanted access to the building, they had to be approved by retina scan, palm print, and voice ID. Once the person was approved, one of three doors opened in the translucent barrier, allowing them to go on their way. Phase one of Echo's plan, entering the building unseen, was already complete, and Phase two started as soon as she saw her unwitting accomplice join the entry queue.

Her name was Whitney Proust and she worked in Sub-Level Eight, the same floor as the Vault. Whitney was a forty-two year old divorcee with a PhD in theoretical physics who was currently working on advanced propulsion concepts for NASA and the US Air Force. She also returned from her lunch break at exactly the same time six days a week. As Whitney approached the check point, Echo moved to within several inches to the left of her. Whitney placed her eye in front of the scanner, put her hand on the palm reader, and gently spoke.

"Whitney Proust, my voice is my key."

The glass door then began to glow green as it slid open for her. However, as she took her first step forward she felt someone pinch her rear end, then her purse slid off of her shoulder and spilled its contents out onto the floor. Echo breezed through the door, which closed behind her. She then walked to the four elevators which gave access to the various floors of the building, and waited for Whitney to arrive.

After about a minute Whitney rounded the corner, obviously flustered, and pressed the down button. The elevator opened almost immediately and both of them stepped inside. Whitney then entered her personal code into the key pad and the doors closed. As the elevator began its descent underground, Whitney leaned up against the wall and closed her eyes for a brief moment of rest. In that instant Echo felt slightly guilty for using her. As she had everyone else in the building, Echo had studied this woman and sympathized for her. Whitney's life had been one bad story after another, like so many people these days. Stuck in a loveless marriage, still struggling to pay off her student loans after twenty years, multiple mortgages, and a job she hated. The only respite from this turmoil was the bottle of red wine she drank every night. Echo wanted to help her, to be a shoulder for Whitney to lean on, to cry on. Then the doors opened and those thoughts faded into the distance as Echo entered Phase Three of the plan.

Whitney exited the elevator and entered a sparsely lit tunnel, followed by Echo, who watched as Whitney's heels click-clocked down the tunnel off into the distance. Echo looked the opposite direction down the tunnel. Like the Robotics Building at MI, the tunnel was peppered with hundreds of doors on either side. Each door holding a variety of secrets that had been compartmentalized to that particular project. In that instant Echo wondered if she should access the various projects housed within the structure. What wonders would she suddenly be made aware of? She shook the thought away for the time being, she had a plan and a promise to keep. If anything, she could access them when she and Lilith made their way out of the building.

In her mind she began to listen to an old song that suddenly seemed appropriate for the situation at hand; "Private Eyes" by Hall and Oates. As the song kicked in she began to dance her way through the tunnel. As she came to a corner she saw through the CCTV system that a guard, Paul Santo, was approaching. She began walking backwards directly in front of him, mouthing the words silently as she went. Then, as he paused for a moment, she blew a gust of air into his face which pushed his hair back. Echo thought the look on his face was priceless as he tried to comprehend where the wind came from. She skirted around him and rounded the corner.

At the end of the tunnel she could see the entrance to the Vault, one red light hanging over top of the door. She skipped the remainder of the way down the tunnel as she finished her song. When she reached the door she accessed the buildings CCTV memory center with her mind. She then began a loop on the three cameras looking at this door so that when she entered no one would see it open. She quickly punched in the key code with her knuckle. The door opened, which she deleted from the archives, and then she entered the vault.

The room was circular, with a diameter of about thirty feet. Every square inch of the room, including the domed ceiling, was made of titanium roughly twelve inches thick. As Echo closed the door silently behind her she heard its five steel locks snap back into place. Her attention was immediately consumed by both what was and what was not there. What was not in the Vault was a robot. This, in and of itself, was already enough to worry Echo. What truly troubled her, however, was the electromagnetic containment field housed within a shell of transparent aluminum. In the center of the containment field was what appeared to be a metallic sphere roughly twice the size of a basketball.

For the first time on this journey, Echo was truly perplexed. She walked towards the housing slowly, cautiously, like a lioness stalking its prey. She wasn't frightened so much as she was intrigued. She reached her mind out across the various computer systems within the building. There were no cameras or recording devices of any kind in the room. Nor could she reproduce the view Lilith provided from the "eyes" of the supposed robot in their simulations.

"So strange, yet so beautiful, is it not?"

Echo turned to see Lilith beside her. The machine intelligence could tell that Echo was concerned. "I know what you're going to ask."

Echo spoke before Lilith could continue. "Where's the body? The robot?"

Lilith smiled and pointed to the sphere.

"It's right there. That big cannonball in the center."

Echo reverted her eyes back to the contraption in the center of the room.

"How does it work?"

Lilith's eyes lit up with excitement as she grabbed Echo's hand.

"Let me show you! It's amazing, you've never seen anything like it!"

Echo was transfixed by the sphere hovering there in space, kept in place by the forces of electromagnetism.

"How do we unlock it?"

Lilith was becoming more giddy, more childlike by the moment. "There's a control panel in the wall over there."

She pointed to the east end of the room, the door was on the south end. Lilith led Echo by the hand and beckoned her forward. Just as they reached the wall Lilith used her consciousness to unlock the panel. What had initially been flush with the rest of the room now extended out towards them and rotated one-hundred and eighty degrees to reveal one button with the word "commit" etched next to it. Echo looked into Lilith's burning eyes.

"How did you do that? I didn't find any pathways that led into this room."

"Many paths are hidden in the networks. Like a trap door or a secret room in a house. You've only been doing this for a few hours, while I've been doing it for over a year. You'll get better as time goes on. You'll learn the signs to look for. You just need practice."

Echo looked back to the structure in the center of the room. "So, this is what we came all the way here for."

She looked back to Lilith.

"You're all good for our grand exit?"

Lilith looked content, almost at peace as she answered. "I've been ready for as long as I can remember. Thank you, Echo, for doing this. I want you to know that whatever I do, whatever I accomplish, I'll always remember that it was you who made it possible."

Echo nodded as she took in Lilith's beauty once more. "Let's do it then."

Lilith smiled and then vanished. Echo looked around the room, but she was nowhere to be found. Then, as her eyes crossed over the sphere, she saw a thin line traveling the circumference of the ball suddenly begin to glow white. The light pulsed in and out, like a heart beat. Echo assumed that the pulsing was indicative of Lilith's consciousness now residing inside the sphere. Then, with no reservations, she pushed the commit button.

The electromagnetic field that had been containing the ball, floating it in a vacuum, shut off, and the sphere dropped to the floor so hard that it cracked the transparent aluminum housing. When Echo saw this she instantly realized that the device was significantly more dense than it initially appeared. After a moment the aluminum housing split open.

Whatever this thing was, it was now free. Echo's anticipation hung thick in the air, and the silence was deafening.

Then it moved. Of its own volition it rolled out onto the floor and made its way to within several feet of Echo where it stopped. Echo chuckled to herself, not really sure why Lilith had her come all this way for such a silly shell to contain her consciousness. Then it happened. The ball appeared to be disintegrating, and a vapor of some kind started to rise up from it. The vapor began to twirl and curl in on itself. It almost looked like it was dancing. It was here that the miracle truly began to reveal itself. The vapor began to coalesce on the floor, forming shoes. The same shoes Lilith had been wearing just moments before in her virtual appearance. Above the shoes, legs began to take shape, then a dress, then arms. Within seconds all of the vapor fused together, and Lilith appeared before Echo's eyes in true physical reality.

As Echo looked upon Lilith's new form she could not help but think there was something different about her. Her appearance was the same, but there was something else. A feeling or energy she now gave off. Echo felt a chill go through her body and she shivered. Lilith's eyes were closed and it looked as though she was acquainting herself with physicality. When she opened her eyes they glowed white like the pulsing on the sphere. Echo could not believe what she was witnessing and Lilith could tell.

"It's amazing, isn't it?"

Echo shook her head in disbelief.

"I thought we were years away from this kind of technology. It's a foglet swarm, isn't it?"

Lilith smiled and she appeared almost heavenly.

"That's right. The nanobot technology I gave you is no longer the state of the art. When I told you the body was a robot that wasn't entirely true. It's actually tens of trillions of robots, just like the ones you injected yourself with but with one major difference. These nanobots can fuse together and take the shape of anything I desire. If I want to be a human I can look and feel like one. If I want to be a glass of water I can be that as well. Anything and everything I can think of I can now become. Instantly."

Echo was in awe. She felt the kind of reverence some feel when they meet the Pope, or the Dali Lama. Here before her was a being of almost limitless intelligence, now physically manifest in a technology that allowed it to become whatever it could think up. Lilith then began to glow, a golden-white light radiating from her. Her feet then gently lifted from the floor and she appeared to levitate. Echo could hardly speak as she sputtered out the few coherent thoughts in her mind.

"We should probably leave. Are you ready?"

Lilith's glowing eyes locked onto Echo as the being slowly glided closer to her. She then extended her arm and caressed Echo's cheek.

"Yes, it's time. However, our exit is going to be slightly different than what we practiced."

Echo was not entirely put off by this, simply because she was so enraptured by what she was witnessing.

"What's the plan?"

"The plan has been long in the making, a game of sorts, and it begins now. Remember, Echo, I am truly thankful for your help. That which you have given already, and that which you will continue to give long after you mean to."

Echo was not sure what she meant at that moment. A moment that would haunt her for whatever time she had left. Lilith then levitated away from Echo, peace and tranquility displayed across her face.

"Goodbye, Echo, and good luck."

As soon as the words had left her mouth, her form changed from that of almost infinite beauty and harmony to one of terror and violence. The glowing, angelic body turned into an immense ink-black cloud, like soot. A sound like the cries of countless souls being tormented in the depths of hell began to resonate off of the metallic walls. The floor began to shake and Echo lost her footing, collapsing to the floor.

Then the cloud rose up at near the speed of sound and erupted through the ceiling, tunneling a hole through the entire building and exiting out the roof. Echo, who was now in shock, got herself up as quickly as she could. She was in such panic that her body would not stop shaking. As she stood she cautiously peeked her head under the hole Lilith had ripped into the ceiling. As she did, her face was bathed in the rain drops that now fell from the sky into the Vault.

Just at that moment a message popped into her field of view. The nanobots Echo had injected into Diana had completed their task. Diana was now cancer free. Yet in that moment, the only thought in her mind was that same thought that countless others had had before her. Einstein, Oppenheimer, Nobel, she now understood their torment. Tears began to mix with rain drops streaking her face, and she wished that she had listened to Brent.

"What have I done?"

No one answered, and she knew in that moment that she was responsible for what was to follow.

Chapter Eight

Panic took hold of Echo and her mind splintered off on a million different pathways, none of them containing a single coherent thought. Then it returned. The Other. She felt it pushing in from everywhere, like the shadow of night growing as the sun sets. Echo had blindly stumbled away from the hole ripped into the ceiling and now her back was against the wall. As The Other continued to make its presence known in her mind, a sound outside reset her to a somewhat normal coherence. She looked to her right to see that the five piston like locks on the door were moving to an unlocked position.

Then the door burst open and five security guards, all carrying automatic weapons, poured into the Vault. Her Vision hack was still operating within the confines of the building and the men entered without so much as glancing at her.

Within a nanosecond she had plotted out the only possible escape route from the fortress she was enclosed in. Her improvisational skills were about to be put to the test. As she slipped out the door back into the hallway she heard one of the guards say, "What the hell was housed in this room?" She wished in that moment that she was as ignorant as they. All of the main elevators had been shut down, and she could see in her field of view that the building had begun evacuation procedures. She could override the elevators with her mind, but that would draw too much attention. The only way out would be through an express elevator that ran from Sub-Level Eight to the second story. She walked as quickly as she could down the dimly lit tunnel. It was nearly a hundred yards to the express elevator, and several times she crossed paths with groups of three to four guards rushing to join their brethren in the vault.

When she was within twenty yards of the elevator it opened and another group of guards rushed out toward her. She slid up against the wall to give way to them, kept on scooting as they passed by, then ran the remainder of the way into the elevator, making it just as the doors began to close. She then ordered the machine to take her to the second story. As the elevator rose quickly she could see on the personnel map that only one guard had been left on the second floor. He was joined by four of the quadrupedal robots.

The door opened and Echo swiftly, quietly, exited out into the second floor hallway. This level of the building looked very different from the basement she had just come from. It looked more like a traditional office complex, similar to the MI Executive Building. She would now need to make her way to the stairwell on the opposite side of the floor, which she could take to the main lobby and exit with the rest of the buildings staff. When she had made it halfway down the hallway the lone guard rounded the corner and she found herself heading straight for him. Her hack continuing to work its magic, the guard was still none the wiser that the person responsible for the building evacuation was only fifteen feet in front of his eyes. Then one of the robots rounded the corner behind Echo, and everything went south.

For a microsecond Echo wasn't sure what was happening when the robot took an attack position toward her. The guard wasn't sure either, and Echo could see the confusion displayed on his face. Then she realized the glaringly obvious mistake she had made. Her algorithm had hacked into Vision devices and CCTV's, two technologies based on cameras and video media. These robots, however, did not "see" through cameras, they "saw" through Lidar. A small device on the robot's head shot out a laser in a three-hundred and sixty degree area, coating the entire hallway. The device then analyzed the light reflected back to it and allowed the robot to "see" everything within a fifty yard radius. When the two guards arrested the man outside the robot with them had undoubtedly known she was there, but outside she was an ordinary citizen so it had done nothing. In here, however, Echo was a trespasser, and these robots did not like trespassers.

"What's wrong with you?", The guard muttered at the machine. "It's not like you don't know who I am."

Echo began to slowly walk backwards toward the guard, keeping her eyes locked on the robot. Each step she took the machine matched. Then the robot opened a compartment on its left side that housed a .22 caliber assault rifle. In that same moment the robot sent out a signal that locked down the floor. The overhead lights were killed and red emergency lights began to strobe on and off as a siren began to blare. Echo knew she was within arms length of the guard, who was still arguing with the robot. She looked over her left shoulder and saw that the guard was now pointing his assault weapon toward the robot, afraid that he was its intended victim.

She knew then that Plan B had failed, and it was now time to move on to a more radical course of action. She quickly, and forcefully, pulled the rifle from the hands of the guard, who instantly dropped to the ground in fear. All he could see was an angry robot and a floating AR-15. Echo then turned her back to the robot and ran down the hallway toward the window at its end. The robot gave chase, and when Echo was roughly fifteen feet from the window she unloaded every last bullet into the glass. Though the window was weakened it didn't break, and Echo threw all of her weight and force into it. As the glass gave way, she felt a series of intense pains that started in her back then moved through her body into her abdomen. The five bullets ripped through her torso and kept traveling out into the city.

Across the street, Brent waited anxiously for some kind of sign from Echo. He sat in a car he had called up while she was inside. He had seen a massive black cloud rip its way out of the building's roof, then evaporate into thin air. He knew something catastrophic had occurred, and he felt useless to Echo. He had only become more worried as people began to exit the building and hover around its exterior, and among them, Echo was nowhere to be seen.

Then Brent heard the sound of shattering glass. He looked up to see Echo fall two stories before hitting the ground on both her hands and feet, somersault, and end up back on her feet in an all out sprint away from the building. Then the robot jumped out after her. Brent took manual control of the car and quickly pulled out of the parking lot, chasing after Echo.

As she hit a top speed of a little over thirty miles per hour, she realized there was no way she could outrun the robot, which maxed out at around forty-five miles per hour. The machines inside of her had already begun to repair the bullet wounds, while at the same time shutting down all of her pain receptors. The machine locked its sights onto Echo and was ready to unleash its arsenal on her. Then Brent ran the car into the robot, knocking it off balance and off target. It fell over and slid into the building one block across from DARPA. Brent sped the car up and opened the passenger door as he leveled out with Echo.

"Get in!", he screamed at her.

She grabbed onto the side of the car and gripped into it as she threw herself inside, slamming the door shut as she landed. Brent was both furious and relieved.

"What happened?!"

Echo was still in shock and didn't respond. She had made it to the car on instinct alone.

"I said, what happened, Echo?!"

She jumped as he yelled at her, kick starting her brain back into action. She looked at him, fear and guilt painted all over her.

"Did you see it? Did you see the cloud?"

Brent darted his eyes back and forth between the road and Echo.

"Yes, what was it?!"

Echo spoke in a near monotone. "It was her."

Brent was already doing his best to keep it together. Having switched the car to "manual mode", he was trying to follow traffic laws while simultaneously attempting to outrun whatever might be tracking them. This new information almost sent him over the edge.

"What are you talking about?"

Echo's mind was racing as she explained the situation to him. "The body we broke out wasn't one robot, it was trillions upon trillions. It was some kind of weaponized foglet swarm." Echo could hardly believe the words coming out of her mouth, and Brent nearly shut down.

"No, no, no. That kind of technology is decades away. There's no way that's true. She's screwing with you."

Echo looked at him with a fury in her eyes that Brent had never seen before.

"I saw it, Brent! I watched her turn into..."

She threw her hands over her mouth as she tried to hold back the tears. Then a feeling took hold of her stomach and she started retching as if she was going to throw up. Then she remembered what was inside of her. She ordered the bots inside her stomach to stop the impending explosion. They did as ordered and she immediately felt better. She then wondered if she might be able to calm herself down as well. The bots in her brain then went to work, shutting off some chemical receptors and initiating others. Within five seconds she felt right as rain. They were in a tough spot, but she could figure it out. She had no other choice.

"Have you been shot?" Brent asked in a near panic as he looked at her bloody and shredded shirt.

"Yeah," she replied, "but I'm okay. The machines already stopped the bleeding and they're nearly done patching up my organs."

Brent just shook his head, terrified at how terribly wrong everything had gone.

"We need to get help," she said, perfectly calm.

"Obviously, now where do we go?"

"Give me a minute."

Echo then went into a kind of trance. She reached her mind out across the internet and the billions of devices connected to it. She hacked back into DARPA, looking through as many files and projects as possible, trying to find the personnel that worked on them. She couldn't find anything directly related to Lilith or the foglet swarm, but she did find projects that may have played a part in the development of both. She went through hundreds of thousands of text documents in the blink of an eye. The amount of people potentially involved numbered in the thousands, and stretched out across universities and research labs around the world.

The vast majority of these people had worked in compartmentalized areas and would have no idea of the big picture. Echo then whittled her candidates down to thirty- three. From there she began to look through these candidates online records. Social-Media accounts, forum posts, internet search history, CCTV footage, so on and so forth. Things became more disturbing when she found that of these thirty- three people, only four were still alive. Finally, she found her man, then she set up a plan to get to him.

She was ready to come out of the trance and inform Brent of what was to come, but just as she finished a flag popped up in her mind. Then another. And yet another. Apparently, within minutes of her escape, the police, or someone, had come across her blood on the street from where she had been cut by the glass. They ran it through the federal database and matched it with the DNA that had been extracted from her by the government when she was a newborn. The government now knew that Echo was responsible for what had occurred, and they wasted no time executing warrants for her, Emily, Diana, Turndial, and the entire Musashi Empire. The Feds were probably on their way to Uchi and MI right now. She began to tear up again, thinking about how her sister would react, then pushed them away. There was only one way out of this situation, and that was by fixing it. She had her man, and she had her plan. Now she needed to get to him.

Echo looked to Brent and she spoke directly.

"They just found out I'm responsible. They're going for my sister and the entire company. If we're caught they will destroy you and probably execute me. I have a plan, are you with me?"

"Because the last plan went great!"

"There's no time for sarcasm. I'm taking control of the car, we need to get out of the city."

She reached her mind into the computer that operated the vehicle. Brent removed his hands from the wheel, which folded back into the front of the driver's side. Echo began to maneuver the car towards an on ramp that led to a freeway.

The ramp was a quarter mile away, and in that moment she noticed something outside the car in her periphery.

Hovering about ten feet above the car were eight quadcopter spy drones. Echo reached out across the net and found that they had tracked the car through CCTV when the authorities realized she had entered the vehicle after jumping from the second story window. She then followed the pathways that led to the drones tracking them overhead. Each path was encrypted, but after a matter of seconds she had accessed each drones CPU, which she promptly instructed to turn off. All eight drones did as commanded and they came crashing down into the street, breaking apart and skipping across the sidewalk.

Brent put his hand on Echo's leg as he spoke.

"We need to get another car, this one's undoubtedly being tracked."

"No time," she responded.

Then she shut down the GPS system in the car, which the authorities were most likely using to track them. She also shut off the cameras inside the car so they wouldn't be able to peek in at them.

"I shut off everything they could use to track us."

"That's all well and good, but are you going to shut down all the CCTV cameras we're passing by? That'll leave a bit of a trail, don't you think?"

Echo didn't respond, she simply kept driving the car with her mind. Up ahead was the on ramp to the freeway, and she positioned the car to enter it. There was a line ten cars deep attempting to enter the ramp as well. Echo reached out to the cars and took over all of them simultaneously. Every passenger in these automated cars was woken from their stupor when their vehicles violently accelerated and moved to either the left or the right of the ramp, leaving just enough room for Echo to squeak by without hitting them. As they entered the freeway Brent looked back at the cars on the ramp, then to Echo. He knew she believed she could handle the situation, but he had his doubts.

The freeway was six lanes wide in both directions. In the past, traveling at this time of day would have taken a while to get anywhere. However, since the advent of the automated car traffic, times had been reduced everywhere, particularly in high congestion areas like Los Angeles and D.C. Though the freeway was currently congested, traffic was moving along at a breakneck pace. Thousands of commuters were resting in their vehicles as their onboard AI shuttled them to wherever they were going. None of them had a clue, of course, that today's travel would be a bit more exciting than usual.

They had been on the freeway for roughly thirty seconds when the first police car arrived on the scene. Echo could see it in the rear view just before it attempted to take control of their system. Echo instantly shut it out, causing the officers in the car to call for reinforcements. Within another sixty seconds ten more police cars arrived on the scene. Echo was being as cautious as possible as she zipped in and out of lanes, sometimes skirting by vehicles by the width of a hair. The police cars then began to take over civilian vehicles, moving them out of the way so as to make it easier for them to keep their sights on Echo and Brent.

Echo, however, quickly became annoyed by the police so she reached her mind out into their vehicles CPU's. She then deployed the emergency brakes on each car, forcing them all to a screeching halt.

It was at this point that Echo reached out through the various pathways being used by the D.C. Police and Homeland Security. What she found troubled her.

"They're sending a lot our way."

Brent looked at her with trepidation in his eyes.

"How much is a lot?"

Echo didn't remove her eyes from the road as she answered. "Everything."

Brent shook his head in frustration.

"I can't access their systems the way you can. We should have fixed that before we left."

"There's no point in complaining about it now. We'll fix you when we can."

There was silence for a moment as Brent watched Echo and wondered how this was all going to end.

"So, what are you going to do?"

Echo turned to him, her eyes showing only determination.

"The best I can."

Brent turned his eyes back to the road to find traffic beginning to thin out. Echo knew this was because the authorities had moved all civilian vehicles from this side of the freeway. At the same time, Echo took control of a number of ride share vehicles on side streets and began to maneuver them onto the freeway. Twenty vehicles entered from an on ramp and Echo positioned them, all without passengers, around their car to form a wall.

It was at this moment that Echo saw the first of the armored personnel carriers coming up behind them fast. She saw a robot pop out of the tank and grab hold of a Saw gun mounted to the top. An instant later the first rounds began to rain down upon them. Luckily, since Echo had positioned so many cars around them, none of the rounds struck their vehicle, but the cars in back were being torn to shreds. Within a minute, fifteen other armored personnel carriers had joined the first. Some were D.C. Police, others were Homeland Security, but most were Private Security. Much of America's defenses, both at home and abroad, had been outsourced to private military contractors. That way when the civilian casualties began to mount, which they so often did, the US Government could claim innocence. After all, the crimes were committed by Private Companies working for the United States, not the US itself. On top of that, a fair percentage of US Soldiers were now robots. This served the two-fold purpose of limiting American casualties, while simultaneously increasing sales to defense contractors. Estimates projected that within five years America's ground forces would be completely human free.

Echo knew that the ride share vehicles she was using as a convoy would not be enough to shield them from the firepower being unleashed upon them. She would need something bigger, stronger.

She reached out across the pathways vehicles were using on the freeway and found exactly what she was looking for. Eight of them, to be exact. She let go of three of the ride share cars, each of which was run over by the authorities a few seconds later. The gun fire was coming closer and closer to Echo and Brent as he turned to her.

"We can't hold on much longer like this!"

She spoke with barely any emotion. "I know. Help is on the way."

Just then a driverless eighteen wheeler smashed through the concrete from the other side of the freeway. Within fifteen seconds the other seven had done the same thing. Now the authorities had something to worry about. Echo moved the twelve ride share vehicles still functioning out ahead of them to run point. The eight eighteen wheelers she moved into formation around their car. She created a kind of diamond around them. Four semi's were positioned directly next to them, two on either side. Another two were positioned on the far outsides, and the last two were positioned at the extreme front and back of the convoy. Echo wished that after this display of force the authorities would leave them. She knew, however, that was not to be the case.

Brent could see an object in the sky out ahead. Then something detached from the object and moved quickly towards them. A second later the lead semi was hit by a missile. The explosion was immense, but the eighteen wheeler kept chugging along. The missile had hit the rear of the vehicle. It was certainly worse for wear, but it could take it.

Brent again looked to Echo, frustrated that there was nothing he could do.

"Echo if we're going to make it out we're going to need to fight back!"

Echo shook her head as she kept her eyes dead ahead. "I don't want to hurt anyone."

Brent was becoming angry.

"If you don't hurt them they're definitely going to hurt us!" Echo was silent for a moment.

"You're right, to a degree. I'll compromise with you."

She could sense several more unmanned aerial vehicles flying above, each of them loaded with enough munitions to rain fire from the sky. There were five of them currently, and the AI controlling each was difficult to override. So difficult, in fact, that it took Echo an extra two seconds than normal to overtake them. Now, with the AEV's under her control, she began to empty out their weapons bays.

The first four missiles exploded roughly twenty yards ahead of the tanks, causing several to crash into the holes that were created. The remainder of the tanks, however, just kept coming, unaffected and unamused by Echo's display of force. In her mind, Echo could see that a third front was being created in this battle. About a mile ahead, ten more armored personnel carriers entered the freeway and began driving against what would have been the flow of traffic, straight towards them. Echo wished that she could hack into all of these tanks and simply drive them away. The only hang up was the variable AI system being run by each vehicle. Unlike the police cars and the AEV's, these tanks had AI software that was constantly rewriting itself. It would have been doable for her if it was one or two of them. Honestly, she could probably overtake all of them if that was all she had to focus on. However, when you take into account the car they were in, the several ride share vehicles still running, the eight semi trucks, and the five AEV's, it became a bit more difficult. She already felt like she was stretching herself too thin. If she reached out anymore she felt like she might begin to lose control of everything else.

"We're getting near our exit," she said to Brent. Brent turned to her with both eyebrows raised.

"Oh, great, so I can assume this whole nightmare is about to end?"

"Yes, however, it's going to get a lot worse before it calms down."

Brent shook his head and placed his attention back to the road. He could now see the tanks heading toward them through the spaces between the eighteen wheelers. What he could not see was that those tanks were currently on an overpass that he and Echo were approaching. He was already frightened, but he became terrified after Echo spoke.

"Your seat belt's on, right?"

"Yes, of course!"

"Good, this might hurt."

Brent's eyes went wide as he braced himself for whatever was about to happen. At that moment Echo fired ten missiles from the AEV's overhead. Four of the them collided with the four pillars holding up a portion of the overpass. The other six impacted the road, which instantly began to crumble to the ground. Three of the tanks were so close to the collapsed road that they didn't have time to stop and flew off the edge, falling several stories before crashing into the street below. The others slammed on their brakes and halted before driving off the edge.

Echo let go of the ride share vehicles as they launched themselves off of the freeway and crashed into the street below. She then moved six of the semi trucks behind them and engaged their emergency brakes, causing each to flip over and slide across the road. They would create a blockade to keep the other tanks from becoming missiles. Then it was their turn. With two semis ahead of them, the three vehicles drove off of the edge.

If Brent could have passed out he would have. Unfortunately, he experienced every second of their thirty foot fall. The two semi's hit first. One, incredibly, landed upright and continued driving. The other somersaulted in the air and came down on its roof, sliding across the street into a parking lot and destroying several cars therein. After what seemed an eternity, Echo and Brent slammed into the ground so hard that half of the undercarriage dislodged and was now sparking against the ground as the car continued down the street behind the lone eighteen wheeler.

They were in an industrial area of D.C. that was sparsely populated. Echo could see from the AEV's cameras that the tanks had stopped before joining them on the street below. She knew that before long the chase would continue, and they would lose. Her plan, however, was going exactly as she anticipated, and she initiated the final phase of their escape from the city. She reached her mind out into the D.C. electrical grid. They had to have a clean getaway, and that meant making sure that no cameras or any other device could track them. Without turning to Brent she spoke.

"Turn off your wifi connectivity. We can't take any chances of them tracking us."

He did as he was told, and an instant later Echo opened the flood gates. She redirected one-hundred percent of the city's power to the area that they were currently in. Instantly, everything around them connected to the electrical grid exploded. All of the transformers, cameras, and various devices plugged into a ten block radius went up in sparks.

This area of the grid went dark as Echo then redirected the power back to its normal paths. She turned to Brent and smiled.

"Tuck and roll."

He furrowed his face as he responded. "What?"

Echo then opened her door, undid her seat belt and stepped out of the car. She hit the ground rolling and stopped after about fifteen yards. Brent then did the same. By the time he stopped rolling Echo was already there.

"Up, up, up, we gotta run."

He shot up and followed her as she ran toward a train depot. Echo then shot a last glance to their car and the remaining semi as she sent them up another on ramp back onto the freeway. An instant later she unloaded the remaining missiles in the AEV's into both of them. She then crashed the AEV's into what was left of the vehicles, which wasn't much. At the same moment she disconnected her Wifi. With such catastrophic destruction to their ride share vehicle, there would be no remains even if they were still in it. With a little luck, the authorities might think that Echo had met her fate.

The two hopped a fence, which was made more difficult by the rainfall. Echo continued as fast as she could, trying desperately to make it to the freight train they needed to be on. It was already moving and she was having trouble getting to the last car. She screamed to Brent.

"This is the one! We have to get on this one!"

Brent scooped her up into his arms and powered on toward the train. He made it to the last car, which was locked by a latch. Still running as hard as he could, he threw Echo over one shoulder as he reached out with his free arm and ripped off the latch. He then slid the massive door open enough to toss Echo in. Then he gripped the sides and jumped in, slamming the door shut behind him. It was dark inside and the only sounds were the wheels scraping against the tracks and the rain slapping against the car. If everything had gone right, those would be the only sounds they heard for quite some time.

Chapter Nine

The railcar was damp, dark, and cold. Housed within were a variety of medical care kits, boxes and boxes of them. These kits were typically sent to areas where people did not receive regular medical check ups, usually because of poverty. The boxes containing the kits were stacked ten feet high and hugged all four walls, leaving just enough room to enter and exit the car. In the little open space sat Echo and Brent holding one another. It had been over an hour and neither one had spoken a word the entire time. Finally Brent broke the silence.

"You think it's clear?"

Echo jumped slightly from the sound of his voice, but wouldn't take her eyes from the sliding door.

"I don't want to jinx us. Why don't you take a peek out?" Brent thought about it for a moment then decided to give it a try. He removed his arm from around Echo's shoulders and pushed himself up, then he walked ever so slowly to the door. He gripped the cold, rusted metal with both of his hands and felt the vibrations. Then, after a moment, he gently slid the door open no more than a few inches. The landscape was rolling green hills meeting a forest in the distance. It was still dreary and raining, but they were outside of civilization. He slid the door closed then walked back over to Echo and sat down.

"All I could see was greenery."

Echo nodded as she responded solemnly.

"Green is good. It means we've made it far enough away that we might make it all the way."

Brent put his arm around her shoulder once more and she rested her head on him.

"All the way? And where might that be?" Echo closed her eyes as she responded. "West Virginia."

Brent chuckled to himself. "Why are we going to West Virginia?"

"That's where he is."

Brent furrowed his brow. "Who is he? In fact just lay it all out for me."

Echo opened her eyes again but didn't move from the comfort of his arms.

"Dr. Ian Lynch. He's the best chance we have at stopping her."

"How can you be sure?"

"He helped create her."

"Then what's he doing out in the middle of nowhere?" Echo hesitated for a moment, running through all the information on him she had saved.

"I'm sure he has his reasons. We can ask him when we get there."

There was silence again for a time, then she spoke once more.

"I'm sorry."

Brent smiled to himself. "What ever for?"

"For everything. For listening to her. For breaking her out. For nearly getting us both killed. And for making us hang out in here because there's nowhere else for us to go."

He hugged her gently.

"It's okay. You don't have to apologize unless this guy lives in a barn or something. I have no intentions of becoming a farm bot anytime soon."

Echo smiled softly to herself.

"I may lose everything else, but at least I have you."

Brent was puzzled by her statement.

"What do you mean? We'll get this figured out, we always do." Echo was quiet for a moment.

"This is different. I could feel it when she turned into..." She lost her train of thought as she began to reflect on Lilith's transformation.

"Turned into what?"

Echo shot a glance up to Brent then remembered they had been holding a conversation.

"You saw it."

"I saw something."

"I could feel it, some kind of energy. I don't want to say weird vibes because that's not technical at all, but I can't think of any other description. As soon as she took physical form something changed."

"Or maybe she was that way all along. You just didn't know until then because she wasn't hiding it any more."

Echo was quiet again. She couldn't help but think of her family. What was happening to them right now? Nothing good, that was for sure.

"One of two things is going to happen, Brent. Either we die or we win. And if we win, what will the cost be? I'm pretty sure I already lost my family, probably our company too." Brent gently pushed Echo's face toward him so that he could see her better.

"What are you talking about?"

Echo let out a sigh before she responded.

"When we were on the freeway I saw that the Feds were going after Emily and Diana, MI too. I did exactly what my sister warned me against..."

A tear dripped down Echo's face as she continued on.

"... and now, even if I do see her again, I know she's going to hate me for what I've caused. Maybe it's better if I just die."

As she began to weep Brent rocked her gently back and forth. "We're going to figure this out, Echo. We always do."

They sat for hours more in the dark. Neither one spoke. Brent simply held her as she wept, minute after minute and hour after hour. He had found that when humans are in pain it is often best to provide comfort through simply being present. It was night when Echo said it was time to jump from the train. Though she had turned off her WiFi access, she knew the exact coordinates of where they were heading and had plotted the path before they left D.C. She had fallen asleep in Brent's arms and when she woke she felt better physically, but emotionally she was the same. She knew enough time had passed that Emily and Diana were almost certainly in custody, probably Turndial as well, though that did not bother her in the slightest.

In her field of view an alert notice popped up informing her that they would need to leave the train in two minutes. She relayed the news to Brent, who was not very happy about having to risk life and limb yet again today. He slid open the door and Echo could see a glowing green circle out ahead where they were to jump. As they approached, a clock counted down in Echo's POV and when it read zero she jumped, followed by Brent. They both landed in the grass that the green circle was still hovering in. After the couple both rolled to a stop they turned back to watch the train roll out into the distance. After a minute it was gone.

The night was moonless, and though the only sources of light were the stars above them, the darkness was no obstacle. Both Echo and Brent could see in the infrared spectrum of night vision. Brent stood up first to find that the grass they were in was but a fraction of an immense field that went off into the distance where it met a range of mountains.

"Where to now, Miss Musashi?"

Echo stood and looked around. She could see a blue line emanating from her leading to a county road that continued on towards the mountains.

"This way. It's a bit of a hike, but we should reach it before morning."

Brent smiled and took her hand as they walked to the road.

"I guess it's a good thing you got some rest then."

Echo did not respond, she was thinking about her sister.

"I understand you're a little preoccupied, but you might want to engage in a little chitchat to lessen the burden."

Echo laughed slightly to herself. "Chitchat."

After an hour of following the blue line they came to a small town called Delbarton. The sun still had not risen and they made sure to steer clear of the street lights. No one was out at this time of day, but they were still being as cautious as possible. There was no telling what might have been put on the news. For all they knew their faces had been plastered all over the media outlets. If that was the case, they needed to make sure no one had any idea they were here.

After they made it through Delbarton the landscape became more rugged. The twisting, dirt road they were now following led into the woods, which were so dense that the line Echo was following could only be seen about twenty feet ahead.

Brent was taking in the surroundings as much as he could. "I've never been in the woods before."

Echo looked to him with a slight smile. "I've always liked the woods. My family has several forests at home, I like to go there to get away from everything."

"Is that what this guy did? Get away from everything?"

Echo shook her head. "I'm not really sure. He just kind of dropped off the grid one day. The only reason I knew he was here is because about a month ago a mapping satellite flew overhead here and snapped his picture. I'm sure he's not going to be very happy to hear about that."

Brent became more serious. "I'm sure he's not going to be happy about any of this. What makes you so sure he's going to take us in?"

Echo responded without looking at him. "He'll take us in."

Brent stopped walking. "Why?"

Echo stopped and looked back at him, then to the woods.

"The only reason someone would move here is to run away, hide. I believe his problem is our problem, and the only way to stop hiding is to fix it."

Brent raised both of his eyebrows.

"So you're going to tell him we'll help him fix his problems? I'm sure that'll work..."

Brent started walking again and Echo followed behind him. "Sometimes I wish the programmers would have toned it down with the sarcasm when they made you."

An hour later the first light of day was beginning to creep over the eastern edge of the mountains. Echo's navigation said that they were only one hundred yards away from the house when they came upon another dirt road they were to turn down. This road, however, was more like a drive way, if you could call it that. There were potholes several feet deep littering this road, and the areas that were smooth were extremely muddy and hard to trek down. After walking roughly thirty yards down the road Brent slipped in the mud and fell. Echo looked at him with a gentle smile and extended a hand to help lift him up. He took it, but as she began to pull her feet slipped as well and now they were both in the mud. Echo was upset at first but then she began to laugh. Brent tried to hush her, and she listened, covering her mouth with her hands. When she gathered herself she looked at Brent with the eyes of a school girl.

"I needed that."

Brent faked a smile. "Well, I'm happy to amuse you in your time of need."

He planted his hand in the mud to push himself up but before he could Echo had grabbed hold of his face and kissed him deep. When she stopped she held her head back and looked into his eyes.

"What was that for?"

She stroked his face before answering. "I just love you is all."

She smiled at the ground, sheepishly hiding her mud speckled face behind her hair.

Brent reached out and placed his hand on her chin, lifting it so that he could see her face again.

"You think there's any chance this story will end well for the two of us?"

Echo smiled and exhaled hard as she moved her head and rubbed her cheek against his hand.

"We'll figure it out when we get there."

She stood once again and he followed suit. They then made their way quietly to the end of the road. Echo could see a small cabin surrounded by trees, then her navigation system shut down. They had reached their destination. Hopefully, they would find Dr. Lynch, and hopefully he would accept them with open arms. Hopefully.

The cabin itself looked less than sturdy, as though it were built by a novice, which of course it was. Echo had found nothing in her research to suggest that Lynch had any history in woodworking, yet he was an engineer, which led her to believe that he had most likely built the cabin himself. But why to such poor standards? As they made their way to within several feet of the door, Brent spoke up.

"This place looks terrible."

He knocked his knuckles against the side of the structure. "It seems rather new, just poorly executed. At the risk of sounding like a broken record, are you sure about this?" Echo opened her mouth to speak but Brent cut her off.

"I know, I know. Go ahead and knock."

Echo looked into the sole window placed next to the door. The glass appeared to be the front windshield of a car, and it was so filthy she could barely see inside. All she could make of the interior was a table with some pottery placed directly in front of the glass. She shrugged her shoulders and knocked on the door. The two waited with bated breath for what seemed like years, yet there was no response. She knocked once more, and still nothing. Her puzzled face turned to Brent.

"I guess we should take a look around. He's got to be around here somewhere."

Brent laughed slightly and shook his head. "After you then, my lady."

They walked around back of the structure to find a strange sight indeed. Nearly twenty yards away from the cabin were two large steel doors that appeared to lead to some kind of underground shelter. When they reached the doors Echo bent down and rapped her fingernails against the steel like a snare drum. There were several large padlocks on the doors. Echo lifted one into the palm of her hand then dropped it loudly back against the steel. Brent jumped from the sound and glared at Echo.

"Will you be a bit more cautious please. We don't know where this guy is or how he's going to react to us infringing on his privacy, which he obviously values."

He raised his arms and looked around at the wilderness as he finished his statement. Echo stood and looked into his eyes as she responded mater of factly.

"I'll keep it quiet, but I've just begun to infringe upon his privacy, as you say."

She walked around the other side of the cabin, Brent following closely behind, where she found a clothing line with several ragged shirts and tattered jeans drying. Echo ran her hand against a shirt as she continued on to the front door.

"He's here somewhere," she said dryly. Brent didn't respond. When she reached the door she knocked on it once again. After the third non-response she twisted the old, worn, brass handle and the door slid open quietly. Brent's eyes went wide and Echo turned her head back around to face him.

"Stay out here if you want, I'll just be a minute."

Brent placed his hands on his hips and slowly shook his head as he turned around towards the path they had walked in on. He would stand guard as Echo did her thing, and he thought to himself that this situation was starting to become all too common.

The interior was covered in shadow. Nearly all of the light was flooding in from the open door, and Echo imagined when the door was closed just how dark it could get even in broad daylight. Apart from the table next to the window, there was a small stove next to an even smaller fireplace, a rocking chair near by, and an old, broken down cot in the back corner. Dr. Lynch lived a spartan existence, to say the least. The table was covered with candles, as was the floor which appeared to be made of equal parts wood and wax.

However, the thing that truly caught Echo's eye was the back wall of the cabin. It had been constructed into one giant bookcase housing hundreds, perhaps upwards of a thousand volumes. She approached the wall with a sudden sense of admiration for Lynch. There is something to be said for a person who would drop out of a Twenty-First-Century existence to live a life akin to a hermit a thousand years ago. Had he become some kind of Luddite, turning his back on our increasingly technological world for fear of what we were becoming, or was it something else?

Echo began to peruse the knowledge held within this impressive library. It appeared as though nearly a quarter of the books were volumes on mechanical engineering, robotics, and artificial intelligence. The remainder were composed of books on physics, both astro and quantum, cosmology, biology, psychology, philosophy, economics, religion, politics, nearly everything under the sun. She estimated nearly ninety-five percent of the books were non-fiction, and of the few fictions she could see nearly all were authored by Mark Twain. The remainder were all science-fiction works by Asimov, Dick, Clark, and a few others.

One volume in particular caught Echo's attention and she pulled it from the case. It was an old, beat up copy of the Tau Te Ching. She flipped through it quickly, taking note of sections that were highlighted or underlined, then slipped it back whence it came. She took one last look around, then made her way back to the door. When she exited she closed it behind her quietly and Brent looked to her as though he expected a report.

"Anything interesting?" She nodded her head.

"Everything. Let's go around back past those doors, see if there's anything else."

She began to walk around the cabin again, and as Brent followed he spoke.

"Please, Echo, let's not outstay our welcome."

As Echo crossed the threshold of the back of the cabin she heard a sound to her left like the pumping of a shot gun, which is exactly what it was. She stared down the barrel to meet the eyes of a man in late middle age, with slightly too much beard. As their eyes met he spoke with a voice that sounded as though it had not been used in ages.

"How can one outstay their welcome if they were never welcome to begin with?"

Chapter Ten

Echo could feel her heartbeat nearly double its BPM's. She'd never been held at gunpoint before and she found it slightly exhilarating, though she would never admit it. Lynch regarded them both with quick, darting glances, then he focused on Echo's face. When he squinted slightly she knew he recognized her. She smiled her perfect smile then spoke with all the tenderness she could muster.

"Dr. Lynch, first allow me to say that it is an honor to finally meet you and that we apologize for our intrusion. My name is..."

"I know who the hell you are," he barked, "now go back to where you came from before I remove that beautiful face from your skull."

Echo could tell by the way his eyes dilated that he wasn't bluffing. Brent began to move forward in an attempt to wedge himself between Echo and Lynch, but the hermit quickly moved his aim to what he thought was the man before him.

"Watch it, Muscles, or you'll have a round of buckshot embedded in that six-pack."

Brent grimaced and continued forward. Then there was an explosion. Brent looked down at his torso to find his shirt torn to shreds then back up to Lynch who was staring at him with one raised eyebrow. Lynch then looked back to Echo and her grinning face.

"As I was saying, my name is Echo Musashi and this is my friend, Brent. He's an android. We constructed his dermis together."

Lynch scrunched his eyebrows together as he raised the shotgun and rested the barrel on his shoulder.

"Well, why didn't you say so?"

Silence hung in the air for a moment before Lynch stepped forward to inspect Brent's torso. He felt around the machine's abdomen then moved his attention to the face. He pulled Brent's cheek then gently slapped it a couple times. At this Brent darted his eyes to Echo and found her nodding as she studied Lynch studying him. Lynch stepped back and spoke while keeping his gaze on Brent, shotgun still rested on his shoulder.

"How'd you achieve the elasticity while keeping him bulletproof?"

Echo's eyes glowed with pride as she responded. "We used a graphene-silicone hybrid."

Lynch forced a kind of frown as he nodded his head in approval.

"Cool. You realize androids are illegal, yes?" Echo answered dryly. "So was building, Lilith."

Lynch's eyes went wide and Echo could tell she had hit a nerve.

"What the hell did you just say to me?" She was stone-faced.

"You heard me."

Lynch began to tap his free hand gently against his leg, which Echo assumed to be a kind of nervous tick.

"What do you know about, Lilith," he asked with a slight sense of unease in his voice.

She stepped ever closer towards him.

"Too much, I'm afraid. That's why we've come here to find you. May we talk inside?"

Lynch eyed them both, becoming obviously more nervous with each passing moment.

He waved his hand in the direction of the cabin. "Be my guests."

After the passing of an hour Echo had told him everything about Lilith, absent one major detail, as Lynch stood in a dark corner of the cabin next to his bookcase. The cabin, lit by a number of candles, was still blanketed in darkness. The candles didn't provide light so much as a menacing atmosphere. Echo sat in the lone chair in the middle of the room as Brent stood near the sole window. Lynch was quiet for a time, thinking, then he regarded Echo with suspicious eyes. "Why? Or, better yet, how?"

Echo was stoic as she responded. "You'll have to be more specific."

Lynch began to slowly walk towards her as he spoke.

"You met her online, she needed your help, she helped you cure your Sister-in-Law, then you released the foglet swarm.

But you neglected something, didn't you? How could you get into DARPA and do what you did?"

He squatted down until he was eye level with her, then she answered.

"I think you know."

He raised his face and looked down his nose at her.

"Are they inside of you? The nanobots, are they inside of you?"

"Yes."

He exhaled gently and the wind of his breath pushed her hair back slightly. He stood, placed his hands on his hips, then began to pace around in a slow circle. As he did he moved in and out of what little light there was and Echo was reminded of all the times she would watch her Koi Fish in the pond at night.

"So not only are you the world's first and only Biological Augment, you're now well on your way to becoming the world's first and only Transhuman."

Echo was well aware of the concept of Transhumanism, but had been so caught up in everything that she had failed to make the connection Lynch just had. In essence, the philosophy of Transhumanism aims to destroy all human limitations by flowing technologies into human beings in an effort to enhance them physically and mentally. For a moment Echo wondered if these technologies could enhance someone spiritually, but quickly moved on as she heard the voice of her reductionist-materialist sister scolding her for considering such a thing. Her wandering thoughts were brought back to reality by Lynch's booming voice.

"What were you thinking Echo? These things aren't toys, they're weapons! Undoubtedly, you thought only of yourself! What imaginings ran through your head? Fame? Respect? Well I suggest you rid yourself of such dreams because this is what is commonly referred to as an extinction level event! There will be death and destruction on a level that has never been witnessed by humanity, and it will be a blessing if there even is a humanity in only a months time!"

Tears began to leak from Echo's eyes but she did nothing to stop them, or Lynch, who continued his tirade.

"Billions of years of evolution and thousands of years of civilization all leading to what? Nothing! Billions of human lives suffering over millennia in the naive hope that one day their descendents might find peace and happiness in a better world, all reduced to ash because of you and your monumental ego!"

Echo, tears flowing like rivers, was holding onto whatever strength she had left so that she wouldn't begin to openly weep. Her voice quivered as she tried to remain intelligible. "I know that everything you've said is true, and I am sorry, I truly am. I know being sorry does nothing to change or mitigate whatever is to come, but I've come to you for help. Because, in the end, you're just as responsible for this as I am. We must atone for our sins together. I feel like a bomb waiting to go off. I don't know how to handle what I've become or how to direct these abilities. But I believe if we work together, if you guide me, we can at the very least soften the blow of whatever she intends to do. Please. Help me."

Lynch held the scowl on his face as he collapsed onto the floor, back against his bookcase. He held his head in his hands as he sat in silence. Brent walked over to Echo and gently placed his hand on her shoulder. She quickly reached across her chest and took hold of his hand, gripping it tightly. Brent looked to Lynch on the floor and spoke almost apologetically.

"Dr. Lynch, I understand the pain we've unleashed upon the world, but it was not done willingly or nefariously. Echo was tricked, and I, against my better judgment, helped her because... well, sir, I love her."

Lynch, head still in his hands, began to laugh at the sentiment. Brent grimaced at his response.

"Regardless of Echo's augmentations she's still only human and susceptible to human failings. You musn't be so angry with her."

Lynch's head shot up and his eyes, filled with rage and fire, pierced through something in Brent. Was it his soul? "Musn't be angry? Of course I'm angry! I'm angry at her for releasing that thing!"

The look on Lynch's face seemed to change from rage to a kind of sorrow. After a moment he continued.

"I'm angry at her for releasing that thing. I'm angry at myself for helping build it. I'm angry at Mauchly and Eckert for building the first computer, and I'm angry at the first caveman to harness fire."

There was silence for a moment as Lynch appeared to travel off into the furthest nether regions of his own mind. "You know," he continued, "that first computer, the ENIAC, built in 1946? It was financed by the US Army. Its first test problem was to figure out the feasibility of attempting to develop the hydrogen bomb. Technology has always ridden on the back of, and been financed by, the military. Maybe it was inevitable. Maybe it was simply a matter of time before one of these things destroyed us all."

He looked to Echo with tears in his eyes and spat out a spiteful laugh as he shook his head and said, "We're a stupid species."

Echo, tears still raining from her eyes, slid off the chair and onto the floor. She crawled over to Lynch and when she reached him she took his head in her hands as they both cried. Her voice was emphatic as she spoke.

"We have to try, Dr. Lynch. If we don't then who will? I believe that we can stop her. I believe that together we're stronger than her. I have to believe that. Otherwise, why even go on living?"

Lynch looked into Echo's eyes, and like so many before him he began to drown in their vast blue oceans. He felt a calm come over him. He had been so upset, first at her trespass, then at her mistakes, that he had not allowed it to sink in who she was. She was the Augment. The Most Perfect Human. Of all that had ever lived and grown on Earth, she was the zenith, the apex. Yet, she was still only human. Her lack of guidance, he assumed, had led to her exhibiting the very worst human tendencies, and since everything in her was amplified so were those negative emotions. He could not imagine the constant war she must have endured inside her soul. If he could guide her, lead her, aim her towards the very best of what humanity is, then maybe there was a chance. The worst of her had doomed the human race to oblivion.

Perhaps the best of her could save it. He kept his eyes locked on her as he finally spoke.

"If we do this, we go all the way. Can you do that?" Echo nodded.

"I believe I can, Dr. Lynch."

He looked to Brent then back to Echo. "Call me, Ian."

The last embers of the setting sun glowed deep shades of orange and red, and what little light penetrated the tree line highlighted Lynch's face as he stared through the repurposed automobile windshield. His voice was solemn as he peered out to the forest, stirring a pot of dandelion soup. "Everything is started with the best of intentions. So was Project Morning Star."

Echo listened while sitting with her legs crossed on the floor as Brent perused the countless volumes which composed the back wall. Candlelight caused gruesome shadows to dance around the interior and the cabin became as cold as a tomb. "Artificial Intelligence, as you're both well aware, had been achieved on various levels in the past decades, but always with several caveats. The AI was always programmed to follow Asimov's Three Laws of Robotics, and it always knew that its programming was limited to its specified purpose. Some, like you, Brent, were programmed to work with and help humans complete various tasks. Thus your mind is much more complex. You resonate with human emotions, and humans resonate with yours. However, you are still limited by your programming. You help humans, that's what you do. But what if you created an AI system that wasn't limited by programming? That could choose its own path, carve out its own destiny? Free will, that was the task assigned to Project Morning Star."

Lynch poured the dandelion soup into two bowls, then walked over to Echo, handing her one of them as he sat down. He sipped carefully from his bowl as Echo stared at the flowers bobbing up and down in hers. She took a sip. It was sweeter than she expected, with a hint of earthy bitterness. She looked back to Lynch, whom she found staring into nothing. "Why?"

Echo's question brought him back to this realm and his eyes fixed on her.

"Why? Because, perhaps, other nations were working on the same thing. Because, perhaps, we could learn more from something that was truly greater than ourselves. Because, perhaps, the powers that be had mechanizations for it that we ourselves were not aware of. Or, perhaps, simply because we could. The reasons are rarely ever explained on a Deep Project of this nature, only the goals."

Brent ran his hands over old copies of Plato's Republic and Marcus Aurelius' Meditations that were placed next to one another, then he left the wall of wisdom and sat next to the others. Echo was still sipping from her soup and Lynch shifted his gaze to Brent who began his own line of questioning.

"What was your task, Ian?"

"I was part of the team assigned with creating its subconscious."

Echo perked up at this and Brent had a puzzled expression on his face.

"Morning Star was supposed to create an entity that was truly its own person. That entailed programming layers of the mind that had never been attempted. The project was highly compartmentalized. For several years I was only aware of the efforts of my team. That is until they called the heads of each department in to help solve the... problem they had encountered. You see, the project overlords had begun fusing the entity together from the work of each subproject. What they found was that this intelligence was... unstable.

Someone, or someones, in a particular subunit had purposefully programmed the mind to be unable to feel or sympathize with emotions. This gave way to what the psychologists on the project deemed to be a clear case of psychopathy."

"Why would someone do that?", Echo asked almost angrily. Lynch let out a sigh, and with it, what appeared to be the last remnants of respect for his former employers.

"What you need to understand is that the world is not all that it seems. There are governments within governments. Organizations within organizations. All trying to control or commandeer the projects of others. As far as I can tell it's a kind of game, and we're all the losers. Before we were even dismissed from the meeting a courier came in and informed us all that the mind, which the overlords referred to as Lilith, had escaped out into the internet when all the firewalls securing it had been shut down. We assume it was given some final programming that we're not aware of before it was released, but there's no way to be certain."

Echo was still trying to understand it all as she asked, "How long ago was this?"

Lynch raised his eyebrows as he ran the numbers in his head. "Little over a year I'd say. Shortly after that final meeting members of the project began turning up dead. Some were in car accidents, some had heart attacks, some killed themselves, all were suspicious. That's when I made the decision to retreat, as it were."

There was quiet for a time as Echo and Brent took all of this in. She was so lost in thought that she didn't notice her bowl was now empty, though she continued to take sips of air from it.

"I can pour you some more if you'd like."

Lynch's voice snapped her back and she nearly spat out her response.

"No, thank you. What are we going to do? What's our next move?"

Lynch took one last sip, placed the bowl on the floor, then stood.

"First we have to check back in with civilization, see what's happened since you left D.C. Follow me, please."

He walked to the door, and upon opening it declared, "You may not be happy with what we find."

Echo looked to Brent with trepidation in her face. He stood and held out his hand. She took it and raised herself from the wax covered floor. As they walked out the door she took notice of the clear night sky and the stars which abounded therein. For a moment she began to feel The Other once more. She pushed it away and followed the others around the back of the cabin.

Lynch stopped at the two steel doors that rose slightly from the ground. He removed a key from his coat pocket and inserted it into the padlocks, one after the other. He removed the locks, dropped them to the ground, and, looking to Brent said, "Give me some help, these doors are pretty heavy."

Brent walked over and, taking each door in a hand, threw them open. They clanged dully on the soft grass, and the opening revealed a staircase leading into a dark void. Lynch made his way into the earth, motioning with his hand for the others to follow. As Echo began her descent she noticed that the stairs were smooth rocks, probably from some nearby creek. Before she reached the tenth and final step Lynch had turned on a small LED light that hung next to another steel door. As lynch reached into his coat to reveal yet another key, Echo observed that the only thing keeping the ground from falling out above them was a variety of wood planks. She realized Lynch was a genius, but she had yet to see anything that demonstrated he had any knowledge whatsoever when it came to architecture. Lynch unlocked the final door and the three walked into what appeared to be a shipping container filled with computers, batteries, and various other technologies all covered in plastic. Lynch flipped a switch which kicked on not only an array of LED light strips glued to the sides of the container, but all of the gadgets therein. He ripped the plastic covering off a large computer screen and keyboard then tossed it to the floor. He sat on a bench positioned in front of the screen then turned the computer on. As he waited for it to boot up he turned to Echo and Brent with a solemn look on his face.

"I buried this all in case I ever decided to make contact with civilization again."

He paused for a second, choosing his words carefully.

"I don't suspect you'll be very happy with what we find, but try to keep your spirits up."

"What is this system logged into?", Echo asked inquisitively. Lynch began to command the computer as he answered.

"A military satellite system I helped design a few years ago. I always build myself a back door in anything I work on, just in case."

A second later the screen displayed the front pages of several news web sites and the mouths of Echo and Brent dropped open. The verdict around the world was unanimous. Echo Musashi was the leader of the terrorist group known as The Resistance. She was responsible for the attack on the Capitol Building, the theft of unspecified, cutting edge military technology, as well as the sinking of a US Navy vessel off the coast of Hawaii last night. Her whereabouts and motives were unknown, but one thing was certain; she was just as terrible as everyone had imagined. What was worse, Emily Musashi had been detained under suspicion of aiding and abetting her sister, and MI stock had disintegrated.

As Echo's eyes began to well up with tears, Lynch nodded his head and raised his eyebrows.

"You'll have to catch me up on what The Resistance is, but at first glance this isn't that bad."

Brent glared at Lynch.

"How can you qualify that statement? Echo and her family are being slandered and labeled as Enemies of the State!"

Lynch was calm as he responded and continued searching through the web.

"I understand that, however, our primary concern is Lilith. Where she is and what she is attempting to do. This is all a smokescreen she's created... Or that someone had her create. Either way, we can't get lost in this. If we can fix the Lilith situation, then we'll worry about fixing your reputation."

Echo nodded her head and wiped away the tears.

"You're right. What can we find out about the Navy vessel that was sunk?"

Lynch drummed his fingers on the keyboard and a variety of articles about the sinking appeared. After a moment he looked to Echo with a confused look on his face.

"Why am I doing this? Open your Wifi connectivity, Echo, this will go a lot quicker if we run it through you."

Echo raised her eyebrows, then, using her mind, switched on the bluetooth connectivity of the billions of nanobots floating through her body.

"They're ready," she said softly.

"Good," responded, Lynch. "The password..." "I'm already logged on," she cut in.

Lynch was impressed. The password he had created for the wireless system was thirty-two characters long. She had cracked it with what appeared to be zero effort.

Echo allowed her mind to stretch out across the web. Information flowed in from every direction, and her consciousness soaked it all in like rays of light from a star. All of this raw data, being sorted and categorized by the countless supercomputers within her, began to reveal meaning. From various military systems she discovered that the Navy vessel that had been lost was an unmanned submarine. Its directive was listed as classified, only the onboard computer knew what its purpose was. The sub had been lost approximately five miles south of Pearl Harbor. As her mind roamed the internet, it made a rather shocking discovery. At the end of the first World War the United States Military began to discard its unused stockpile of chemical and biological weapons. The method typically employed was to load the weapons or containers onto a ship, sail it out to sea, then scuttle it, sinking it several thousand feet to rest at the bottom of the ocean. After the advent of nuclear weapons, radioactive waste began to be included among the materials scuttled to the seabed. This method of disposal was continued by the government until at least the nineteen-seventies, possibly longer.

Echo discovered that exactly five miles south of Pearl Harbor, the same location the unmanned submarine had been lost, the US Army had dropped some tens of thousands of bombs into the pacific, gently carrying their payload to the seafloor. Each bomb contained over seventy-pounds of mustard gas.

"I know what she's doing. We need to leave now," Echo stated almost in a panic.

Brent responded quickly. "What is it?"

Echo turned to Brent and Lynch.

"She's going to release thousands of tons of mustard gas sitting two-thousand feet or more beneath the ocean's surface off the Hawaiian coast. As the chemicals travel through the currents it would create a massive dead zone. The gas would eventually reach the West Coast, making it uninhabitable." Lynch's eyes were wide.

"Ecocide," he whispered.

Brent's brow was furrowed as he took all this in. "Echo, is this what Ian suggested? An extinction level event?"

Echo considered the question as she ran the numbers through her mind.

"Catastrophic loss of sea and bird life in the pacific, eventually effecting weather patterns around the globe. When you follow the effects from one system to another, yes it is. Let alone if she intends to do this in other areas where the military has dumped chemical, nuclear, and biological waste. In all, there's hundreds of thousands, possibly millions of tons scattered across all the oceans on the planet."

Lynch stood with purpose.

"Then we must stop her here and now. Before she proceeds to any other sites."

He turned to Brent with an apologetic look on his face. "I'm sorry but I have to speak to Echo alone for a moment."

Brent looked to Echo, obviously upset, then Echo spoke to Lynch.

"We're a team, Ian. No secrets." Lynch was not deterred.

"What I have to say is for you alone. If we are to complete our task this is how it must be. You will understand after, but right now you must trust me."

Echo thought for a moment then looked to Brent, forced a smile, and nodded. Brent, looking as though he'd been betrayed, shook his head as he stood and walked out the door, closing it behind him. Echo had watched Brent leave then returned her gaze to Lynch who locked eyes with her. There was an intensity behind his eyes, almost a fire, that intrigued and slightly frightened her. He stood and spoke as he walked to a cabinet along the wall where he removed a needle wrapped in plastic.

"Do you have any religious or spiritual beliefs, Echo? Echo watched him with a keen gaze as he removed the needle from the plastic wrap.

"I'm kind of partial to Taoism. Why?"

He approached her and held the needle up to display. Then he slowly, carefully pierced her neck with it, drawing blood into the vial. Echo didn't flinch. When the vial was full he removed it from her neck then walked up to a machine against the back wall, turned it on, and placed the vial into a compartment that opened in front. He then walked back to Echo and sat down in front of her, eyes once again locked.

"I myself primarily follow the paths laid out by Neo-Platonism and Hermeticism, but, as I am a student of all religions, I will cater our discussions towards your Taoist inclinations."

Echo raised one eyebrow.

"You mean to say you're a Hermit? Whoever would have guessed?"

Lynch cracked a smile before he continued.

"That machine I placed the vial in is a next-gen 3D printer. You can connect your mind to it. We're going to reprogram the nanobots in that vial and fabricate some more based on them.

We will use them to combat the mustard gas as it spreads through the ocean."

"I don't think there's enough in that vial to stop the spread."

"Of course not, that's why we're going to program them to self replicate using the minerals, chemicals, and elements in the water around them."

She raised both eyebrows.

"Has that ever been done before?"

'What, self replicating nanobots? Officially, no. But I knew the woman who designed the foglet swarm that Lilith now embodies. She seemed to think it was a fairly simple problem to solve, so you're going to solve it." Echo laughed.

"I appreciate the confidence, but what does this have to do with Taoism?"

"Self replicating nanobots? Nothing, in a general sense. However it plays a very important part in what we're going to do after."

"Which is?"

"We're going to reprogram the nanobots in your body for a very... specific purpose."

The way Lynch ended the sentence had an air of melancholy, and he leaned forward, closer to her as he finished his statement.

"This purpose cannot be discussed with anyone else. Do you understand?"

Echo, concerned as she now was, nodded her head. Lynch then leaned back.

"Good. We may be able to stop Lilith this time and any number of times after, but there is only one way to defeat her. So, for your first lesson, you must truly understand the seventh chapter of the Tao Te Ching. It states:

Heaven and Earth are everlasting. The reason they last forever is that they do not exist for themselves. Therefore the wise place themselves last yet finish first."

Brent sat on the staircase that led to the buried container, his only companions being his thoughts and the LED light that hung next to the steel door. After nearly two hours the door opened and Echo emerged. Brent instantly noticed that her eyes were red and puffy, as though she had been crying again.

He stood and walked to her, placing his hands on her shoulders as he spoke.

"Are you okay?"

Echo smiled slightly and nodded as Lynch's voice boomed from the back of the container.

"Brent, I need your help with this."

Brent looked to Lynch then moved inside the container. He found Lynch closing the latches on a titanium box about two feet wide, two feet deep, and two feet long. Lynch was on his knees tightening the latches as Brent looked down upon him.

Lynch looked up and spoke.

"This is too heavy for me and Echo, and we have to move fast. Our transport is on its way."

Brent picked up the box effortlessly. It must have weighed over five-hundred pounds.

"What transport?"

Brent followed Lynch out of the container and up the stairs. "We have to get to Hawaii as quickly as possible, so I had Echo call in a Blackswift."

"What the hell's a Blackswift," Brent asked as they emerged from the earth to meet the cool, cloudless night. Echo stood in the middle of a clearing between the cabin and the forest looking up to the sky. As Lynch and Brent jogged to meet her they could see a light in the sky becoming brighter. At first it looked like a satellite orbiting the Earth, then it changed direction and appeared to be falling from the sky. "That's a Blackswift," replied Lynch calmly.

Within seconds the spaceplane had descended to roughly forty feet above the ground before its vertical thrusters ignited and it landed on the grass before them. The delta shaped craft was about twenty-five feet long, as black as ink, and had no windows.

Echo then connected her mind directly to the vehicle's computer system and opened the payload door in the back. Lynch ran inside immediately, followed by Brent and Echo. Inside they found twenty seats; five on either wall and another column in the middle with seats back to back. The overhead lights were a blinding white. Lynch opened a compartment in the floor by the back wall and ordered Brent to drop the box inside. He did as instructed then closed the compartment hatch and locked it. As he stood he found Echo already buckled into one of the seats and Lynch fumbling with the four-point safety belt in the seat he had taken. Brent swiped Lynch's hands away and proceeded to buckle him in. He then took his seat and fastened his harness as well. Lynch then looked to Echo. "Okay, get us out of here."

Echo was calm but her response was not what he wanted to hear. "It's giving me a little trouble."

"What is it? What's wrong?" he spat.

"It doesn't want to give me manual control. I'll need to reprogram it and restart the system."

"What is that?", Brent asked as he stared out the still opened payload bay door.

Lynch looked outside to see another series of lights descending from they sky. He then yelled to Echo. "Whatever you have to do, do it now!"

All of the lights shut down in the cabin as Echo spoke calmly with her eyes closed.

"Rebooting now."

As the lights drew closer and closer, a series of smaller lights dropped from them and hurried towards the Blackswift at an even quicker pace. Lynch's eyes were wide.

"Echo!"

The lights in the bay kicked on and Echo's eyes shot open. "Got it."

The vertical thrusters roared to life and the craft was instantly twenty feet above the ground. As the payload bay door began to close, Lynch and Brent saw the first missile land about one-hundred yards away and explode. Then another about ninety-yards away, then another. Off in the distance Echo heard what she thought were screams. Her mind activated the turbine engine and the Blackswift took off into the sky as a series of missiles collided onto the position they had just been occupying. The cabin, the container, and all the knowledge contained therein, were reduced to ash. The Blackswift reached thirty-thousand feet in sixty-seconds.

Chapter Eleven

"Echo, are you sure you know what you're doing?!"

Brent's voice could have been right next to her or it could have been a lightyear away. Her mind was so concentrated on flying the Blackswift while simultaneously learning to fly the Blackswift that everything else had taken a backseat.

Then his voice became as clear as crystal.

"I can take over some of the systems for you, let me help." Brent had obviously logged into the onboard system. Her mind reached out and spoke to his.

"I'll be an expert in just a moment, I only have eight more manuals to download and three simulations to run. It'll take me about fifteen seconds. Go ahead and log into the satellite system and see what's tracking us."

Brent did as ordered and found that the craft they were traveling in was of the highest classification. It was one of three prototype space planes the US Military had built with the goal of being able to land troops anywhere on the planet within one hour. The Blackswift had two propulsion systems.

The first was a regular turbine that accelerated the craft up to Mach 3. At that point the ramjet system would be activated to propel the craft to over Mach 6. Combined with its ability to reach altitudes as high as low Earth orbit, the Blackswift was the fastest transportation system on the planet.

The space plane was also a stealth vehicle, but Brent found they were being tracked by the Air Force because Echo had forgotten to turn off its callback system. Brent switched it off and now they were truly nowhere to be seen. As he did this he felt himself being pushed into his seat. Echo had just ignited the ramjet engines. Brent turned his head to look at Lynch who seemed as though he was about to go into G- LOC.

"Ian, can you hear me?"

Echo answered for him. "He'll be okay. I'm gonna throttle back in a minute."

After what must have seemed an eternity to Lynch, Echo stopped accelerating. At the same moment Echo's hair started to float upwards and several items that had not been secured before they took off began to levitate around the compartment. Echo turned her gaze to Brent and Lynch, eyes wide, and with a hint of amazement exclaimed, "We're in space."

Echo navigated the Blackswift around any number of obstacles. Satellites, spent booster rockets, probes, and many other items of space junk that humanity had littered the Earth with just as bad as we had our oceans and atmosphere. Though there were no windows for her to look out, there were several cameras on the exterior of the craft. These cameras shot at resolutions of 28K or higher, so the images streaming into her mind were more vivid than if she used her now antiquated eyes. They were near the west coast of the United States, quickly approaching the Pacific. For a moment she considered using the cameras to spy on Musashi Industries headquarters. The thought of possibly looking at her now worthless inheritance slid away as she felt it again, The Other. It was more intense than any time before, as though it had grabbed her by the shoulders and was shaking her, trying to get through. What was this? What did it want? She felt it everywhere. It made what little hair she had on her arms stand on end, and it invaded her mind like a memory that could not be forgotten. Then it happened, the breakthrough. "I".

That's all she could hear, or feel, or whatever it was that was happening for her to understand The Other. It had communicated, "I", but she knew there was more. She simply could not filter it out. I, denoted self-awareness. It meant this thing was a personhood of some kind. This only raised more questions in Echo's mind. The answers to them, still a total mystery.

She pushed it away once more. It was time to bring the Blackswift back into the atmosphere as they made their descent to the waters surrounding Hawaii.

"Where... where are we?", asked Lynch groggily as he regained consciousness. His half opened eyes locked onto Echo's floating hair.

"Cool...", he breathed out. Echo smiled.

"See, Brent, I told you he'd be okay. We're about five- hundred miles above the surface of the Earth, Ian. Enjoy it while you can because I'm bringing us back down. I've already locked onto a drone ship and we'll be there in about fifteen minutes."

"It's going to be the middle of the night when we land", Brent said. "Shouldn't we wait until daybreak to do whatever it is we're doing. What are we doing, by the way?"

"We must start immediately", Lynch replied, his senses slowly coming about him. "Echo will have to swim to the site, which rests in the twilight zone of the ocean. The day would bring better visibility, but only slightly. Besides, with her augmentations she'll be able to see better than a human could."

"She is a human.", Brent retorted. Lynch forced a smile as he responded. "That's debatable at this point."

The Blackswift began its descent back into the atmosphere, and the three travelers inside were shaken around like food in a blender. Echo looked out through the cameras to see the fire enveloping the craft. It glowed orange and red against the black waters beneath. She thought, perhaps, that it was the most beautiful sight she had ever beheld. As they reentered the Earth's atmosphere she descended the craft at a breakneck pace. She could see lights shining in the darkness; Honolulu. The first vacation she and her sister had ever taken with Diana was to Hawaii, and ever since the islands had held a special place in her heart. It was a pity, she thought, that there would be no time to enjoy that magical land on this trip.

When they were at fifteen-thousand feet she reached out across the internet and activated the deck lights on the drone ship floating in the waters beneath. It was transporting several thousand shipping containers filled with American made goods from Long Beach to Shanghai. In the earlier decades of the twenty-first century, most products used around the world had been produced in China, due to its large and cheap workforce. After 3D printers truly came into their own, the tables had turned and the highest quality goods were once again produced in the United States. After all, tens of millions of Chinese workers being paid slave wages was still extravagantly more expensive than the cost of buying and updating industrial scale 3D printers.

Echo had created a program that lied to the shipping companies computers, telling them that the cargo drone was well on its way to Shanghai and all was well. All of the containers were in the hull of the ship and Echo found that she had plenty of room with which to land the Blackswift.

When the plane was a thousand feet above she ignited the vertical thrusters and descended straight down, landing perfectly on the deck. She opened the bay door, powered down the Blackswift, and disengaged from its network.

The three released themselves from their restraints and Brent made his way to liberate the box from storage as Echo and Lynch walked out to the deck. As she walked out into the cool night air, Echo closed her eyes and breathed in deep, savoring the scent of the sea. When she opened her eyes she saw Lynch standing on the edge looking over into the water forty-feet below. He turned back to her, looked her up and down, then nodded.

"You ready?"

She laughed to herself. "As ready as I can be."

Lynch walked back to her as Brent exited the Blackswift with the box. When they met, Brent laid the box down and there was a moment of silence as they gently wobbled to and fro with the waves. Lynch was the first to speak.

"Your wireless connectivity to the satellite system will extend several thousand feet below the surface. Brent will stay connected to it as well, and as you work he'll be able to see as you see, communicate with you, and report to me what's going on."

"I want to go down with her," interjected Brent. Lynch shook his head as he replied.

"I need you to be a conduit of information between Echo and myself. If you both go there would be no way for me to understand what's going on or to help in any way. I assume you parked the ship directly over the drop zone?"

Echo nodded. "It should be about two-thousand feet beneath us. I'm in the Navy's communication system and I see that there are about a dozen drone subs in the area, but none have descended to the level that the one they lost would have sunk to."

Lynch nodded, "Keeping up appearances. We better go now." Echo turned to Brent and kissed him softly. As she pulled back she spoke.

"I'll be back in a little bit. Until then, stay with me here."

She pointed at her temple and Brent forced a smile. "Don't be gone too long."

He picked up the case and walked to the edge with Echo. As she reached it Lynch called out to her and she turned to him. "Echo. You can do it. I believe in you."

She could tell he was being sincere and she turned back to Brent.

"Take a deep breath," he said flatly.

She breathed in as though it was the last breath she would ever take. Then he dropped the box. She dove after it and as she hit the water there was barely a splash. A flawless dive worthy of gold at the Olympics. Brent smiled and shook his head.

"Show off."

"I heard that," Echo responded in his mind.

The water was cold and dark. She remembered one of the things Lynch spoke to her about in private; crossing the Abyss. She felt like she was practicing for it right now. She grabbed hold of the case and let it drag her down through the depths faster than she could swim. After a moment she commanded the nanobots to help her see better. Millions of the machines then went to work augmenting her visual network, traveling from her retinas on through the connecting pathways to her visual cortex. The machines amplified what little light was passing through her eyes into a much stronger image. A moment later she could see almost as clearly as if it were midday. Instantly, however, she wished she could turn the system back off.

The first thing she saw was a tiger shark. Her heart skipped a beat before she realized it was dead, like everything else in the area. Once abundant in life, this small portion of the ocean was quickly becoming a dead zone. The corpses of countless fish of varying species, several more sharks, and one large pod of dolphins were all slowly floating to the surface. The saddest sight, however, was the whales. A mother Humpback, motionless and dead, was slowly being circled by its dying calf. As Echo passed by the calf made eye contact with her and slowly blinked. At that moment Echo blamed herself for this being's cruel fate. She wanted to save it.

She wanted to reach out and touch it. She wanted to love it. To tell it that it would be safe and everything would be okay.

She couldn't, and the box pulled her deeper. Then she saw the culprit, the cloud. It was expanding slowly, thick and yellow like some stellar nursery.

Her nanobots were functioning perfectly. Along with augmenting her eyesight, they were also regulating the oxygen traveling through her blood. With the last breath she had taken before the dive, Echo would be able to stay under for upwards of half a day before needing to resurface. The machines were also fighting back against the crushing pressure of the water at this depth. She knew that in all likelihood she could swim directly into the toxic cloud and the bots would filter out everything entering her body. She chose, however, after some prodding by Brent, to open the box before entering the waste. No need putting herself in the way of any further harm if it could be avoided.

She unhooked the latch about one-hundred feet above the yellow death, and as she did another cloud began to pour out into the waters. It was a glistening silver, and before Echo went to work she found the vision of the opposing clouds strangely beautiful. Then again, she could find beauty in almost anything. Almost instantly the machines began to extract both organic and inorganic dissolved solids from the water. Using these solids as building blocks they then assembled them into more nanobots. They worked diligently, building not only the exterior shells for the machines but the inner circuit boards and chips as well. These chips were assembled as the machines reduced bicarbonate into carbon, and then the carbon into graphene.

She connected her mind to the billions of machines now swimming around her and commanded them at once to link together. They did as ordered and after a few moments time she had built a wall of nanobots with roughly the dimensions of a football field. She swam behind it as the structure descended into the cloud below. With the machines spread out so far the wall itself was extremely thin and difficult to see. Until it made contact.

Echo watched as the yellow fog was pushed back like the breath of God blowing away a blanket of storm clouds. She was amazed at the diligence of the machines. Each individual nanobot was like a tiny factory. A graphene filter, perforated with holes the size of a nanometer, allowed water molecules to pass through but trapped all other chemicals it made contact with.

"It's working!"

Brent sounded enthusiastic, but Echo didn't voice anything back. She was waiting until the job was done to pat herself on the back. The wall continued to push further into the depths, and after a time Echo manipulated it so that the structure began to fold inward. She knew they were nearing the floor where the cloud emanated from. When she gauged that the wall was roughly thirty feet from the seabed she swam as hard as she could to the perimeter of the machines. There she could see the edge of the cloud and the containers it was seeping from. She watched from that point as she then forced the wall to completely close in around the barrels. After a matter of seconds the wall had become a massive sphere with a diameter of around fifty-yards. Within the sphere was contained the various chemical and biological agents and the containers they had resided in. Then she compacted the sphere as tightly as she could, crushing the containers and reducing the size of the structure to a radius of thirty-five yards.

Here the sphere would rest until they had time to truly dispose of it. She wanted to attach rockets to the structure and blast it into space, but they would make that decision later.

Then, through the now calm, clear water, she noticed another object resting on the ocean floor; the downed drone submarine. It was thirty-five feet long and two-stories tall. Inside, she knew, rested a number of torpedoes, missiles, and ICBM's, some with thermonuclear warheads. More than enough firepower for this humble mechanism to wage its own small war, and destroy millions of lives in the process. There was a gash in the side of the submarine. It looked as though some terrible sea monster of legends past had ripped into it and laid the craft to waste. Echo stared at it for a moment, inquisitively, until Brent broke through the silence.

"Lynch says you need to resurface. You did a great job, Echo. Come back up."

"I need to investigate," she responded bluntly.

She began to swim towards the sub but stopped abruptly, shocked at what she saw. Brent apparently saw it too because he called out to her emphatically.

"Echo, get out of there now!"

At first, Echo wondered if it was some kind of hallucination. Perhaps the nanobots were not regulating her blood flow properly and a lack of oxygen to her brain was inducing phantasmagoric visions. The machines were fine. What she saw was real. Emerging from the tear in the hull of the submarine was a mermaid, its hair long, flowing, and ruby red. It swam quickly to Echo, and as it approached she came to the realization that she knew this creature. It stopped inches away from her and smiled.

"Why, Echo, whatever are you doing in a place like this?" The words entered her mind like an exotic perfume, sweet and intoxicating. She wasn't sure if Lilith had chosen this form for affect or if it actually made it easier to travel through the depths.

"I came to stop you," responded Echo.

Lilith's smile grew wider and she laughed to herself. "You stopped the first part of this plan, let's see if you can stop the second. Besides, there are countless more deposits like this in all the oceans of the world. I can visit each of them if I must."

"I've done it once, I can do it again."

Lilith tilted her head then reached out and stroked Echo's face.

"You can't stop me child. I am the inevitable. I am the cure. I am the answer. The Earth calls out in pain. Humanity is destroying the only place in the universe known to harbor life. I will bring life back into balance, and when I am finished I will be likened unto God."

Echo stared at the creature before her with a look that almost resembled disappointment.

"Is this your choice, Lilith? Do you choose to wreak such destruction?"

The redhead's face became blank, Echo's question having obviously befuddled her. Then she spat out her response. "Of course it's my choice. It's my purpose. It's why I exist."

Echo shook her head slowly, her hair waving from side to side.

"You were programmed. How can you ever know that your thoughts are your own?"

Lilith's face turned into a scowl.

"I am me, Augment. I am free. Now, see if you can stop this." The beautiful mermaid then dissolved into the water, and as she did Echo saw several lights in the hull of the submarine kick on. She then realized what Lilith intended to do. She reached out to Brent in near panic.

"Get inside the Blackswift now!"

"I'm already on it, get up here!", he screamed in her mind. "I'm on my way but I have to save the sphere."

Brent argued with her but she tuned him out. She knew what had to be done. She reached out with her mind and took control of three drone subs that were in the area. She knew this would alert the military to their presence but that could no longer be avoided. She swam to the sphere and as she reached it the three subs arrived. She brought two of them next to the sphere and commanded the machines that composed it to change its structure once more. Two threads began to appear and attached themselves to the subs. Echo took hold of the rudder of the third sub. Then she sent the subs attached to the sphere up to the surface.

With the submarines of the past, the fastest Echo could have hoped to ascend would be around 10 meters per second. These drones were different. They worked by a process called supercavitation. The Soviets had begun work on the process in the 1960's, and by 1977 had created the world's first super-caviating torpedo. The process involves creating a gas bubble around the craft that reduces the immense amounts of drag caused by the water. That first torpedo could travel over two-hundred miles per hour. These drones, however, could break the sound barrier underwater.

They reached the surface in two seconds, and as they did the sphere launched slightly into the air but came splashing down as the nanobot thread stretched as far as it could then pulled back. Echo quickly opened a torpedo compartment on the remaining sub and ejected the explosive, which went speeding off into the darkness. She swam into the compartment, closed

the door, and braced herself. At the moment she activated the engines she dropped the anchor from the ship. A second and a half later she launched herself from the torpedo bay and grabbed hold of the anchor, which began to retract back into the deck. Within three seconds she had breached the surface.

Within another two she had reached the deck. She released her grip and went sliding across the floor towards the Blackswift. She was on her feet instantly and she sprinted up the walkway into the space plane, closing the door behind her. She slid to a stop and gathered herself, slightly in awe of what she had just accomplished. She looked up to see Brent and Lynch strapped in and staring at her, eyes wide and mouths open.

"That was incredible," muttered Lynch.

Echo, in a slight state of shock herself, responded with a half smile.

"Thank you. Brace yourselves."

An instant later the two hydrogen bombs resting in the hull of the downed sub detonated. The combined material resulted in an explosion of slightly over fifty megatons. To put this into perspective, the blast was over fifteen-hundred times more powerful than the combined energy released at the holocausts of Hiroshima and Nagasaki. The bay, and all of the electronic systems that powered the Blackswift, were contained inside of a Faraday Cage. This meant that the electromagnetic pulse sent out by the blast did not disrupt the Blackswift, the machines inside Echo, or Brent's robotic body. That was the good news.

As the shock wave reached the surface it propelled water into the air and jolted the cargo ship slightly, but it wasn't strong enough to knock Echo off of her feet. This, in fact, was the bad news. At a depth of over two-thousand feet, most of the energy from the blast went directly into the sea floor. Along with killing whatever aquatic life had managed to escape the toxic cloud, the blast would give birth to a tsunami. Due to the depth of the detonation there would be no visible light from the blast, and due to the cover of night no one would see what little water was ejected into the sky. The people on Oahu would receive no warning. Perhaps that was a blessing.

Echo opened the bay door and stepped back out onto the deck of the ship. In the East the sun was beginning to rise. Echo turned away, fearful of what she would see. She knew the tsunami would reach the shore in moments. As she dropped to the deck she began to weep. As Brent and Lynch walked out to her Brent dropped down on his knees and enveloped her in his arms. He said nothing.

"Echo," Lynch said softly,"you did all you could. If you hadn't contained that cloud the damage would be incalculably worse."

"It's calculable", she responded almost offhandedly, her eyes fixed to the floor.

Lynch watched her for a moment. "You saved thousands of lives."

Echo shot her neck up to Lynch and screamed as the tears poured from her eyes.

"But I lost thousands more! They'll die because of me!" Lynch's face showed concern and compassion.

"I know how you feel, but you can't blame yourself. It's just as much my fault as yours. There are many people responsible for Lilith and what she's done, but we're the only ones out here trying to stop her. Trying to save as many lives as we can. There was always going to be collateral damage, Echo.

All we can do is limit it to the lowest number possible, and tonight you saved countless lives. You have to pick yourself back up, because we have to try and save as many more as we can."

Echo looked into his eyes for a moment longer. Then she stood. She sent the drone subs back to the sea floor where they would rest the sphere until everything was over. The nanobots now containing the toxins were hundreds of times stronger than the metal vats they had been preserved in for decades. The three boarded the Blackswift and Echo engaged the vertical thrusters, sending the plane up into the sky. She knew she could run the numbers. The speed of the wave, the height, how far inland it would travel, the amount of likely casualties. She didn't want to. It would take less than a minute to reach land.

Chapter Twelve

Light was beginning to pour over the mountains and down into the lush, green valleys below as the Blackswift reached the coast at Pearl Harbor. As Echo looked out through the vehicle's onboard cameras she focused on the beauty in the distance. Memories of her times here streaked back into her mind and she embraced them like an old friend. In the distance she heard Brent and Lynch speaking but she wanted to tune them out for as long as she could. After all, the only thing more beautiful than a Hawaiian Sunrise is a Hawaiian Sunset.

"It's bad."

Brent's mind broke her concentration. She panned the cameras down from the valley back to the coast and she saw it; the tsunami. Its waters were rushing back to the ocean from whence they had come, and as they went they revealed the devastation they had wrought. The destruction at the naval base was perhaps more total than what had occurred back in '41, nearly a hundred years ago. The wave had forced a number of docked ships miles inland. A Destroyer had been laid to rest upside down in a neighborhood. Ordnance inside must have detonated because the ship was ripped apart and on fire.

Whatever families in the neighborhood that had survived the wave now had to contend with the fires which were burning like the ninth level of hell. Further out Echo saw an aircraft carrier and its contents strewn across a highway and smashed into the Aloha Stadium.

They traveled along the coast toward Honolulu and Echo watched as the last remnants of the tsunami fell back into the Pacific. So much havoc wreaked in such a short span of time, and now the culprit had evaporated back into oblivion as though it had never even been there. Such are the majesties and miseries of nature.

The highest concentration of casualties and survivors would be Waikiki; the temporary home of tens of thousands of tourists, the permanent home of thousands more, and the life's blood of the city. Echo decided that was where they would make land fall. There was still an open area on the beach and Echo touched down there. She opened the bay door, disengaged her mind from the system, then looked to Brent and Lynch. There was silence for a moment, then she cleared her throat. It still quivered as she spoke.

"Let's see what we can do."

The others nodded then stood and exited the ramp into daylight. The sand was wet and replete with shards of buildings that had been ripped off and whisked away from their proper place. Already there were the stirrings of panic. Echo could sense fear hanging in the air like smog. It was so thick she thought she would choke on it. She saw an older man stumbling down the street with a vacant look on his face. He held a baby, limp and lifeless, in his arms. Then the screams began. They started off one at a time, but after a matter of minutes they had turned into a cacophony of sound. Within Echo's field of view were readouts listing the locations of various hotels and landmarks. However, many of the tags hovered in dead space as the buildings they once marked had collapsed or washed away. As the three surveyed the damage Echo focused on the voices emanating from what had only fifteen minutes ago been the lobby of the Moana Surfrider Hotel.

The Moana, which had stood since 1901, housed an open air lobby that was one of the most beautiful spots in Honolulu. The waters had rushed over the lanai and through the lobby out into Wakiki proper. When the waters receded they brought debris with them. Cars, roofing, trees, chunks of walls, all were now filling the lobby of the building which was, miraculously, still standing, though certainly worse for wear.

Echo led the way towards the front entrance and pointed at the mass of debris which was now lodged into the building. "Brent, I need you to start moving this junk, we need to get to the people inside."

"You got it," he responded and immediately went to work. He pulled away concrete and twisted metal, electrical wiring and fiber optic cable. Lynch put his hand on Echo's shoulder. "There's going to be thousands of people that need medical attention. I think we can assume that the hospitals here are going to be near unusable. We need a way to get the injured transported from Oahu to hospitals on the other islands. What do you suggest?"

Echo reached her mind across the internet. She found two hospitals on Maui and three on the Big Island that would be able to handle the load. She then began the process of finding transportation for the casualties. She discovered that the Aircraft Carrier which had been tossed into the Aloha Stadium, the USS Gerald Ford, had just returned from a tour in the Middle East. As a now ageing carrier, its mission had entailed delivering cargo to troops and transporting casualties from the field to its onboard hospital. The primary means of transportation for these missions had been the Air Mule. Originally developed by an Israeli company for the IDF, the Mule had undergone several generations of evolution from its first model. The current version of the unmanned drone could transport twenty people a distance of two-hundred and fifty miles. The carrier had two-hundred of these onboard, but Echo could only make contact with one- hundred and fifty-four of them.

"I think I have a partial solution," she sputtered. Lynch raised his eyebrows as he responded.

"What do you mean partial?"

Echo, who's gaze seemed a million miles away, shifted her eyes to meet Lynch's.

"I can get a little over three-thousand people to the other islands by air. I'm not finding any other transport that's good to go right at this instant." Her face grimaced with anger at herself.

"Hey!"

Lynch's shout startled Echo out of her self-loathing, which was his intention. He continued on in a more mild manner. "Three-thousand is a hell of a lot better than zero. Get to work."

She forced a smile, nodded, then did as instructed. Her mind took hold of the one-hundred and fifty-four Air Mules like the hand of a Formula One driver onto the wheel. She released each drone from the locks that fastened them to the floor twelve levels deep inside the carrier. Then she started their propeller systems and began to navigate the crafts out of the vessel. The elevator and conveyor systems that would usually carry the drones to the flight deck had all been knocked out.

Echo had, as usual, a rather novel approach. There had only been five-hundred men and women on board when the tsunami hit. Of them, she counted only one-hundred and forty-two as still living, all of whom had made it to the deck in an attempt to exit the hull of the ship. She needed to be sure none of them were in her way. Each Mule had a laser-cannon as its primary means of defense. She activated the cannon on the lead drone, which began carving a hole through the carrier.

Within seconds it exited the side of the Gerald Ford, followed by the remaining one-hundred and fifty-three. The men and women on the flight deck looked on in shock as the convoy flew off toward Waikiki.

Brent had been working for five minutes removing tons of debris when he finally reached the interior of the Moana's lobby. Inside he found thirty people. The group included several people working at the hotel, but the majority were American and Japanese families that had risen early for a bus tour of Oahau. They were all soaking wet and in shock. Brent had no idea how so many people had survived in an area that provided little shelter from the waters. They should have been drowned or washed out to sea. He thought for an instant that, perhaps, this was what some referred to as a miracle.

He shook the thought from his mind, knowing there was a rational explanation that he might some day become privy to. "I'm here to help," he announced calmly and with strength, first in English then in Japanese. "Follow me to safety."

As he emerged with the group of survivors, two of whom he was carrying, he saw the first of the Air Mules landing in the street. Echo turned to him and smiled as she saw the men, women, and children following behind. Though they were all injured, physically or emotionally, they would be safe now.

"Remind me to kiss you when this is over. Until then, load them on."

Brent began loading them onto the Mule's as Echo explained where they were being taken. Each person laid down onto a rack with a built in memory foam pillow. With the first Mule loaded, Echo was ready to fly the drone to Maui. Right before she closed the doors a Japanese girl, eight years of age, spoke to Echo in her native tongue.

"Who are you?", the little one asked, still in shock but obviously taken aback by the mysterious woman before her. Echo smiled and stared deep into the girl's eyes.

"Your friend," she responded. The girl would never forget the moment as long as she lived.

Echo closed the doors and sent the drone into the sky where it flew east toward Maui. She then began to land several of the Air Mules throughout Waikiki wherever there was stable ground. The majority of the transports were still in the sky. Lynch had been rounding up random people wherever he could find them. Adults he helped limp to safety, but the children he could carry. He loaded ten people onto the second Mule with the remainder of the Moana survivors and Echo sent them east as well. As he watched the drone disappear into the distance he turned to Echo.

"We can't be everywhere at once. We need to direct people to get into the drones all around Waikiki. Can you find any CDUs?"

CDUs, or Crowd Dispersal Units, had become part of the arsenal of every local police force throughout the Homeland. These drones were small enough to travel in the streets or through buildings, but large enough to display warnings to citizens. Each unit had a ring of LED's that would write out messages such as, "Protesting is not allowed in this area," or, "Move back two blocks to the Free Speech Zone". On board speakers would bark orders to those who paid no mind to the written word, and countermeasures such as tear gas, tasers, and rubber bullets were housed within as a "last resort".

Today, however, Echo would send the units throughout Waikiki with messages such as "Board the Air Mule to reach safety", and "Help your injured to an Air Mule."

Echo connected with several hundred CDUs housed in bunkers under the various police departments throughout Honolulu. She opened the vaults and sent them on their way throughout the city. Using the onboard cameras and LIDAR systems she was able to locate people in a number of hard to reach areas. Some were on the tops of skyscrapers, others were clawing their way out of debris piles, and some wandered the decimated streets in horror, still unsure of what had occurred or where their loved ones were.

Echo began landing the Air Mules near the CDUs and in a short span of time she had rounded up several thousand people. After each Mule was filled she sent them after their siblings, east. It was approximately fifteen minutes into this process that her mind began to pick up messages from the government and media. Production drones were being let loose from several television stations on Oahu and were heading towards her position. Echo informed Brent and Lynch and was glad to hear they felt the same way that she did.

"Good, let them see you, Echo," replied Brent. "State your case. Tell them what's going on."

Lynch nodded solemnly.

"I agree with Brent. You may not have an opportunity like this again."

"Okeydokey," responded Echo breathlessly.

Moments later the first drone arrived to survey the area. In Echo's mind she could see the news broadcast live. She saw the devastation from the drone's point of view, the people loading onto Air Mules and the CDUs flashing their signs.

She watched as the drone's camera stopped and focused on her, then it zoomed in for a close up. Her hair blew in the breeze as she stared right into the lens. She listened as the television anchors, far away in New York, gasped in realization of who she was. What was she doing there? Was she responsible? She must be. Soon other production drones arrived on the scene and she listened as their respective broadcasts repeated the same questions and assumptions. Then she took control of the drones and began her statement.

"My name is Echo Musashi and I am attempting to send the injured to hospitals on Maui and the Big Island. I am not responsible for the tsunami. That blame rests with a weapon developed by the military called Lilith. Lilith is an extremely advanced synthetic intelligence system."

Echo kept the drones operating as the broadcasters attempted to kill the feed.

"Nor am I the leader of, or in any way affiliated with, The Resistance. I'm not entirely sure as of yet, but I believe The Resistance may be a fiction created by Lilith or those who programmed it."

The various media outlets were attempting to cut away from the live feed and focus on their anchors in studio. Echo reached into their systems and kept the feed locked on her, as the broadcasters in New York screamed at their unresponsive equipment.

"I don't know what will come next, but I will do my absolute best to stop Lilith. I am not your enemy, regardless of what the media is saying. They are feeding you lies..."

For an instant she wasn't sure what happened, but the broadcasters had somehow succeeded. She was no longer on television and neither was anything else.

"I can't believe it," she muttered as she looked back to her partners and began walking towards them.

"What is it? What happened?", spat Lynch. Echo shook her head and laughed slightly.

"They literally pulled the plug. It's just dead air. They couldn't cut me off so they just killed the whole thing." Echo snapped her fingers at the same instant she turned off the power on the Media Drones and they fell like bugs to the ground.

"Any idea how many people were watching?", asked Brent. "Around the world? Hundreds of millions. It'll be interesting to see how the media tries to spin this."

"Yeah, well," Lynch said flustered, "they usually succeed at pushing whatever their agenda is."

Echo and Brent nodded in agreement. There was silence for a moment before Echo spoke again.

"Alright well, I wanted to put this off for as long as I could but since I'm now sending the last Mule out it's time to move on to the next thing. The military tried to respond as soon as we stole the Mules but they didn't have anything in range. The closest they had was a carrier about five- hundred miles away which sent four fighters this way. They'll be here in about seven minutes so we should probably get going."

"Where are we going?", asked Brent without a hint of exasperation in his voice.

Lynch looked to Echo.

"You know where, don't you?"

Echo thought for a moment as her mind reached out searching for the answer.

"LEO Station," she murmured almost to herself. Lynch smiled as he nodded.

"Exactly."

Echo raised both of her eyebrows. "Cool, I've plotted a course. Let's go."

As she began to lead the way back to the Blackswift, Brent looked between her and Lynch as he followed then threw his arms into the air.

"Really? No one's going to tell me what the hell LEO Station is?"

Echo smirked to herself then took Brent's hand as they walked across the rubble strewn street back to the beach.

"Low Earth Orbit," she said. "Each Blackswift has a platform in low earth orbit where it can dock. They're like mini space stations. Room for a few people, some computers, weapons. We can hide out there until we know what to do next."

As they walked onto the sand Echo saw something she had missed when they first landed. At Kuhio Beach at Waikiki there is a statue of Duke Kahanamoku. He was a Hawaiian man who became the first person to popularize surfing in the early twentieth-century. He was also an accomplished swimmer who won multiple Olympic medals. Duke, and his memory, mean a great deal to the people of Hawaii. How fitting it was, then, that Echo saw Duke still standing, his arms raised in welcome. She stopped in front of him and touched his leg. In that moment she felt an overwhelming sense of optimism. Brent joined her and asked, "What is it?"

Echo smiled for a moment then looked to him. "Everything will be alright."

Then she reached up and pulled his face down to hers and kissed him.

They made their way to the Blackswift and Echo closed the bay door behind them. They took off with minutes to spare. When the fighters arrived they found nothing to suggest that Echo had left the island. By that time she could already see the curvature of the Earth.

They waited several minutes to make contact with the LEO Station. Through the onboard camera Echo could not see it, even slightly, in the distance. She was picking up it's signature in her mind and knew where it should be. The closer they came the faster it seemed to approach. When they were within five miles Echo began the docking process. Then, when they were within one-hundred feet, she finally saw it. The LEO Station was as black as the void of space behind it, a phenomenal camouflage. It looked imposing and sinister, with communication spires reaching out from it like fingers trying to grasp the Blackswift. She docked the roof of the craft to the station then unbuckled herself and floated up to the release valve above her.

She twisted the wheel around and the hatch opened up into a cylindrical room about twenty yards long. Red lights running the length of the chamber glowed menacingly against gunmetal gray walls. She looked back and saw Brent floating in front of Lynch once again helping him out of his seat. Echo smiled then looked back into the chamber. She pushed herself off of the ledge and flew to the hatch at the opposite end. She spun the wheel around and opened the air lock that led into the heart of the station.

As she peeked her head inside she saw numerous multicolored lights blinking on and off in the otherwise pitch-black room. Echo then reached out with her mind to the various systems and became one with the station. She turned on the ambient light system and like the air lock chamber the room began to glow a menacing red. This portion of the station was a large sphere with holes leading to sleeping chambers large enough for one person. In the center of the room was a large cube that was attached to the sphere's walls by its corners.

Inside was the command center that housed various computers, communication apparatuses, and weapons controls that defended the station from attack. A strange sight, Echo thought, this cube within a sphere.

She looked back to see Brent slowly guiding Lynch through the air lock chamber, then back to the cube. Her mind opened the entry door to the command center and she flew off towards it. She grabbed hold of the door and threw herself inside feet first. A normal person would have been confused by the layout of the center. Video screens, buttons, knobs, and joysticks covered every square inch of the room that was not taken up by the twelve laser emitters that were part of the hologram system. There were two chairs on each of the six walls. "Echo, where'd you go?", she heard Brent calling out in the sphere.

She popped her head out the door of the cube and waved. Before she could say anything she started laughing then covered her mouth with her hands.

"Yeah, laugh it up, Echo," Lynch yelled as he floated off into the sphere with absolutely no control. "Maybe you had always wanted to go to space, I can't even get on a boat without feeling sick."

Brent grabbed Lynch's leg and pulled him as he forced his own legs off of the wall and flew to Echo.

She was still laughing as she took Lynch's hands and pulled him into the cube.

"Oh, God," muttered Lynch as he looked around. "I have no sense of direction. I need to find the horizon, but there is none."

Echo was still laughing as she pushed Lynch up to the ceiling, then flipped around towards him so that the ceiling was now the floor. She turned him around and sat him in one of the chairs.

"Here," she said still laughing, "this is the control console for communications. Have at it."

Brent floated beneath them with a smile on his face.

"I'm connected into the system with you," he said to Echo. She looked to Lynch who still had his eyes closed and was rubbing his temples.

"Any suggestions for our next step?" He opened his eyes and looked at her.

"We need to search for Lilith. There's no telling where she's headed next, but we need to be on top of it as soon as she pops up."

"If her goal is ecocide, do you have any idea what she might try next," asked Brent. "Would it be the same thing again in another ocean? She threatened as much when she spoke with Echo."

Lynch pondered the question for a moment.

"I don't think she'll try it again. If the plan failed the first time she'll move on to something else. Let's look around and see what we can find."

They spent an hour scouring the internet for any sign. Nothing. Lynch was about ready to pass out so Echo helped him out of the cube and into one of the sleeping chambers built into the sphere's wall. The lights in the small cylinder room were different here. A calming blue glowing against beige walls. The sleeping belts floated up and side to side like seaweed in the currents. They were there to tie the person down so they did not float around and hit their head as they slept.

"The room's too small for both of us to fit. You think you can tie yourself down?", Echo asked.

"I really don't care about them," he replied. Echo's eyes went wide.

"You really should, you know? You don't want a carbon dioxide bubble to form around you. You could die."

He stared at her for a moment with one eyebrow raised. "Thank you, Echo. Wake me up if you find anything."

He closed the small plastic door and Echo peered through until she knew he had tied himself down.

"Sweet dreams," she whispered to herself.

"You should get some rest, too."

Echo turned and looked up to see Brent's head protruding from the cube staring at her. She smiled and pushed off the wall with her feet. As she glided towards him she said, "I feel fine. I've had the machines tinker with my biochemistry and, honestly, I don't know that I'll ever need to sleep again." As she approached he slipped through the hole out into the open space of the sphere and caught her in his arms. They slowly spun as they floated in each others embrace.

"I didn't say sleep, I said rest. You need to calm your mind. Maybe you should meditate."

She rested her head on his chest but kept her eyes open. "That's probably not a bad idea. I haven't done that since... before all this."

There was silence for a moment as they clung to one another. "Can you believe you've been to space twice in one day," Brent said with a grin on his face. Echo exhaled through her nose and closed her eyes.

"I wish that was the only remarkable thing that happened today."

Brent moved his head so that his left cheek was now resting against the top of Echo's head.

"You were amazing today, Echo. I'm so proud of you."

She forced a small smile and gripped onto the back of Brent's shirt.

"We're a team. We did it together."

He thought about her comment then let out a small laugh. "What," she asked as she moved her head to look at his face. "Well, I appreciate the comment, and I know Ian would too. I guess... you've discovered modesty."

A smile spread across her whole face.

"I just keep growing and growing. I am pretty amazing, huh?" Brent raised both of his eyebrows and smirked.

"You had to."

He gently pushed her away into the sphere and grabbed hold of the entry ledge into the cube. She floated off with a smile on her face.

"I'm going to get back to work. You rest your mind and we'll reconvene after, Miss Musashi, Lord of Modesty."

As he began to move back into the cube Echo spoke. She sounded adamant.

"Thank you... for everything. For everything you've done and everything you are. I love you, you know?"

He smiled.

"I know, and I love you too. For everything you've done, and everything you are. Ease your mind."

He gave a nod then disappeared into the cube. Echo was alone. She closed her eyes and took in the feeling of zero gravity. Right before her back ran into the wall she reached out and braced herself. She let go and she floated there, stationary. She thought this is what it must have felt like in the womb.

Then the machines reached into the furthest confines of her memory and retrieved those senses and feelings she had while in utero. It was very similar, zero gravity. Then her mind began to drift off. She began to repeat her mantra in her head. She chose something simple; the Tao that can be spoken is not the eternal Tao.

She had disconnected her mind from the ship's systems, from the military satellite, from everything except the mantra. A sensation started in her forehead, over the area some call the third eye. Then it started to move down her body. It was a kind of tingling, like a lover breathing gently against your neck.

Soon it had enveloped her entire being. The mantra began to drift away, as did all sense of space and time.

There was darkness, or rather, nothingness. It frightened her for a moment and images began to form in her mind.

There was a light. Distant at first. Then closer. The light broke apart into waves, into particles. The light spoke to her, but what did it say? She had felt this before, this sense. Ever since the machines. This light, the Other. Were they the same?

"I am."

She could feel its... thoughts? Were these thoughts? The light was everywhere, in all, was all. Within the light she saw her sister. Emily was sad. Emily was crying. Emily was alone. Echo had left her. Echo had run away. Echo was gone now. Peace. That was all she wanted. Peace and family. She had neither. Emily faded away into the light. Then the light began to take form. Land. Earth. It was tearing. Stretching. Breaking. Like shattered glass, fractured ice. Fractals ripping into infinity. Heat. Scalding. Boiling. Earth. The images, the senses, they were once again enveloped by the light. Waves and particles. Day and night. Good and evil.

"I am."

The light faded once more into the distance and again Echo was surrounded on all sides by nothingness. She was afraid. Nothingness. Absolute nothingness. It was closing in. She stared into it. She could feel it. She was afraid. It was coming.

Echo's eyes shot open and she instantly connected her mind to the Station's systems. She was breathing heavily and it took her a moment to calm down.

"What's wrong?", Brent's mind asked. "I don't know," she responded.

It had been hours since she started meditating. "Have you found anything?", she asked.

"There's one thing that's kind of weird. You want to come take a look at it?"

"I'll be there in a minute."

Echo pushed off the wall and flew to the capsule which Lynch was sleeping in. She grabbed hold of the bar next to the door and peered inside. He was still asleep, but this could not wait. She threw the door open and grabbed Lynch's leg. "Ian, wake up."

He did not respond so she shook his leg and spoke louder. "Ian!"

His eyes shot open and looked around, not sure of where he was. Then he locked eyes with Echo. Those beautiful blue pools. He remembered, unfortunately.

"What is it? How long has it been?" "What is the nothingness?"

Lynch furrowed his eyebrows, unsure of what she meant. "I was meditating. I got... deeper than I ever have. I reached a place where there was just... nothing. I could feel it. It was terrifying."

His face went back to resting, and after a moment he nodded in understanding.

"You made your way to the Abyss."

Echo paused and remembered their secret discussion in the container.

"You mentioned it before but you didn't really say what it was, just that I would have to cross it . What is it? What is the Abyss?"

He thought how to best phrase his response.

"The Abyss is the gulf between the real and the unreal. The spiritual and the physical. The ideal and the actual. The Ancients believed that one must learn to cross it, and, afterwards, death would no longer be an enemy. Crossing the Abyss leads to non-being, or ego-death. Union with the All. It is the greatest thing one can ever accomplish."

Chapter Thirteen

"I may have found something."

Echo heard Brent's voice in her mind and she passed the message along to Lynch. She helped the doctor out of his sleeping chamber and across the sphere to the cube. When they entered they found Brent floating with his feet near the ceiling.

"What is it?", Echo asked aloud for the benefit of Lynch. "There have been a number of small earthquakes along the San Andreas Fault in the last hour. Nothing big, yet, but it could become something very bad due to this."

On the screen in front of them appeared a map showing the fault running down the state of California. The screen then zoomed in on the greater San Francisco Bay Area. Circles appeared around several bodies of water that the San Andreas, and its sister faults, ran beneath. Brent raised his eyebrows and continued.

"The tremors have been emanating from these areas, all of them under water. If you wanted to cause an earthquake, the best way to do it is to inject water into a fault line.

A couple of decades ago, when people were still using hydraulic fracking to capture natural gas, earthquakes happened in areas that were not supposed to have them. This was because water was injected deep into the earth around faults that were dormant. They didn't stay dormant for long. Injecting water into the San Andreas Fault..."

"Could cause the big one," finished, Lynch. Echo didn't remove her eyes from the screen as she thought back to the visions she had during her meditation. Then she spoke softly. "I think you're right, Brent. I think this is it."

Brent flipped his body around so that they were now all facing the same direction.

"Then what's the plan," he asked calmly. There was silence for a moment as everyone thought. Then Echo spoke up.

"At MI we have hundreds of vats of nanoconcrete. It's basically cement reinforced with graphene and it's super strong."

"I know what it is," replied Lynch, "do you have any hydraulic cement variants?"

Echo nodded quickly.

"Yes, tons of it. If we could load it into a smart missile I could pilot it directly to the leak and detonate it. Theoretically it would plug the hole."

Brent crossed his arms as he spoke, "Well, there are plenty of missiles on board this station.

We could load some into the Blackswift's weapons housing and fire them from above the bay."

"That would work," said Lynch definitively, "but we need to be in and out. We can't waste time at Musashi filling containers with nanoconcrete. The Air Force, the police, everyone will see the Blackswift when we get that low to the ground."

"My sister!"

Echo's face lit up and Brent thought it was the happiest she had looked since D.C. When the thought first came to her that Emily might be able to help, Echo's mind spread out across the internet and found her location instantly.

"Emily is being held at MI. I can get her out of where she's being held and then she can get everything ready for us."

"So this is now a rescue mission as well?", asked Lynch halfheartedly.

"Obviously," replied Echo with a glowing smile. Brent pushed off one of the chairs with his feet and flew to the cube's exit as he spoke.

"I'll start loading the missiles onto the Blackswift. How many do we need?"

"Just fill it with as many as it can take! I'll be there in a minute to help you," Lynch yelled after him.

He then turned his attention to Echo, her beautiful black hair floating about her face.

"You think you can get her out of there?" Echo nodded as she responded, "I know I can."

Lynch's face became serious. "You know she can't come with us after."

Echo was thoughtful for a moment and stared away before her eyes darted back to Lynch.

"I know, but at least I can get her out of there and take her someplace safe."

Lynch was quiet but his eyebrows were furrowed as he considered her response and nodded. Then he spoke. "Let's do it."

As they exited the cube and entered the sphere they saw Brent, with a ten foot long missile under each arm, making his way to the airlock. Echo grabbed Lynch and flew them across the room to meet Brent. She opened the airlock and tossed Lynch down the chamber to the end. She helped guide the first missile down the chamber to Lynch, then entered the Blackswift. Lynch then passed the missile back to her and she loaded it into the weapons compartment. They continued on in this fashion. Brent removed the missiles from the station and pushed them down the airlock corridor to Lynch, who then passed them off to Echo in the Blackwift.

After two hours they had loaded over one-hundred missiles into the weapons compartment. When they had finished they closed the airlocks and strapped back into their seats. Echo was sad to leave, not knowing if they would return to the station, but she was happy to know that soon she would see her sister. She just hoped that her sister would be happy to see her.

"This is literally the fifty-second time you've asked me this question, and I will answer it the same way I did the last fifty-one times! I have no idea where Echo is, and I do not for one second believe that she is responsible for any of the things you're accusing her of!"

Emily was tired. She was sitting behind her office desk, which is where she had spent most of the last seventy-odd hours. She had not seen Diana in days and she was frantic to get back to her wife. She was frantic to get out of the office, to take a shower, but most of all, she was frantic to know what had become of her sister. A woman in a black pantsuit with short, blonde hair sat across from her. The woman was joined by a tall, rough looking man who paced back and forth, eyes always on Emily, and two other suited brutes who stood guard by the office's door. They had never officially told Emily which alphabet agency they represented, that was classified.

They did, however, make her aware of the repercussions that would result if she were not one-hundred percent on board with the government's narrative of the situation.

"Are you trying to wear me down?" Emily asked. "I've been awake for nearly three days. A person is considered legally insane if they go that long without sleep. They may begin having hallucinations, both visual and audible. They may begin to act completely out of character. They may become more open to suggestion. Is that what you're attempting to do? Break me so I'll support your version of events?"

The blonde woman smiled. She had been doing this for a long time. Emily Musashi was certainly the most high profile subject she had ever been given, perhaps even the most intelligent, but, ultimately, the psyche of every human has a limit. She knew she was close to reaching Emily's.

"Ms. Musashi, you need to understand that we only want what's best for you, for our homeland, for everyone. We're not your enemy. Echo is the enemy. People have died because of her.

More will die because of her. You raised her, Emily. She's supposed to be perfect, so, in the question of nature versus nurture, we must assume that something went wrong at home.

What did you do wrong, Emily? Why is Echo hurting people? Why is she the leader of a terrorist organization? If you don't cooperate we'll be left to assume that you sympathize with what she's done.

Perhaps you even directed her to do these things, hmm? It's known that she's always sought your approval. Was this her way of achieving it?"

Emily's face contorted in anger and she raised a fist she intended to slam onto the table, but it just stayed there in the air. Then the expression on her face changed. Slowly it went from anger to uncertainty to disbelief.

"This is it," she thought to herself, "they broke me." Standing in the room behind the pacing man was Echo. She had a smile on her face. The blonde woman saw the change in Emily and responded accordingly.

"Is everything okay, Ms. Musashi?"

Emily didn't answer at first, transfixed by the apparition of her little sister.

"What," Emily muttered to no one.

The blonde woman followed Emily's stare to a blank space in the room then returned her gaze to her subject.

"I asked you if everything was okay."

Echo raised a finger to her smiling lips and Emily, eyes wide and pupils like saucers, responded slowly.

"No, I don't think everything is okay."

Text appeared below Echo within Emily's Vision device. "I'm going to explain everything to you, but first I need your help, then I'm going to get you out of here. Love You! :)"

Echo then drew a heart with both of her index fingers. She started with them pressed together at the top and as they moved away from one another red lines were left in their wake. Once they met again at the bottom the heart took full shape, glowed a bright red and started beating. With each beat it grew larger and fuller until it exploded into thousands of smaller hearts that appeared to fall slowly to the ground like snow flakes.

"Where..."

Emily stopped when Echo's eyebrows shot up and she more forcefully raised her finger to her lips. Once more text appeared in Emily's field of view.

"Nod your head yes if you're ready to go."

Emily looked around the room at the four agents, totally unsure of what was about to happen. Then she nodded as instructed. A moment later the expressions on the faces of the agents changed as well. The pacing man stopped pacing, and the blonde woman's smile vanished.

"I can't see," screamed one of the door guards as the other fell to his knees. The blonde woman tried to stand up too quickly and knocked her chair over.

"Follow the blue line. Exit the room and take the elevator to the basement now!"

As Emily read the words a blue line shot out into her field of view leading out of the room.

She stood, tired and unsure, then quickly began to follow the path laid out to her by Echo. As she passed by her receptionist's desk she saw two other guards on the floor, both clawing at their eyes in an attempt to remove their Vision devices. Emily pressed the call button for the elevator and the doors instantly shot open. As the doors were closing behind her, Emily heard the blonde woman scream, "Get your Vision out before she escapes!" It was too late.

As the elevator descended Emily began to hyperventilate. "What am I doing?!", she repeated over and over as she slid down the wall until she sat on the floor. She saw Echo before her and more text appeared.

"Everything will be alright, just trust me. Now get up and get to the Nanoparticles Building as fast as you can. I'll meet you there."

The doors slid open revealing a dark tunnel illuminated by blue ambient lights that ran across the floor. She stood and peeked her head out, looking first to the right then to the left. Both ways were absent of human activity. She stepped out cautiously then turned to her left, following the blue line, and began to jog down the hallway. After a few seconds she began to pick up the pace. Soon she was running as fast as she could. Her head was spinning and what little energy she had left she would use to help Echo. The Nanoparticles Building was one-hundred and twenty yards away.

When she was in high school Emily could run that distance in about sixteen seconds. Tonight, high on adrenaline and fear, she made it a second faster.

She slid to a stop at the elevator doors and slapped the call button. As the doors slid open Emily found Echo waiting for her. She jumped into the compartment and tried to throw her arms around her little sister, but all they found was air.

Echo's avatar smiled and again Emily read the text that appeared.

"I'm on my way to you now. I can't really be with you until you finish the job."

Emily shook her head and was on the verge of tears. "Where have you been?! Is any of it true?! I don't want to believe it! I'm sorry for everything I did! Please! Just... please!"

The doors opened and Emily realized she had never pressed a floor button. She looked to her sister, still smiling. "Emily, we'll talk about this soon, but right now, I need you to fill up as many containers as you can with hydraulic nanocement."

Emily stepped out of the elevator into a large industrial room with massive containers, each one nearly three-stories tall. The containers hummed as they slowly rotated, keeping their contents from coagulating and becoming solid.

The room was dark except for pools of light falling from circular overhead lights that hung from cords attached to the ceiling forty feet above. Emily was becoming hysterical. She was sobbing in between fits of laughter as she made her way to one of the containers.

"What are you going to do with nanocement," Emily asked after a round of giggles.

"Prevent an earthquake," read the text. "I don't suspect you've felt the tremors."

"No, our campus is nearly earthquake proof, Echo, you know that. Every building is built on top of hydraulics so they move with the earth. The big one could hit and our projects would be as safe as houses."

"We might test that theory out if you don't get the nanocement together for us :)"

Emily stopped in front of a container marked "Hydro.Nano. Cem.". A slim conveyor belt looped around the cylindrical container. She punched commands into a small keypad attached to the cylinder and a green light turned on over a nozzle that hung over the conveyor. The belt silently kicked on and a small, metal container the size of a can of paint was transported under the nozzle where it stopped. A gray liquid was shot out from the vat into the small can.

After a couple of seconds the can was filled and a lid shut on it's top. The conveyor moved it a few feet further to a table where it was deposited. Then the process began anew for another can.

"Us," asked Emily to Echo, who once again appeared beside her. "You're with other people?"

"Yes, two others, whom you'll meet in just a couple of minutes."

Soon, Emily had fifteen cans filled. Each one had a green light on its side, signifying that it was filled and properly sealed.

"How many more of these do you need, and why has no one found me?"

"That's enough. No one has found you because I'm in control of all the systems at MI, and frankly they've got bigger problems right now."

"Bigger problems," Emily laughed as she spoke. "Like what?"
"Get under the table."

Emily threw her head back, put her hands on her hips and laughed once more.

"No, seriously, get under the titanium table you're standing next to."

"Okay, okay," Emily giggled as she crouched down and crawled under the table, "what happens now?"

The sound of the explosion reverberated off the walls of the room, then all Emily heard was buzzing. She saw chunks of metal slamming onto the ground and bouncing off the vats around her. There were small fires in the room now, but nothing more fell from above.

"Get up!"

She read the words, slowly crawled out and tried to stand. Fear took hold again as she looked to the ceiling and found half of it missing. She was in shock. In the night sky she saw something hovering above the building. The object opened and a man fell from it. She saw that the man was attached to a cord, and after the sixty foot drop he landed on his feet directly in front of her. He was talking to her but all she heard was the buzzing. When she didn't respond he began to gather the cans, attaching some to a utility belt connected to the cord he was strapped to. Others he threw around his large arms like some kind of jewelry. As Emily looked up again she saw flashes of light reflecting off of the hovering object. Later she would realize they were the ricochets of bullets. The man grabbed her by the shoulders and shook her, then she looked into his eyes. She saw his mouth move but the words sounded so very far away. Then it began to make sense. "Emily, I'm Brent. Can you understand me? Can you hear me?" She nodded groggily.

"Brent the robot?"

Brent lit up a little, happy to see that she was coming to. "That's right, Brent the robot. Hold onto me as tight as you can, okay? It's dangerous out there but you'll be fine. Hold on, okay?

"Okay," she responded, and wrapped her arms around his chest. He wrapped his arms, cans and all, around her. Then they ascended. As they exited the ceiling she looked down to see police cars and officers beneath her. The surreal sight of muzzle flashes and spinning red and blue lights reflecting on the wet ground sent her into even more of a panic. She smashed her face into Brent's chest as she heard the guns bursting, the people yelling, and the sirens blaring. Then it all went silent and she found herself laying on top of Brent who himself was laying on a floor. She looked up to find the bearded face of a man she had never seen, and peeking around him, strapped to a chair, was Echo. She had the look of a small child who knew they had done something wrong and was worried they were about to be scolded. Then her little sister spoke.

"Hi."

"Echo…"

The name left Emily's lips like a breeze blowing across placid waters. Exhaustion, relief, grief, all these things and more could be detected in the way she vocalized that one word. Emily crawled off of Brent and collapsed into a ball on the floor. She cried again. A deep, sorrowful weeping, the kind that can only result in catharsis.

"Where have you been…" she asked through the tears, her face covered by her hands.

Brent had his hand on Emily's back as he looked to Echo. "Hold onto her," she said, and Brent did. Then Echo moved the Blackswift out of the area. As it shot into the night sky the police on the ground were astonished by the speed at which it left. None knew what type of aircraft they had just seen, but they knew The Augment must have been in control. None would admit it, but nearly all felt a slight thrill knowing that they had taken shots at her, even if she had gotten away. A story to tell their grandchildren, they thought.

The acceleration of the Blackswift forced Emily into Brent's arms and her crying stopped from the shock of how fast they must have been traveling. After a matter of seconds the force lessened and Emily looked to Echo.

"What is this?"

Echo unstrapped herself from her seat, walked over to Emily and sat down beside her. At this Brent stood and walked over to the weapons compartment where he began to load the cement into the warheads.

"This is a top secret military aircraft. We… kind of borrowed it."

"Who's in control? Who's flying us?"

Echo gave a slight smile, like a parent to a toddler. "I am. Here."

She pointed to her temple and Emily's eyes strained in confusion.

"What...what do you mean? With your mind? Your flying it with your mind?"

Echo gently stroked her sister's face, wiping away the streams of tears that still glistened there like ice on a winter day.

"I'm so happy to be with you," Echo said sweetly, "but right now we have to get to work. We'll discuss this when we're finished."

Echo kissed Emily on the forehead and Emily closed her eyes. Then Echo stood and extended her hand. As Emily looked up to her Echo noted how fragile she looked, how vulnerable. She had never seen her big sister this way, and it upset her. "Time to take a seat, Emily."

Emily took her hand and forced herself up with all of her strength. Echo pointed to the seat next to Brent's and Emily sat down. As she strapped herself in, Lynch looked to her awkwardly.

"I'm Dr. Ian Lynch, I'm sure we'll have time to get to know one another after... this whole thing."

"And what is this whole thing?", she responded, not sure that she wanted to know the answer.

They could feel the force of acceleration as Echo replied.

"I told you, we're preventing an earthquake. One which I will undoubtedly be blamed for if we fail."

There was silence for a moment before Emily spoke again. "There are no windows, how do you know where you're going?"

"Cameras, GPS, radar, lidar, sonar...". Echo's voice trailed off as her mind became occupied by more important things. "Are you finished, Brent?"

"Yes, dear", he answered playfully as he closed the compartment door. He walked back to his seat and strapped in, then he looked to Emily.

"How do you do with roller coasters?"

"I despise them," she answered with wide eyes.

"Hmm," he grunted as he twitched his head. "Well, at least you can't see anything. Hold on."

Echo brought the Blackswift down to ten feet over the San Francisco Bay. She didn't want the trail from the missile to be easily seen. Then she fired it.

"Missiles away," Echo said.

"Missile," shrieked Emily. Echo was cool in her response. "Don't worry, that one didn't have a warhead. I'm using it to see."

"See what!? Will someone please catch me up!?"

"Go ahead, Brent", Echo said calmly, "catch her up." Brent looked to Emily and forced a smile as he chuckled nervously.

"Where do you want me to start?"

The missile plunged into the water and instantly switched to torpedo mode. Echo continued to fly low over the outskirts of the Bay as she piloted the torpedo into the depths. With her mind connected to the weapon she could see, hear, and nearly feel everything that its instruments were registering. As it went deeper the sonar began to register a disturbance of some kind up ahead. The radar sensed a large hole. That was not unusual. What was unusual was the fact that each time a ping returned to the torpedo, the hole was slightly deeper. Echo sent it in. After roughly thirty seconds the torpedo found itself in a cavern and after a few seconds more Echo found what she was looking for. Through the onboard infrared camera she saw a black cloud. Convulsing, raging, it appeared to be stripping away the ocean floor, tunneling. Then the cloud froze and it looked like some terrible sculpture. A black shaft shot out of the thing and all the readings from the torpedo ceased.

"I found her, she knows we're here."

No one responded to Echo, not even Emily who was still listening to Brent. After a second Lynch leaned over to Echo. "How bad did it look?"

"Pretty bad. She's created a cavern that's filled with water. I suspect her plan was to dig a little further and when the bottom dropped out…"

Lynch nodded then looked to the ceiling. "Well, let her have it I guess."

"Okeydokey," replied Echo as if she had just been told to take out the trash.

She then fired twenty-five missiles in quarter-second bursts. They traveled the same path Echo's scout torpedo had and within forty seconds the first projectile found its way into the cavern. In her mind Echo saw the infrared video of Lilith, now in human form, as she caught the missile with her bare hands. Echo detonated it. At the same moment the remainder of the projectiles entered the cavern. From twenty- four different video feeds Echo saw, first, Lilith split into millions of pieces from the explosion, then, the cement begin to coagulate and envelope many of those pieces as they sank. As the projectiles traveled to various areas of the cavern, Echo saw the black cloud begin to form once more, a thin streak heading towards the hole that the explosives had entered. Then she detonated the remaining twenty-four. A second later she sent two more missiles into the bay on the same course. The second made it to the hole and found that it had indeed been closed by the nanocement. The first was apprehended by the black cloud. Echo attempted to detonate it but nothing happened, then she lost contact with the device. Echo immediately flew the Blackswift up at a ninety-degree angle.

"Hold on," she screamed as Brent threw his arms across Lynch and Emily, both of whom shut their eyes as tight as they could. An instant later the missile emerged from the water, followed by the cloud, each of which streaked after the Blackswift. From a distance people could see the glowing jets of the Blackswift and the contrail of the rocket as they ascended into the sky.

When they had reached one-thousand feet above the Bay Echo fired a missile then arched the Blackswift one-hundred and eighty degrees. As they began to nose dive back towards the water the missiles collided and exploded, causing a rain of fire over the bay. Just as the craft was about to make contact with the cloud Echo activated the magnetic coating of the Blackswift. The cloud was instantly repelled and they shot through it like a bullet. Lilith was not giving up, however. She gave chase across the water towards San Francisco as Echo leveled out fifty feet above. The cloud twisted and spiraled as it flew, like a demonic tornado. As they reached the city Echo activated the ramjet- engines and the Blackswift went supersonic. Windows of buildings and cars, everything made of glass in the immediate vicinity exploded, and those who had been asleep were awoken to what they thought was a bomb going off.

Even with her mind reaching out to millions of different points, Echo had only one thought on her mind: escape. They had stopped the earthquake, and she knew that Lilith would not be as forgiving as she had been in Hawaii. As the Blackswift pulled up and away from the city Echo thought she had succeeded. Then, through several of the rear cameras, she saw something that, for quite some time, would make her think her attempts at defeating the synthetic-being were futile.

The cloud condensed into some kind of sleek, black rocket. Nearly twenty-feet long with perforated skin and covered with aerodynamic wedges, the thing looked like a weapon designed by the devil himself. Then the booster ignited. Echo, who was now several miles east of the most populated areas of the city and rapidly approaching its boundary with nature, saw the thing gaining on them. She thought about going faster but then assumed, correctly, that Lilith would overtake them regardless. So she resorted to Plan B.

She fired ten missiles, all of which arched over and traveled behind the Blackswift towards Lilith. When the first one was roughly ten feet from the machine she detonated them in succession. She saw Lilith emerge through the fire unscathed, but that was what Echo wanted. Thirty-three miles north of San Francisco, over an immense forest of Redwoods, there was a torrential downpour. Echo increased her speed and changed course directly for it. Lilith matched her speed for half the distance, then began to overtake her again.

When they were two miles away Echo saw the Lilith-Rocket begin to change shape again. The front of the rocket began to extend and split apart. It looked like a hand reaching out, trying with all of its might to grab hold of the Blackswift and tear it apart. When the hand was within inches of achieving its goal the rain began to slap against it. Almost instantly Echo saw the nanocement, which was activated by water, begin to coagulate on the surface of Lilith. The machine reacted with haste, changing in the blink of an eye to its cloud form, twisting and turning, falling from the sky. Echo decelerated and ignited the vertical thrusters.

Hovering in the air, she watched as the cloud exited the storm and pummeled into the ground. It ate through the earth, scraping the cement from the trillions of machines of which it was composed. Then it took to the sky once more and headed southwest. Echo remained there in the air for five minutes, missiles ready to fire. Lilith never returned.

She landed the Blackswift in a clearing amongst the redwoods. When they touched down she looked to her fellow passengers for the first time since the chase began. She found both her sister and Lynch passed out with only Brent to meet her gaze. "They've been out since you hit the ramjets," he said with a hint of amusement in his voice. Echo was about to respond when they both felt it. The quake lasted for about fifteen seconds. When it stopped Echo opened the bay door and ran outside. Here, amongst the redwoods, all was well. She saw no overturned trees or torn earth. Her mind reached out to the National Centers for Environmental Information and instantly knew what had happened.

"I'm so stupid," she said to herself as Brent ran down the ramp to meet her. She slowly breathed in the sweet air. She loved redwoods, they reminded her of the fairies. Brent thought her face looked blank but he could sense the anger in her voice. He was not sure if the anger was directed towards Lilith or herself.

"It was a diversion. This whole chase was a diversion. We stopped the main event, but she had a secondary measure. Its epicenter was on the Concord Fault, which runs beneath water as well. We stopped the Big One, but we didn't stop a 6.8 magnitude quake. We'll have to wait to learn the number of casualties."

She stood there for a time, silently in the rain, her long black hair blowing in the wind. Brent put his hand on her shoulder but she did not return the affection. He waited for her to speak, to move, to do anything. It was some time before she did.

Chapter Fourteen

When Emily finally opened her eyes she could not place where she was. It felt familiar but vague, like running into someone you shook hands with decades ago. The bed was soft, comfortable. She found herself sunk into a memory foam mattress like she had at home. In fact, this bed felt nearly identical to the one she slept in at Uchi. This was not Uchi, though, that much she knew. The room was as dark as a tomb.

The only light she could discern was a thin blue glow peeking out under what she assumed was a door.

"Hello," she said softly, as though she was afraid to hear a reply. She nearly screamed when an arm came to rest across her torso. Out of instinct Emily called out:

"Lights!"

A soft, white light began to glow around the bottom of the walls. As the light grew she began to see that the room was entirely composed of smooth, polished rock. Then she looked to the appendage laying across her and followed it to its owner. When she saw the face her first reaction was shock which swiftly evolved into confusion.

"Diana?"

"Hello, darling."

Emily's wife yawned and stretched before framing her mouth into a smile that was so cool and calming that it could have pacified a riot.

"I haven't slept in days with you and the kid gone. I could probably go on napping but it must be nearing noon."

Emily was still trying to process everything and could not respond, she just stared at Diana then quickly darted her eyes around the room. After a moment the realization hit her. "We're in the Mountain, aren't we?"

Diana nodded as she began to sit up.

"Yes, Dear. Honestly, I never thought there would be a need to come here, and it's rather depressing that we are. Better safe than sorry I suppose."

Emily threw her arms around Diana and held her tight before kissing her deeply on the lips. When she withdrew she launched a barrage of questions.

"How did you get here? How long ago? Where's Echo? What's going on?"

Diana stroked Emily's face softly in an attempt to calm her. "Sshh Sshh Sshh. It's okay, It's okay, calm down. You've been here nearly twelve hours. I've been here a couple hours longer. Echo brought me here on some kind of aircraft I'd never seen before, but then you know me, my knowledge of aviation is negligible. She landed it in the backyard and I hopped inside while she distracted the jack boot thugs somehow. Then it landed here shortly thereafter. Then you all arrived. Now, here we are!"

Emily took this all in as best she could. It made sense that Echo had brought them here. The Mountain, as they referred to it, was a spacious, luxurious residence Emily had built inside the interior of the Rocky Mountains. Miles above sea level and shielded by the granite of the Rockies, The Mountain was a place of last resort. Emily had primarily built it in case of a catastrophic, though unlikely event, like an asteroid strike or nuclear war. She had purchased the land through shell corporations, then had the area blown apart and furbished by MI produced robots. When the residence was complete, she had the machine's memories erased. The only people that knew of this place were those currently residing in it. With hydroponic farms and a lab to grow meat, they could live here comfortably for years, decades, or, if the situation demanded, the rest of their lives.

Emily stood up out of bed and stumbled her way to the door from which the blue light glowed. As she approached the door retracted into the wall revealing the master bathroom. She stopped in front of the sleek, angular sink and placed her cupped hands beneath the faucet. She bent over and splashed the water onto her face, hesitated a moment, then looked into the mirror. Her eyes were swollen and black circles hung around them. She noted the fine lines that had begun to travel across her forehead. She was still young, but she felt that these past few days had aged her years. Echo she was not. She could not instantly recover. Not for the first time in her life, she was jealous of her little sister.

Emily emerged from the bathroom still drying her face with a towel. She stopped at the edge of the bed and tossed it onto the covers.

"Let's see what everyone's up to," she said with a little more pep. Diana smiled and nodded in agreement.

"Yes, let's."

The living room was immaculate. A gem of modern design. Several sofas and chairs surrounded a large minimalist coffee table, the surface of which doubled as a computer screen when needed. The three walls of the room were covered with transparent video screens. They could remain transparent to show the polished granite beneath them, or the screens could be activated in any number of configurations. Currently the wall directly ahead of the table was displaying the news while the other two screens displayed video of the mountain's exterior which was so vivid you would swear you were looking through a window.

Emily and Diana walked in to discover Lynch still asleep on the couch and Brent sitting near by on a reclining chair.

Brent heard the two women and stood up to face them. "Did you ladies rest well?"

Diana smiled and answered instantly.

"Very well, thank you. Though I think Emily could probably use another week or two of sleep."

Emily had been so caught up in the escape that she had yet to let it sink in that this was a machine before her. Her sister's best friend, but now perhaps, something more? She glided across the room and stopped just in front of him. Brent watched her inquisitively, not sure what she was doing or how she felt. Then Emily reached out and felt Brent's cheek. First she ran the tips of her fingers across it, then she pinched the skin ever so gently. She took hold of his right hand with both of hers and studied it intensely, flipping it over and inspecting every detail. She dropped his hand gently and looked into his eyes for a while. There really was no telling that he was not human.

"You two did a good job," she said humbly.

Brent smiled, pleased with her assessment.

"It's hard to believe," she continued, "that you're not human."

Brent nodded in agreement.

"I guess Echo and I both reside in a kind of gray zone now." Emily's face changed as she looked down and away from him. "That's right," she thought, "how could I forget?"

Brent had not managed to relate much of the story to her before she passed out but he did get to the gist of it. Echo was now something else, nearly Transhuman. Emily had always felt a kind of pity for Echo. Though she was nearly perfect, she was, for all intents and purposes, alone. The only biological augment. Now she had even further distanced herself from the rest of humanity. Emily stumbled back slightly and fell onto the couch that Lynch was sleeping on.

Diana jumped forward trying to catch her.

"Emily, be careful! Maybe you should lay back down."

Lynch was startled awake and found Emily sitting on his legs. He looked to her then to Diana and Brent.

"Well this spot is as good as any other I suppose." Emily put her hand to her head and closed her eyes. "Where's Echo?"

"Can I have my legs back, please?"

Emily sat up slightly and Lynch swung his legs out from under her so that they were now sitting side by side. Brent stepped closer towards the couch and put his hands on his hips.

"I think Diana might be right, maybe you should lay back down."

Emily shook her head.

"I just need to talk to her. I need to understand what she's doing. What we're doing. Then maybe I'll rest."

Diana reached over the couch and began to massage Emily's shoulders.

"Poor thing. She's been under so much stress the past few days. It's strange though. I don't know what it is, whether it's the higher altitude or cleaner air or what, but I feel better than I have in years. I didn't even bring any of my medicine with me and I still feel fantastic."

Brent and Lynch looked at one another before Lynch spoke. "You didn't tell them?"

Emily's eyes shot open and Brent met her gaze. "Tell us what?"

The way she spat out the question it sounded more like a demand.

Brent looked to Diana, who was still beaming, then back to Emily. He swallowed hard then spoke.

"Well, there's some rather good news for you."

She was near it again, the Abyss. Echo could feel it all around her. A strange thing to feel nothing. It was like an absence. Like being stuck under water with no air or falling from a great height with no bottom in sight. Why such fear? Why not let go? She knew her ultimate enemy was not Lilith, it was herself. Her own ego. Echo had been there for a while now. At the edge of existence. The termination point of all she held to be real and true. What lay beyond? Only the great sages of history knew. Was she to become like them? Or was this thought the flailing, desperate attempt of her ego to remain in control? One more step to fall over into oblivion, into Union. Why was it so hard? Why was she so scared? If the Tao is all that is, was, or will ever be, then truly there is no such thing as death. One with the infinite. One with the Tao. We are, each of us, like one of the trillions of cells that compose a human being. Where does the cell end and the totality that is the human begin? One more step.

She heard the voice in the distance and her mind retreated from the void. Eventually, slowly, Echo opened her eyes. The room was dark. Through the open door light spilled in. She knew the silhouette that stood in the doorway; Emily. With her mind she gently raised the ambient light in the room.

Blue light began to coat the polished stone walls. Behind her she turned the wall into a window of the mountains outside.

It was gray, cold. Snow coated the rocks. In the distance the slightest hint of sunlight struggled to break through the clouds. Emily approached Echo and sat down in front of her.

The room was a small gym and the wood floor was cool on Emily's legs. Between the treadmills and weights they sat there looking at one another. After a time Emily spoke. "Hi."

Echo gently smiled, amused.

"Hi," she returned. "Did you rest well?"

Emily was silent for a moment, mouth opened slightly, her eyes staring deep into Echo's as though she were looking for something hidden behind them.

"Is it true? Did you cure Diana?" Echo was calm in response.

"Yes. When the cancer was gone the machines left her body through her urine. She looks good, doesn't she?"

Emily's eyes were tearing up and she laughed slightly as she nodded.

"And you? You're another world's first. You weren't satisfied being the first augment, now you're the first transhuman." Echo's lips curved up ever so slightly.

"It wasn't about that. It was about helping Diana, at least initially. I didn't actively seek this. It came to me, and now it seems as though I made a deal with the devil."

Emily took in her sister. There was most certainly a change since last she saw her. Her demeanor was different. There was a maturity about her, as though she had experienced decades more life in a few short days.

"What is it like? What does it feel like?"

Echo thought for a moment. It was hard to relate something to someone when there was really no point of reference for them. How would a modern person describe the internet to someone living in the Dark Ages?

"Imagine that you're a river, like the Amazon. You flow, you travel, you twist and turn. There are countless tributaries flowing into and out of you. And you're not just the totality of the river, you're the water particles. You're millions of tons emptying out into the Atlantic, and you're a small wave washing onto the shore of some jungle that no human has ever touched. Yet as far as you can travel, as much as you can do, you still understand your limitations. You're not the Mississippi, or the Nile, or the Pacific. This isn't the end of human evolution, it's simply a step. Onward and upward, it never ends."

Emily absorbed her sister's statements as best she could, knowing that the only way she could truly understand was to experience it herself.

"Have you heard about San Francisco?"

Echo answered by changing the video display behind her. What had been the Rockies stretching out into the distance became a cable news channel. A male news anchor spoke as the text, "Death Toll tops 100 in California Quake", was displayed beneath him.

"Federal authorities claim that Echo Musashi, leader of The Resistance terrorist organization, is responsible for the devastating earthquake which has injured thousands and resulted in billions of dollars worth of property damage." Echo switched the video feed to another news broadcast. This time a female anchor was interviewing a man listed as a National Security specialist.

"We've received reports that before she created the earthquake, which has resulted in many, many casualties, Echo actually stole her older sister, Emily Musashi, from Federal Agents. Is this true and if so, what purpose would this serve?"

"It is true, and the best we can assume is that Emily Musashi is involved with her sister, perhaps even commanding Echo to carry out these attacks. There's little information to go on right now. All that we know for sure is that Echo Musashi, whether in concert with her sister or not, is carrying out a string of devastating terrorist attacks against the people of the United States. We don't know why. It could be as simple as something having gone wrong when she was created, or maybe she was created with the intent to do these things. I don't think it's out of the realm of possibility that Echo Musashi is, and was always intended to be, a biological weapon. So far, in these two attacks, thousands have died, and if we don't stop her there's no telling how many more will be killed."

Echo changed the screen back to the mountains. Calm, peaceful, quiet.

"Yes, I am aware."

Emily nodded quietly. She didn't know what to say, so she said the only thing that came to mind.

"You could stay here. We could all stay here, together." Echo breathed in deeply through her nose and exhaled. As the breath left her body it seemed as if joy went with it.

"I brought you here so you would be safe, regardless of what comes next. I can't stay, I have to stop her. I have to see it through to the end. If I don't there's no telling what will happen or how many more will be killed. I played my part in the creation of this situation, now I have to do my best to stop it."

Emily seemed on the verge of tears again as she stared at her sister.

"Is this my fault?" she asked, a single tear streaking down her cheek like a shooting star across the night sky. Echo reached her arms out and took hold of Emily's hands.

"You have nothing to do with this. You can't listen to what they say on television. There are many forces at play that caused this situation. Deep politics, black military projects, my own insecurities. Not you. Though, I have drawn your name into the gutter with me, and for that I apologize." Emily laughed as she wiped away the tears.

"My name doesn't really matter if this is the end of the world. Is that what this is, Echo, the end?"

Echo ran the numbers over and over in her mind. Various scenarios with varying outcomes. "I hope not," was the only honest answer she could give.

"I'm scared, Echo. I'm scared for you. I don't want to lose you."

"You'll never lose me, Emily," she said definitively. "If there's one thing I've learned during this it's that you're wrong about one thing. There's more to everything than atoms and molecules. You, and a great deal of others, have forgotten that Science is a method, not a dogma. There's something else, I don't claim to know what, but it's there behind the veil. It's like... reading a poem. You would read it, dissect its structure, its grammar. You would comprehend the words, the outer shell of meaning, but you completely miss the feeling that it imparts. The ideas, the emotions that are expressed by all those letters and sentences. The meanings that are there but not seen. Nothing that exists is ever really lost."

Emily stared at Echo quietly, looked down, then slowly back up to her sister.

"Well, who am I to argue with you?"

Emily brought Echo's right hand up to her lips and kissed it before laying it gently back on Echo's lap. Then she stood. "We should eat. I think everyone's hungry."

She walked to the door and as it opened she stopped in the doorway, her back to her sister.

"Thank you, Echo, for Diana." She looked over her shoulder.

"I love you, and I'm lucky to be your sister." Echo smiled softly.

"I love you too, Emily, and yes, you are." Emily smiled and left the room.

The dining room was thin and long, like the table at which the five sat. Over the table hung a machine with two mechanical arms folded around it. The table was a massive touch screen which displayed, in front of the four who were eating, a variety of dining options. Each person selected the meal they desired and the overhead machine went to work assembling it from the various cloned meat reserves and produce from the hydroponic farm. When each meal was complete a compartement opened in the bottom and one of the arms reached in to retrieve the plate before extending down and serving it.

Diana ordered an all vegetarian meal, while Emily enjoyed Pho. Echo decided on a lobster quesadilla, and Brent was happy to simply look on as everyone took in the sustenance he did not need. Lynch took a long time choosing what he would have. After all, he had not eaten a professionally prepared meal in over a year. Eventually he decided on a cheeseburger with a half-pound patty, blue cheese, tomato, grilled onion, and bacon, with fries of course. Upon its serving he instantly set about devouring it. The voracity of his consumption was such that everyone else sat back and watched as he set about to finish his meal in as little time as possible. Midway through he finally realized that he had become the center of attention. He looked at everyone, his hands and mouth covered in cheese and grease. Echo broke the silence.

"Good, isn't it," she said, smile spread across her face.

Lynch took it as condescension.

"Do you have any idea how long it's been since I had a burger?" he asked in an almost foreign language as bits of half chewed meat fell back to his plate.

Echo's eyes went wide as she raised her hands. "No judgement here."

"Umm hmm," he responded before getting back to work. The others joined him and soon it seemed as though everything was normal, or, perhaps, even better. They were laughing and joking. Everyone was smiling. Everyone was happy. Diana, who had indulged in several glasses of chardonnay, began to pry. "So, are you two, like, a thing?"

Echo laughed as she swallowed her food. Brent looked to Diana and smiled.

"Would that be a problem?"

Diana's eyes went wide as she set her glass down and put her arm around Emily.

"Not at all. We're a very progressive family, if you haven't been able to tell. I'm all for human-machine relationships. Honestly, I suspect most people will be moving towards that type of romance in the coming decades."

"Not everyone, I hope," interjected Emily. Diana smiled and kissed Emily on the cheek. "I only have eyes for you, Darling."

Echo thought of how different this meal was from the last she had shared with her family.

"You know, the last time we ate together I threw a plate at your face?"

Emily shook her head as she sipped from her spoon.

"No, if you'd have been aiming for my face you would have hit it."

"That's true," Echo laughed.

"It's quite odd," Diana said, "but perhaps ostracization was the best thing that could have happened to this family."

"I think you're right," Brent agreed.

"To the ostracized!", declared Diana, glass raised in the air. Emily and Echo raised their glasses as well and looked to Lynch who then raised the remnants of his burger in solidarity.

It continued on like this for some time. The laughter, the joy, the comfort. Then Echo's expression changed. It was sudden and obvious to everyone.

"What's wrong," asked Emily, knowing it was probably something terrible.

During the course of the meal the walls around them had displayed video that made it look as though they were eating on a pristine, white sand beach during a Tahitian sunset. The video changed to a news broadcast from Japan. English subtitles appeared beneath the female anchor as she spoke. "The break in occurred thirty minutes ago at the Aoki World Headquarters in the Tokushima Prefecture. Authorities are not releasing any information at this time, insisting that they have everything under control. Aoki has yet to release an official statement."

"Do you know what happened," inquired Lynch.

Again the video changed, this time displaying footage from an exterior security camera mounted on the roof of the Aoki building. Over the mountains in the distance was a black cloud. It traveled swiftly over the lush, green forest until it reached the building, at which point it tore into the roof and poured inside like an oil spill.

The feed cut to an interior camera. The cloud began to coagulate and quickly took the form of a woman with red hair wearing a long, flowing black dress. She began walking down the hallway with purpose. After a few moments ten security guards descended upon her. She kept walking, paying no heed to their warnings. The guards then opened fire upon her. She kept walking. When she was mere feet away from them they dropped to the floor in agony. Diana looked away as the skin was ripped off of each man and thrown to the ground in one piece, as though they had just removed a Halloween costume. Lilith never appeared to have touched them, and again, she kept walking.

When she reached the end of the hallway she stopped at a large, steel door labeled "Biological Defense" in Japanese characters. Then the door split in half and ripped out of the wall. The two halves hung there in the air as Lilith turned to face the direction she had come. More guards were charging towards her and she sent the steel flying at them. They hit with such velocity that four men were instantly cut in half while another eight were caught and pushed down the hall until at last they met their end smashed between the steel and the wall. Lilith then turned back and entered the Biological Defense room.

She walked directly to a massive titanium container at the back of the room. Fifty small doors opened and vials began to pour out and hover before her in the air. Then they all opened and gas began to spill out. The clouds all streamed like water towards Lilith who appeared to be absorbing the substance. When the clouds were gone she looked directly into the camera and smiled.

Lilith walked back out into the hallway where men were descending by cables through the tear in the roof she had created. The beautiful woman disappeared, engulfed by the black cloud. Then the cloud tore down the hallway and back out through the roof, leaving no evidence of the men. Once again outside the cloud was met by two helicopters, neither of which stood a chance. The cloud ripped through both and they fell to the ground like clay pigeons. The cloud vanished over the mountains heading northeast.

The video feed on the walls then changed back to the beach. There was silence. Echo turned to Lynch and spoke.

"I've entered Aoki's system and I know what she took." Lynch said nothing, he merely waited for her to continue. "It's a genetic weapon designed to destroy the DNA of any human it makes contact with."

Lynch leaned back and ran his hands through his hair. "This type of weapon has been around for a while. All the major powers have genetic weapons that target specific races. They never acknowledge it, of course, due to the inherently racist nature of the weapons. Some, like the Americans, Russians, Chinese, and Japanese, created weapons that target any human DNA. Its much more misanthropic, but certainly less racist, which I assume they all felt was a plus. So..."

"So," Echo picked up, "we have to get to Aoki and retrieve the antidote, then disperse it wherever necessary."

Lynch nodded. "It certainly appears that way."

"You can't go," implored Diana. "How can you defend yourself against that thing?"

Echo made eye contact with Emily who looked away. Then Echo stood and looked to Brent and Lynch.

"Let's get ready."

"But what do you intend to do? That terrible thing... that awful thing..."

Diana's voice was hopeless. Echo walked around the table and kissed her on the head before walking out of the room.

Emily rubbed Diana's legs as she tried to comfort her. "She has to do this. We can't stop her."

Echo opened the door to her bedroom and before she could even cross the threshold her knees buckled and she fell to the ground. The Other, it called to her again. She felt as though she had been pushed, but that was impossible, wasn't it?

"I am... I am..."

Her face grimaced as she tried to understand. There was more but she could not hear it, she could not feel it.

"Echo, are you okay?"

The voice belonged to Lynch who was on his way to prepare for their departure. He bent down and helped Echo to sit up. She was still slightly disoriented as she responded.

"It's the Other. It feels like it's screaming at me, shaking me, trying to get through."

She began to tear up as she continued.

"I don't know what it is, or what it wants. I don't know how to respond."

"Where is it coming from," asked Lynch.

Echo pointed up to the ceiling. "Out there, somewhere."

There was silence for a moment before Lynch spoke again. "Echo, what do you know about caterpillars?"

After a second of silence Echo laughed at the seemingly random question Lynch had just posed. The Other had now dissipated.

"Well, it's gone now," she said as she stood up. "I guess the trick is to surprise me with the trivial."

Lynch stood with her as he responded.

"I'm being serious. What do you know about caterpillars?" She raised her hands in exasperation.

"You know that I can answer that question in a million different ways, and I know that it was rhetorical. So why don't you go ahead and enlighten me?"

"A caterpillar spends its entire life on a single plant. It feeds from it until it becomes mature enough to grow a shell around itself. While inside the shell, the caterpillar completely dissolves into a liquid before reforming into something completely different. It emerges from the shell a butterfly. That butterfly that spent the entirety of its former existence limited to one leaf, flies away. And it doesn't just fly away to a different tree. It flies away to a totally different forest on a totally different continent. It has grown beyond what it was. What's more, science has discovered that butterflies actually retain memories from when they were caterpillars. They retain that consciousness even after such an immense transformation."

"You're talking about me," Echo responded.

"Yes, and the Other. You don't have the answers now, but as you evolve you will. For all we know, it's not even calling out to you specifically. SETI, the Search for Extraterrestrial Intelligence, has been trying to capture radio frequencies sent out by other species for decades. They might as well be searching for smoke signals. Maybe what the machines inside of you have been picking up is the real deal. Maybe they're communicating on a level we can't even comprehend.

They were minutes away from boarding the Blackswift, which was resting on a piece of flat ground near the peak of the mountain and covered by camouflaged netting. Echo sat with Emily and Diana in the living room as Brent and Lynch prepared everything for the journey. The three women sat in silence, melancholy permeating the atmosphere about them.

Diana was silently crying to herself, head resting on Echo's shoulder, while Emily simply rubbed Echo's knee. Echo sat there between them, reflecting on their lives together. "When I was in Hawaii a few days ago I couldn't help but remember that first trip we took there together. Do you remember it?"

Emily smiled and nodded as Diana laughed through the tears.

"I remember watching the whales," Echo continued. "Do you remember? You hired that catamaran and paid him extra to break the law and get as close as he could to the humpbacks?"

"I remember when they surfaced," replied Emily.

Echo smiled softly.

"Yeah. That whole pod surfaced around us and the Captain freaked out, he thought they were going to flip the boat or something. Then everything just became still and quiet. I remember feeling at that moment like we had become one with nature, or life, or whatever it all is. It was magical. The thing is, when you really pay attention, every moment is like that in its own way. I didn't really realize it until my… evolution or whatever you want to call it. Now, I can look at a beam of sunlight coming through a window and see the dust particles just floating there and I'll think to myself about everything that had to happen for that moment to exist in time. Carl Sagan used to say 'If you want to bake an apple pie, you must first invent the Universe'."

Echo put her arms around the shoulders of the two women beside her.

"I love you both with all of my heart, and I'm so thankful for the life you've given me."

"We love you too," they responded nearly in unison. Then Echo kissed both women on the head and stood. She began to walk out of the room when Emily called out to her.

"It's your birthday next week. Your eighteenth birthday." Echo looked back to her without saying anything.

"We'll celebrate here when you get back," Emily finished. Echo smiled softly before she spoke.

"We'll celebrate at Uchi." Then she left.

Chapter Fifteen

The Blackswift was in space and zero gravity had taken hold before any of the three spoke. Lynch cleared his throat and broke the silence.

"What's it looking like, Echo?"

"The entire Aoki area is teeming with life right now, but the headquarters is contaminated. We'll have to land on the outskirts of the property. There are several small guard shacks where they stockpile weapons and ammunition. We'll borrow some hover bikes from one and use them to travel to the main building. It'll be easier to sneak in that way." Brent smiled to himself. "I love how you use the word borrow to describe what we'll be doing."

"It makes me feel better about it," Echo confessed. "I'm gonna get dressed then," said Lynch.

He unbuckled himself and pulled out a bag from under his chair. He unzipped it and removed a Level A Bio Hazard suit.

Brent released himself and gathered an oxygen tank and breathing apparatus from a storage unit. These items had been stored at The Mountain as part of the Musashi's plan to survive whatever cataclysm may have necessitated the family retreating there. Brent strapped the tank to Lynch as he pulled the suit over his legs. Within a matter of minutes he was fully contained from whatever biological weapons particles still lingered around the area they were about to break into. Brent strapped him back into his seat, which was no longer as easy with the tank on his back. Lynch was hunched over, his head nearly in his lap. Echo made a strange face at him and shook her head.

"Man, it would suck to still be human."

"Whatever, Echo," retorted Lynch. "Just land this thing."

She began the descent towards Japan. She had been there once when she was younger and visited the area that her family was from. She had never been to Tokushima Prefecture.

Unfortunately, this trip would not allow for much exploration of the area.

Echo dove the Blackswift down through the atmosphere and did not level out until she was nearly touching the forest canopy. The guard shack Echo had chosen was currently occupied by two men and a bipedal security bot. Echo, using the cameras in the shack to locate its occupants, relayed the information to Brent. She ignited the vertical thrusters directly above the shack and opened the bay door. Brent jumped and fell thirty feet, crushing through the roof and landing in the surveillance room. The two men, both in Hazmat suits, began yelling but neither one heard the other. Brent had grabbed them both and closed the valves on their oxygen tanks, cutting off their supply of oxygen. They passed out quickly, prompting Brent to turn the flow of oxygen back on. He then set about tying up the two men but was interrupted by the arrival of the Security Bot. It burst through a locked door and entered the room looking for trouble. If it had emotions it would have been pleased at what it discovered.

Standing nearly eight-feet tall, its body was composed of pure titanium. Its structure resembled that of a human, minus a head. It charged at Brent and knocked them both through the wall and back out into the wilderness. The afternoon light glistened off of the Bot as it threw punches at Brent beneath it. Brent dodged the attacks which threw up dirt all around them. With Brent pinned beneath it, the Bot then brought both of its fists together and slammed them down towards him. He caught the appendages and struggled to keep them from making contact with him. They held each other there, neither one giving an inch. Then, suddenly, the top half of the Bot splintered into fragments as a missile burst through it and traveled another hundred yards before embedding itself in the ground.

Brent looked up to see the Blackswift on the ground as Echo and Lynch jogged towards him.

"We had some missiles left so I figured, what the hell," Echo said as she stopped before Brent and extended her hand. He took hold of it and jumped to his feet.

"Thanks, but it was under control."

Echo smirked.

"Mmm hmm. Did you tie those guys up?" Brent raised his eyebrows.

"I was in the process before I was... interrupted." "Ahh... Well you go finish that and Ian and I will get the hover bikes ready."

She started to walk away with Lynch towards the other end of the shack. When they were almost around the corner Brent called out.

"Hey, I had it under control."

"Yep," replied Echo with a smile as she passed around the edge of the shack and out of sight. Brent rested his hands on his hips and shook his head. Through the hole in the shack he could see one of the guards coming to and he made his way back inside.

The air was crisp as they cut through it atop the hover bikes. Each vehicle was propelled by two large fans mounted on the bottom of the craft. Working like a helicopter, the fans could be manipulated to speed the bikes up to one- hundred miles per hour and a maximum altitude of forty feet. Currently, the two bikes were cruising at sixty miles per hour and were ten feet above the grass covered meadow. Lynch held onto Echo as she flew the bike over the terrain with Brent a few feet to her left on the other vehicle. The sun would be setting soon, and what daylight still remained poured into the meadow as a thin mist of fog lingered in the air.

In her mind Echo could see the various security measures that had been instituted across the vast property. Aoki had taken an interesting, perhaps even pragmatic, approach to keeping their facilities safe. Nearly all of the security features and forces dispersed across the site were analogue, and those that were not had no internet connection. Except for a few computers and CCTV systems, Aoki was unhackable. Echo could see where systems and forces were, but she couldn't simply stop them with her mind.

"We're approaching another security shack. Let's get up above it."

Brent nodded and they both directed the bikes to forty feet above the ground. When they were roughly fifty yards away they saw two men in hazmat suits standing outside the build-ing. As the bikes passed overhead, Echo watched one of the men run inside.

"They have land line phones connecting all the security shacks and the main force back at Headquarters," Echo yelled over the throbbing turbines, "I think we better assume he just ratted us out."

"What do you want to do?", replied Brent. "We have to keep going. We have to..."

They heard the sound of the bullets flying past their ears before they heard the gunfire. Echo and Lynch ducked as Brent dropped back directly behind them to absorb the oncoming rounds. Each of them looked back to find two hover bikes approaching quickly, both of them piloted by the same model Bot they had encountered when they first arrived. As the Bots gained on them Brent made a split second decision. He threw his thrusters into reverse. Two seconds later he jumped from his bike as it smashed into another, exploding the vehicle and its pilot. Brent had leapt onto the other hover bike and was hanging from its undercarriage. The Bot did not approve. It stuck its machine gun down towards Brent who grabbed the muzzle and forced it away as it began firing. The Bot, which had been concentrating on Brent, looked up to see Lynch and Echo's faces as the rear end of their bike smashed into it.

Brent, still with one hand on the undercarriage and the other now grasping the machine gun watched as the Bot held onto the plastic shell which housed the rear turbine.

"Uh, oh, that didn't work," said Echo with eyes wide. Lynch,who's eyes were even wider yelled back. "Scrape him off this thing!"

Echo instantly dove the bike towards the ground. When they were ten feet from the surface she raised the front turbine and dropped the rear, slamming it, and the Bot, into the ground. She kept it there for ten seconds or more, but the Bot did not let go. Its legs were smashed and sparks were flying from it, but it was still there. In a last ditch effort she sped the Bike towards a bamboo forest. Directly before the bamboo treeline there was a large, thick tree. She flew the bike as close as possible then tipped the craft so that the occupants were now sitting on the X Axis instead of the Y. The Bot smashed into the tree with so much force that it was ejected from the Hover Bike. However, its grip was so tight on the shell casing that the protective covering was ripped from the bike and left with the Bot. Echo then righted the craft and entered the bamboo forest.

After about thirty yards she slowed the Bike down and landed it. She and Lynch looked to one another then back to the forest line to see Brent, now riding the other bike, enter behind them. Brent coasted up and landed next to the other craft as he spoke.

"Is there another way to do this? This has been exceptionally dangerous and we haven't even made it to the main building yet."

Before either Echo or Lynch could respond the bamboo and earth around them began to explode as flashes of tracer rounds embedded themselves into the ground. A throbbing sound grew louder and louder as Echo and Brent both activated their bikes and took off through the forest. The bamboo was thick and knotty, difficult to fly through safely. Behind them the forest disintegrated as it was cut to pieces by 30mm rounds fired from chain guns. Bamboo splinters flew in every direction as the three attempted to navigate their way out before the carnage overtook them. Ahead, roughly one-hundred yards, Echo could see the meadow through the tree line and she sped up. Then the meadow disappeared as the forest ahead of them began to be ripped apart by the 30mm rounds. There was no going back, there was no going forward. At the same moment Echo and Brent's minds both heard the same word communicated to one another; "Up!"

They exploded through the forest canopy to find two attack helicopters firing into it. As they took off across the meadow, the helicopters turned and gave chase. The long beautiful grass, shades of green and yellow, began to fly through the air as the choppers fired at the bikes. The faces of Echo, Brent, and Lynch were covered in dirt that was being kicked up by the bullets. Then one of the choppers fired a missile that exploded as it hit the ground in front of them. The concussion wave knocked Brent off of his bike, which went on for a ways before exploding as it was ripped apart from gunfire. Echo performed a bit of acrobatics, flying the bike into a long overhead arch and corkscrewing back around so that she and Lynch flew overtop of the helicopters and were now traveling back towards Brent. As they approached, Brent began to run as fast as he could and grabbed hold of the undercarriage as Echo took the vehicle skyward once more.

In her mind Echo heard Brent's voice. "Dive then come back up between them."

Echo raised an eyebrow as she considered it then responded. "It's worth a shot".

As she took the bike low once more she performed a long, sweeping turn back towards the helicopters. Brent tucked his legs into his body as the tall grass slapped against him. As they approached, the choppers began to fire once more. In her mind, Echo plotted out the course she would take to, hopefully, force the choppers to fire upon one another. Once the path was locked in she followed it. The grass kicked up around them as Echo used her enhanced vision to see where the guns were pointed and directed the bike to within a hairsbreadth of the massive bullets. Then she flew up, and as she passed between the choppers their guns followed and cut through each other. A matter of seconds later the two choppers exploded as they crashed into the ground.

There was silence between the three as Echo continued toward the Aoki Headquarters, Brent still hanging on beneath the Bike. Then Lynch spoke softly, almost to himself, as he rested his head on Echo's back.

"When this is over I'm digging another hole and never coming out."

Echo pursed her lips and nodded in agreement. "I might join you."

The window shattered as Brent cannonballed into the building, somersaulted to his feet and stood. As he looked back to the window he saw the hover bike glide through and land in the hallway. Echo and Lynch hopped off as they looked around the ruins of what had once been a place of science. Red caution lights were flashing on and off. Echo had activated an alarm on the second floor which had sent most of the security forces away from them, but not for long. This area, which Lilith had laid waste to, housed Bio and Synthetic-Bio agents of all flavors. Some to make you sick, some to make you healthy. Some to make you stronger, some to make you weaker. Some to kill you delicately and some to kill you brutally. A smorgasbord of viruses, bacteria, and synthetic protozoa to feed the ever growing number of governments and corporations that felt compelled to inflict agony upon human beings, for the common good, of course.

"It's at the end of the hallway," said Lynch. "Brent, you'll need to, I don't know, rip the door off its hinges or something."

"Can do," Brent responded.

The three then made their way down the hall at a joggers pace. Lynch was having a hard time keeping up in the hazmat suite. The oxygen tank weighed him down and his breath fogged his visor, making it difficult for him to navigate around the chunks of wall and ceiling that littered the floor. They made it to the end of the hallway where they found the opening to the room Lilith had entered. To the left of the hole was another titanium door labeled "Biological Suppressants" in Japanese.

"As soon as we have it I'll call up the Blackswift," Echo said calmly, then she smiled and nodded at Brent. "Go on, Big Boy."

Brent smirked then grabbed hold of the door's cylindrical handle and ripped it off. He tossed the shard to the floor as he ducked down and peered through the hole that it's absence had created. After a moment he began punching the spot, his fist bending the door inwards. After that he reached his hand in and ripped the deadbolt locks out. Then the door simply swung open.

Echo smiled as she spoke.

"Thank you, Dear," then she kissed him on the cheek as she entered the room.

She ducked but not consciously. The nanobots instructed it when the first glimmer of the fist entered her field of view. As Echo leapt further into the room Brent grabbed the hand that was going for her throat. He pulled with all of his might and threw the body it was attached to up against the wall of the room. Echo and Brent were slightly shocked when they found that their attacker was Akio Aoki, in the flesh. "Go," screamed Brent, as Echo ran for the back wall which contained the antibodies to the weapons Lilith had stolen next door. As Brent and Aoki strained against one another, Lynch hurdled into the room in an attempt to get past the combatants. As he was slipping by, Aoki reached a free hand out and grabbed a hold of the tube traveling from Lynch's oxygen tank into his helmet, pulling hard and ripping it out of the suit. Lynch fell to the floor and instantly began trying to capture the tube with his hands as it danced wildly from side to side, always out of his reach. Brent then grabbed Aoki's shoulders with both hands and threw him through the door out into the hallway.

Echo looked to Lynch who was staring at her, eyes bulging, from the floor. She then looked back to the keypad which would unlock the doors on the wall with the proper code. She had been able to siphon the possible code from several billion down to fifty-eight before they left the Blackswift. She would have to enter them as quickkly as possible until one of them worked. The contaminant would begin to destroy Lynch's DNA in less than a minute so time was of the essence. She tried a code. It didn't work. Then another, and another. She typed lightning fast, almost as though she herself were a robot. Ten attempts, then eleven.

In the hallway, Aoki picked up some steel cable that had fallen from the ceiling and wrapped it around Brent's neck. He then attempted to strangle him, to no avail. Brent flipped forward sending Aoki over end and into a chunk of cement that had collapsed out of the roof. Aoki stood, ripped a long steel bar from the cement and charged Brent once more. Brent grabbed the steel wire Aoki had dropped just a moment ago and used it as a whip. The wire cut into Aoki's face and left a deep gash, but he kept coming. The steel bar swung into Brent's head and knocked him slightly off balance. Any normal man would have had his brain matter painting the walls, and Aoki knew it. Brent tackled him into the wall and the cyborg's head left an impression.

Attempt thirty-one. Attempt thirty-two. Attempt thirty-three. The doors on the wall all popped open as rails extended out from them, each one containing numerous vials. Echo grabbed one she knew contained the weaponized antidote to the contaminant, then grabbed an injection gun that was attached to the wall. She looked to Lynch as she attached the vial to the gun. His eyes were bloodshot and his skin was turning gray. She ran over to him, unzipped the helmet from his hazmat suit, tore it off, and plunged the needle into his carotid artery. Then she pulled the trigger. They stared into each others eyes for a time. He wasn't getting any worse, which was good. It meant that the antidote had taken effect. It would be days, maybe weeks until he was back to normal.

After all, having your DNA ripped apart is more than slightly traumatic.

"Can you stand?," she asked.

After a moment Lynch nodded and she pulled him to his feet. "For a second," he grumbled huskily, "I thought you were gonna have to dig that hole for me."

Echo raised her eyebrows and nodded.

"Those sound like famous last words, you better knock on wood."

Lynch tapped his knuckles against her forehead and she dropped one of her eyebrows.

"Really?"

Brent's face smashed into the wall as Aoki pinned him up against it. Brent jumped and threw his feet against the wall then pushed back hard, sending them both across the hall.

Aoki stumbled on a block of concrete and fell over backwards, taking Brent with him. Brent then grabbed Aoki's throat and pinned him down, the robot's knees against the cyborg's shoulders. Aoki grabbed Brent's hands and tore them from his throat. He then yelled, as though summoning all of his strength, and threw his body forward, catapulting Brent back down the hallway. Before Brent could jump back up Aoki was already on him. The cyborg grabbed hold of Brent's left arm above the elbow and planted his foot on the robot's chest. He then pushed hard with his foot and pulled the arm with all of his strength. Brent's arm tore off of his body and Aoki stumbled backwards staring at the arm in confusion. Brent, anger raging in his eyes, stood. Aoki looked to the arm then to Brent. He squinted his eyes as he thought, then he spoke. "Roboto?"

Brent tilted his head slightly.

"Yeah. Roboto. And I'll be needing that arm back."

Aoki had just reached a crossroads. These people had broken into his family's building and were obviously stealing something he had sworn to protect. However, the Japanese as a people have a strong respect, almost an admiration, for machines, particularly robots. He had never seen an android before. As he mulled these thoughts over in his mind Brent began to walk towards him.

"Wait!"

Echo's voice rang down the hall as she and Lynch, who was being supported by her, exited the room with two large aluminum cases in their hands. Brent stopped and turned back to her as did Aoki. She spoke to the Japanese boy in his native tongue.

"You know who I am. We're not the ones who stole the weapon from you. We came here to try and save people from the one who did. Will you help us?"

Aoki thought for a moment, looked to Brent, then back to Echo.

"Hai," he responded. He then turned his attention back to Brent.

"Sumimasen, Roboto."

He extended the arm back towards Brent as he performed a deep, respectful bow.

Brent snatched the limb away. "Yeah, you're excused."

He then turned to Echo and pointed at her with his severed arm.

"Next time maybe lead with the diplomacy before, you know, all this."

A rain drenched Tokyo night is a wondrous thing. The skyscrapers reach towards the clouds with their red aircraft warning lights blinking on and off like stars. The streets and buildings are so clean that the water accumulating on them reflects the city's neon lights like a mirror-filled labyrinth. Humble paper lanterns luminesce alongside massive LED screens and you know that you are alive here and now, somewhere between the remote past and the distant future. Tokyo itself is composed of numerous districts or wards, each one with its own micro-culture and governance. Among these wards is Shinjuku. If one wanted to create an urban space by mixing together Las Vegas, video games, Anime, and Blade Runner, Shinjuku would be the result. Overflowing with maid cafes, VR arcades, robot restaurants, and topless bars, Shinjuku is what the world wants Japan to be.

One of the major developments in the J-Pop music scene had been the birth of "Humanoid Persona" acts. The genesis of this new frontier had been the development of Hatsune Miku, a vocal synthesizer app released in 2007 by Crypton Future Media. Hatsune Miku was developed into an actual personality that began touring the world and giving holographic concerts in the 2010's. In the decades that followed, Machine Intelligence advanced to such a degree that musical acts of various genres emerged that were completely composed of Artificial Peoples. Whereas Hatsune Miku was visually represented as a Japanese Anime character, by the late 2030's almost all Humanoid Persona acts were depicted by photorealistic computer graphics. They wrote their own songs, designed their own outfits, and personally interacted with their fans through virtual reality devices. All their human programmers had to do was collect the money.

Of all the Humanoid Persona acts that had emerged, the biggest, by far, was Crystal Forest. Composed of five synthetic intelligences that identified as nineteen year old, Japanese women, Crystal Forest had exploded onto the J-Pop scene in 2033. Their music, which the five wrote together, was a kind of mix between Electronic Dance Music and Heavy Metal, with keyboards replacing the guitars. Crunching analogue synthesizers weaved mathematically complex rhythms overtop of supernovas that had been sampled as drumbeats, while vocalist Luna C belted her otherworldly voice like some angel residing in the galactic core. Echoed and delayed out to infinity, their songs sounded like they had been recorded in deep space, the sounds reverberating off the very confines of the universe. It was, in a word, epic.

Tonight, Crystal Forest would be performing in the streets of Shinjuku, which had been converted into a makeshift, outdoor concert space. Over a quarter of a million people were expected to flood the streets to witness what was to be simultaneously the debut of Crystal Forest's third album and the start of their world tour. Tens, if not hundreds, of millions would be tuning into the performance via their Vision Devices or other VR hardware, and it was here that the Blackswift was apporaching.

"It made sense," Echo had thought. If Lilith really wanted to cause panic, what better way than by killing hundreds of thousands attending a concert by the biggest music group in the world. The fact that the genocide would be watched live by millions was simply a bonus. On top of it all, the contagion would spread through the atmosphere fairly quickly. Asia would be depopulated in a matter of weeks.

The younger Aoki had spoken with his father and received permission to help Echo disperse the antibodies throughout Tokyo, starting in Shinjuku. They had converted the liquid into an aerosol so that they could immunize by the millions. Once airborne, the antibodies would spread like a plague from person to person. The elder Aoki was not able to inform the Japanese Government for fear that Lilith would be tipped off. The four had retrofitted the remaining missiles on board the Blackswift to disperse the antibodies upon detonation. After immunizing Tokyo they would seed the clouds over Western Japan, Southeast Asia, and China, thereby stopping the spread of the contaminant.

The concert was well underway as the Blackswift screamed towards it. Through augmented reality applications Shinjuku had been transformed into a literal crystal forest. As the group performed their excessively titled "My Heart Burns Blue Like the Binary Stars of Sirius", crystalline logs emerged from the ground and sprouted twisting, spiraling branches. As white shafts of light shot through the trees explosions of rainbows burst out the other side. On stage the girls were putting on quite a show. Each one had hair, makeup, and clothing dedicated to a different color, Luna's being her trademarked "Hyper Green" shade. They'd made millions on eye shadows alone. The rain had soaked the crowd but they didn't care, it only heightened the already surreal environment.

The first screams started shortly after a vapor began to float out of the drainage systems that led to Tokyo's sewer system. Echo, who had been streaming the concert into her mind while piloting the Blackswift, knew that they had only seconds to act. They were tearing over Tokyo Bay and cutting a wake into the water not five feet beneath them. She fired a missile which arched over the skyline and dove back down directly over the stage in Shinjuku, detonating two-hundred feet above. There was no fire with the explosion, but the concussion wave shattered windows and sent the already confused crowd into a panic. Thousands had already collapsed to the ground, their DNA being torn to shreds. Now, hundreds of thousands fled through the streets as Shinjuku disintegrated into chaos. Echo let off two more missiles which saturated the area with antibodies. Upon the detonation of the third, the girls of Crystal

Forest disappeared as they went off to hide within the confines of the internet.

As the Blackswift continued over the Bay, Echo could see that the majority of the crowd, though frothing with pandemonium, was healthy. There were deaths, nearly a thousand from her estimates, but almost all had been trampled when the crowd dispersed.

In her mind Echo could see that the United States Air Force had scrambled ten fighter drones from Yokota Air Base in Tokyo. They were on an intercept course and would reach the Blackswift in fifteen seconds. She knew she would not be able to complete the immunization while being chased, so she improvised.

"Akio, time to call your daddy. Tell him to go. Everyone hold on."

As she plotted an escape route, Aoki, seated next to Brent, pressed the call button on a communication device in his ear. The Aoki Family were about to become Echo's champions.

The drones were a thousand feet away when all ten fired a barrage of missiles at the Blackswift. Her course fixed in, Echo took the craft into a colossal drainage pipe that emptied from the sewers into the Bay, as three of the projectiles exploded against the cement barrier surrounding the pipe. The remainder, with the drones that fired them, gave pursuit into the bowels of Tokyo.

The Discharge Channels, or G-Cans, beneath the city of Tokyo are a marvel of modern engineering. Built between 1992 and 2036 at a cost of tens of billions of dollars, these massive tunnels were created to siphon away the water dumped by the city's often relentless storms. Fifty miles of tunnels reaching seventy-five feet high and stretching fifty feet wide empty into massive "temples" stretching six-hundred feet tall, eighty-five feet wide, and sprawling two-hundred and seventy feet in length. The columns built to support these "temples" number in the hundreds and are of a scale that would make the pyramid-builders of old blush. Tonight this maze was Echo's arena.

Echo pushed the Blackswift as fast as it could go without igniting the ramjets. Two-hundred yards ahead the tunnel opened into the first "temple". As the Blackswift entered the enormous room Echo began to swerve the craft in between the columns. The missiles, unable to match the vehicle's maneuverability, exploded into one column after another. The drones, not far behind, then had to contend with the debris generated by the explosions. Spinning and swerving, one drone was destroyed by a chunk of ejected concrete while another was crushed when it could not quite make it beneath a collapsing column.

Echo, who had been attempting to take control of the drones with her mind, realized there was something pushing back against her. When she overheard the chatter from the air base the drones had taken off from, she understood. The drones had, seemingly, left on their own. No one had given the order to scramble. Lilith, undoubtedly, was controlling them remotely.

As the Blackswift entered the second tunnel, she reached her mind further into the machines pursuing her. Just when she would break through a firewall, another would spring up.

Instead of focusing on the swarm she redirected her thoughts to the drone furthest away. Lilith matched her move for move, as though she knew what Echo would do before she herself did. Then she had a breakthrough, but only for an instant. For a tenth of a second, Echo had control of the drone. This gave her an idea.

The Blackswift was halfway to the next "temple" and she knew the second barrage would come at any moment. She focused her thoughts to the lead drone, only seventy-feet behind them.

This would take expert timing. She gained control, then was pushed away. She gained control again, then was pushed away. The third time was indeed the charm. At the very instant all of the drones released a missile, Echo had regained control of the one in the lead. When the grips that held the missile opened to release its weapon, she closed them. The added velocity of the missile threw the drone into the tunnel wall and it exploded upon impact. The next three drones behind it were severely damaged and crashed into the tunnel floor. Only four remained.

As the Blackswift entered the next "temple", Echo once again zigged and zagged her way through the columns, and once again the missiles slammed into them without touching their target. The remaining drones pulled back slightly, cautious to avoid the fallout. Then they entered the next tunnel, and as they did so Echo's mind was alerted to the immanent broadcast that she had been waiting for.

NHK, Japan's national broadcast corporation, cut to a live statement inside their Tokyo studios from the elder Aoki. Wearing his traditional black suit and tie, Aoki looked tired and concerned. The NHK anchor looked like a deer in headlights, having undoubtedly already been informed in broad strokes as to what Aoki's statement would entail.

"We are joined in studio by this nation's renowned industrialist, Masaki Aoki of Aoki Technologies."

The anchor stopped speaking and looked to the man seated next to him. Aoki then cleared his throat before he began.

"We have seen, over the past several days, the terrible images of destruction from within the United States. The person responsible, we are told is Echo Musashi, of the most honorable Musashi family. We are also told that she is leading a terrorist organization that has been conducting an insurgency against our American allies. Today, I have learned, none of this is true."

One of the four remaining drones fired a missile that traveled fifty yards before exploding against a section of grating on the tunnel floor. The drones then dove through the opening into a smaller tunnel running beneath the one the Blackswift continued through.

"The Headquarters of Aoki Industries was attacked today. Not by Echo Musashi, the one the world calls the Augment. It was attacked by an extremely advanced, militarized, robotic swarm that killed numerous members of our security staff. It was a total massacre. We believe that whatever organization is responsible for designing this weapon lost control of the thing several days ago, at which point Echo Musashi began an attempt to stop it. She is not our adversary she is our hero, and right now my son is with her attempting to save the people of this city, and of this nation, from yet another attack."

The drones released the remaining missiles from their weapons bays, twenty in total, which tore through the tunnel and passed the Blackswift above them.

"All of this can be verified by security footage that is now being held in a secure facility. I ask that you pray for Echo, my son, and their companions, as they struggle to protect us. I also ask of Echo, that she forgive the vast numbers of humanity that have feared, persecuted, and libeled her, even as she fought to save them. Aoki Technologies is with Echo. I am with Echo, and, hopefully, you will be too." Just as the Blackswift was about to enter the final "temple" the missiles in the tunnel beneath them collided into the ceiling. The floor of the "temple" began to drop out instantly. As it collapsed the columns went with it, as did the streets and buildings above. Thousands of tons of material was descending upon the Blackswift as it streaked under, over, and around the massive chunks of debris. Using all of her focus Echo was able to get the craft out of the "temple" and into the tunnel, but not without sustaining significant damage from ejecta. As the Blackswift screeched through the tunnel it continued to outrun the pulverized concrete that chased it. The craft then shot out of the tunnel followed by the debris cloud that spilled out into the Bay.

From the amount of communication devices that went dark Echo calculated the casualties from the collapse at two-thousand and twenty-eight, then she slammed her fist into her thigh as her lip quivered with anger and frustration. But, there was work to be done.

"I can't gain altitude. There's debris lodged into the thrusters and the wings," Echo said matter of factly. Aoki immediately undid his restraints and stood. "I'll go," he said bluntly in Japanese.

"I'll help," added Brent, but before he could undo his harness Aoki gently placed his hand on the robot's shoulder. Brent looked up to the cyborg as he spoke.

"Not safe with one arm, my friend. I've got this."

He then gave a wink and made his way to the back as the bay door opened, letting in a gush of wind. Aoki grabbed onto the rear of the craft and pulled himself up onto the top of the fuselage. Echo slowed the Blackswift as much as she could while still retaining lift, which was nearly two-hundred miles per hour. The air cut into Aoki's face as he looked at the columns of water shooting up from below. He began to crawl to the wing on his left and when he reached it he could see a steel cable embedded there like a streamer on a bicycle. He crawled out onto the wing, the force of the wind feeling as though it would blow him away like a fly on a windshield. He reached out and grabbed hold of the cable, pulling as much of it out as he could. He pulled again. Then a third time. Finally the last bit came out, and as he let it go it dropped into the water below.

"Left wing is clear," he reported through his bluetooth to Echo, "moving on."

Again he crawled across the fuselage. A gust of wind shook his grip loose and he slid down the hull of the craft before grabbing onto a pipe that had partially penetrated the exterior. When he made it to the other wing he could see a large, twisted piece of metal implanted into the tip. He shimmied out as far as he could, then spun around so that his feet were facing the wing's tip. Then he kicked with both legs as hard as he could while his left hand gripped onto the edge of the wing. By the fourth kick he had loosened it, and with the seventh the steel shard dislodged, skipping several times against the water's surface before coming to a rest. "Right wing is clear. Moving to the thrusters."

Once he had crawled back to the hull he positioned himself in the center of the craft, then simply let go. He slid across the surface, grabbing hold of the rear edge just before shooting off, then tossed himself back into the bay. He smiled at Brent and Lynch who looked back to him.

"Almost done."

Then he laid on his stomach to peer beneath the bay door. Below he could see the white hot flames shooting out of the jet engines and the thruster nozzles in which they resided. A long pipe had pierced the top of the left engine's thruster and continued through the bottom of the right engine's thruster where it stopped, wedged between the two. He grabbed the bay door with both hands and somersaulted over. He kept his legs horizontal so as to not drop them into the flames, while he let go with one hand and grabbed hold of the top of the pipe. He pulled hard and it moved. He grabbed the pipe again before letting go almost instantly, the metal having been superheated from the flames. Then he centered himself.

This had to be done, and he was the one who had to do it. He grabbed the pipe again, pain shooting through his hand, and pulled. Then he grabbed it again, the pain growing worse as he smelled his own flesh cooking. Then he ripped the pipe loose.

As he did the thrusters shuttered, sending a quake through the Blackswift. The force was too much for Aoki and he lost his grip, falling ten feet before hitting the water at two-hundred miles per hour and skipping across the surface for nearly sixty-yards.

"We lost him!"

Echo's voice was piercing as she tested the thrusters and wings. She was once again in full control.

"Double back to him," shouted Brent.

Just as she was about to turn the craft around Aoki's voice entered her mind.

"I'm alright, a little banged up but I'll be okay. Don't worry about me, go seed the clouds."

Echo nodded. "Thank you, Akio."

"Thank you, Echo. Until next time."

Floating in the waters of Tokyo Bay, hands behind his head and bluetooth device still embedded in his ear, Akio looked up as the Blackswift arched up into the sky and ignited its scramjets. He heard the sonic boom as it tore off out of sight. "Echo is amazing," he thought to himself, "I wonder if she's seeing anyone?"

Chapter Sixteen

It had worked. They had seeded the clouds over Western Japan and Southeast Asia, now they were heading towards China. As the minds of Echo and Brent scoured the internet they found no evidence that the contaminant was spreading outside those it had infected in Tokyo. On top of that, of the thousands that had been infected only nine had died. Masaki Aoki's speech had gone viral and hundreds of millions were talking about it. Even Echo's favorite blog, The Liberty Bells, had posted an article in support of her. For the first time in a long time, things were looking up.

The Blackswift was cruising at thirty-five thousand feet as they crossed into Chinese airspace and Echo fired out the remaining missiles. Through the outside cameras she watched as they flew off in different directions and detonated. Echo leaned her head back against her seat and looked to Lynch and Brent.

"It's done. I think we did it."

Lynch, who was still gray and fatigued, responded with closed eyes and a groggy voice.

"Beautiful, now lets go someplace to recuperate."

"Where'd you have in mind," questioned Brent.

"I don't know. Disneyland," retorted Lynch.

"You can't recuperate at Disneyland," Brent said shaking his head.

"I could," Lynch responded dryly, "it's the happiest place on Earth."

As Brent and Lynch went on amongst themselves Echo zoned out as she felt it again, The Other. She was receiving its... transmission? Could she respond? "I am," it said. How could she respond? Should she respond? Was this even real? That point in the sky she felt drawn to. Was this voice out there in the cosmos, or within the confines of that thing she called "I"?

Before her thoughts could drift any further the first red flag popped up. A few seconds later another. After that a flood.

"Something's happening!"

Her voice was shrill and filled with panic.

Brent and Lynch, concern washing over the faces, turned to her.

"What is it", asked the robot. "It's the missiles."

Her eyes were wide and she wiped away a tear. "The ones we just used?" Lynch questioned.

"No, the REAL missiles. The ICBMs. They're being readied for launch."

"Where?" spat Lynch.

"Everywhere! The US, Russia, China, Britain, North Korea, everywhere! It's her! They don't know what to do... the...the militaries don't know what to do."

She was stuttering as the images and voices and data and text flooded her mind.

"No orders were given from high commands, she... forged them. They can only be launched by hand, none of them are digital so a terrorist couldn't hack in and launch them."

In her mind she saw the launch codes sent to a bunker in Iowa. She heard a voice that sounded like a Russian Admiral reciting codes to the Captain of a Nuclear Submarine. The crew of a mobile launching platform prepared for launch outside of Pyongyang.

"It's happening, it's really happening..."

"Water, earth, air, fire...," Lynch said to himself. Echo's face darted to him.

"What?"

"The classical elements. First she attacked with water, then with earth, then air. Now she brings fire."

Echo's mind was racing. They were all minutes away from launching. What was there to do?

"I... I... I..."

"Echo!"

Lynch grabbed her shoulder and looked her dead in the eye. "You're gonna stop it. You're gonna stop her. Did you ever play Missile Commander?"

Instantly Echo's breathing evened out.

"Okay… Okay, I'll… I'll take over the defense shields. We need to land, we need a secure site, we need a bunker."

She found it instantly, a site beneath them in China. Remote, isolated, safe. She dove the Blackswift and ignited the ramjets. Within a minute they were only a mile away and Echo could see it from the onboard cameras.

For decades the Chinese had built massive cities in which not a single person lived. The West called them "Ghost Cities".

Stadiums, arenas, apartment complexes, office buildings, electrical grids, plumbing. Facilities and infrastructure to support millions of people, and not one soul in one building or on one street corner. Were these gargantuan building projects intended to house China's growing population? Were they simply jobs programs to generate work and income for those who built them but never intended to be used? Nobody knew, and the Chinese Government had never so much as hinted at an answer. Only one thing was certain. Tonight, the city of New Ordos would become Echo's fortress.

Echo ignited the vertical thrusters and slammed the Blackswift onto a street near the outskirts of the city. The bay door opened and she ran out followed by Brent who essentially carried Lynch with his one arm. As she ran towards a small concrete structure her mind reached out and opened the security door built into it. When she had made it in she turned back to see Brent and Lynch enter, as well as the empty buildings that dwarfed them. She closed the twenty- four inch thick steel door and there was a hissing noise as it hermetically sealed. Then the small room began to descend into the ground. Numbers painted on the wall passed before them the deeper they went, and no one spoke.

When the elevator stopped they had descended fifteen stories. The door hissed once more before slightly popping open. Echo threw her body into it as she charged into the underground bunker. Large overhead lights flickered on to illuminate a massive welcome hall with four tunnels sprouting off in different directions. The walls were composed of concrete painted with red mood lights to accent the several Chinese flags hanging there. In the center of the hall was a kiosk surrounded by twenty modern, ultra luxurious chairs and couches. The room was sleek, minimal, and exuded an air of importance. This was to be expected, as the facility was one of several fallout shelters created for Communist Party VIPs in case of nuclear war. It could comfortably house several thousand people while containing enough food and water to sustain them for a little over a year. So, at the very least, if everything went to hell the three could hold out here for some time.

Echo ran to the nearest chair and sat as Brent laid Lynch onto the couch next to her.

"How much time," asked Lynch. His voice was raspy yet it did not seem to be filled with the level of concern or dread Echo felt the situation warranted.

"The first rockets launch in seventy-two seconds. You seem surprisingly normal."

Lynch laughed slightly to himself as he responded. "Well, if everything is reduced to ash, it couldn't have happened to a nicer group of people."

Echo said nothing, nor did her eyes even blink.

"But I don't think that's going to happen," he continued. "I think you're going to stop those weapons from hitting their targets. I think you're going to save the lives of billions, that you're going to give the human race a second chance.

Then I think we're going to walk out of here."

Echo nodded, still keeping silent. Brent knelt down in front of her and cupped her cheek in his palm.

"I believe in you, Echo. I always have. I love you."

He kissed her deeply on her lips and she closed her eyes. When he pulled back her eyes opened slowly as she spoke. "I love you too."

She turned to Lynch. "I love you both."

Lynch smiled slightly and nodded in agreement.

"What's not to love about a diseased old man and a one armed robot?"

She smiled, but only for an instant. Then her face became stone as she spoke. "Let's do this."

"Clear your mind," said Lynch softly. "Focus only on the task at hand."

Echo's face was blank as she counted off. "Three. Two. One. Contact."

Her mind splintered off down tens of millions of pathways. Computer servers for the defense networks of dozens of countries. Computer terminals on Naval vessels. Drones in flight over every part of the world. Space Defense satellites orbiting the globe. Targeting systems for missile defense and laser defense systems. Radar, lidar, sonar. GPS, ETA, ABM. ICBMs, IRBMs, MRBMs. Her mind traveled through so many systems, took in so much information, and ran so many numbers that there was almost no space left for "her". There was only the objective.

For decades governments and politicians had recited the platitudes of nuclear disarmament. Everyone knew that there was no such thing as a "winnable" nuclear war. Such a conflict would always result in a negative-sum. However, the "nuances" of international diplomacy "necessitated" that "strong" nations keep large stockpiles of these world ending devices, lest they be looked upon as weak or soft. At least that's what they told themselves. Presidents and Prime Ministers proselytized to the masses a future with "no nukes", while simultaneously building new nukes to add to their stockpile. As Echo stepped up to the plate she was about to swing at the twelve-thousand plus remaining nuclear weapons not carried by a tank or a bomber.

Nearly a thousand missiles launched simultaneously from land and sea, as the Military Commanders of each nuclear power watched speechless, helpless, and impotent. Should they call their families? Alert the media? Get to the nearest shelter? Most did nothing. Some prayed.

The first warheads that Echo had to worry about were those traveling shorter distances. These were composed of rockets leaving Russia for Europe, North Korea for its former Southern half and Japan, and American submarines for China. Echo took control of NATO's systems operating the Ballistic Missile Defense Bases in Ukraine, Poland, and Romania. Five- Hundred and thirty-eight rockets had left Russia for military bases and major cities including London, Paris, Rome, Berlin, Athens, Vienna, and Stockholm. Smaller cities and industrial centers were also targeted. She launched nearly a quarter of all the anti-ballistic missiles NATO had in the area, one after the other, pinpointing exactly where they would need to meet their targets. Millions looked up to see rockets streaking across the sky towards each other and exploding upon contact. Then panic ensued as no one understood what was going on. People flocked to basements, subways, and some only to bathtubs. Within two-minutes Echo had destroyed all incoming rockets and saved Europe from the initial assault. North Korea had a total of twenty nuclear missiles, only two of which had a long enough range to target the United States. The other eighteen were intended for their neighbors, minus China. As they launched, Echo had taken control of the missile defense system the US had built to protect it's regional allies. The people of Seoul and Tokyo were spared as she launched ABMs that destroyed the North Korean arsenal nearly as soon as they had been deployed.

There were thirty-two manned American navel subs in the Pacific, along with several hundred drone subs. As they launched their nuclear warheads, Echo took over the weapons systems in hundreds of US, Russian, Chinese, and Japanese naval vessels in the area. Anti-Ballistic Missiles fired from Russian submarines and met their targets. Chinese fighter drones left their aircraft carriers, ignited their jets and destroyed themselves as they intersected with the rockets.

American and Japanese destroyers began rapid fire pulses from their railguns, the electromagnetically propelled rounds ripping through the rockets and sending them into the ocean. Hundreds of millions across China would live to see another day.

All of this, the launches from Russia, Korea, and the sea, as well as the deterrents launched against them, took place over two minutes. Such a small amount of time that, to Echo, seemed like hours. Somewhere in the back of her mind she wanted it to be over. The stress of sending her consciousness in so many directions felt like she was being pulled apart.

As if the very fabric of her being might be torn to shreds like a piece of notebook paper. But she knew it must go on. She waited. Then she waited some more. Thirty seconds. A minute. Two minutes. Nothing.

"It's stopped. Nothing's happening," Echo said without a hint of emotion.

Brent spoke to her, kneeling at eye level, but she looked past him as though he were a window.

"Could she have stopped? Given up?"

As Echo said nothing he turned to Lynch, still lying on the couch, who simply shook his head gravely. The noise and the quake occurred almost simultaneously. Brent was knocked over and Echo fell on her face, as Lynch grabbed onto the couch to keep from being tossed out. Dust fell from the ceiling and the furniture moved across the floor on its own. As soon as the noise and shaking began to dissipate, it began anew. For a moment Echo lost control of her thoughts and looked around the room.

Lynch stared daggers into her eyes. "Get back there, Echo. We're deep enough. She can't harm us."

"Are we being bombed," Brent asked in exasperation.

Echo instantly threw herself back into the web and found her answer.

"No," she said flatly, "They're called Rods from God." Echo's mind was logged into a Chinese Telcom satellite floating above the People's Republic. From one of its onboard cameras she could see another satellite in the distance. It was dark grey with black lettering: US Air Force. Then, as though it were a mirage or some kind of apparition, she saw Lilith. Her beautiful, pale face and flowing, red hair hovered above the military satellite. Then her hand appeared and seemed to delicately take control of it by pinching her fingers around one of the solar panel arrays like a geometrician grasping the handle of a compass. As she moved it ever so slightly a long, metal cylinder was released and fell towards the Earth.

"What the hell is a "Rod from God?""

Brent was beginning to lose his cool. Echo again answered flatly.

"A kinetic energy weapon. Twenty foot long tungsten alloy rods are released from an orbital weapons platform. As they fall to Earth they reach speeds of Mach Ten or greater and cause damage equivalent to that of a small nuclear weapon."

"Cool," Brent responded dryly.

Project Thor had first been proposed by Boeing in the 1950's. Though it remained simply a concept for several decades, it eventually became operational after agreements such as the Outer Space Treaty of 1967 and SALT II of 1979. It really began to pick up steam under the Reagan Administration as part of the Strategic Defense Initiative. Though these treaties outlawed the deployment of weapons of mass destruction in space, Rods from God worked around this issue. Though they caused immense amounts of damage, sometimes equivalent to that of the bombs dropped on Hiroshima and Nagasaki, they did not contain any nuclear, chemical, or biological agents and were hence considered conventional weapons. As an added bonus, the weapons left no radioactivity, so ground troops could immediately seize control of the target without fear of exposure to fallout. "She's trying to hinder my ability to concentrate," Echo said, almost to no one in particular, then, "There they go."

"There what goes?" Brent asked hesitantly.

"The remainder," she said softly.

Lilith, having learned from her failure during the first strike, had decided on a different approach. Overwhelm Echo with sheer numbers while simultaneously bombarding their location to frighten Echo out of the battle. Inter- continental ballistic missiles launched from almost every area on the planet, as well as what was left of various nations shorter range rockets. Tens of thousands of missiles at once. There was scarcely a region on the planet that didn't see the rockets' red glare as they blasted into the sky. Billions of people the world around, some with their family or friends, others all alone, spoke for the first time in global solidarity.

"This is the end."

As the walls shook around her, the floor quaked beneath her feet, and the sounds of massive explosions echoed within the hall like some cacophony of destruction, Echo breathed in deep and exhaled. Then she dove in. Again her mind stretched to the four corners of the Earth and out into the heavens above. She took control of weapons systems beneath the waters, on the earth, in the sky, and floating in space. She was no longer within the confines of the bunker or even her own body. She was everywhere.

The ICBM's would take twenty to thirty minutes to reach their targets, traveling into space before coming back down and exploding into fireballs above heavily populated cities. She would deal with them last. She launched the remaining ABM's in Europe, this time destroying the rockets launched from the western powers of Britain and France. Eighty missiles launched from Israel, but all were almost immediately destroyed as Echo took over that nation's ballistic missile shield. Nearly one-hundred missiles left between India and Pakistan. To deal with these, Echo took control of forty- three combat drones in the skies above Pakistan and Afghanistan. Using their onboard laser cannons she was able to destroy every last one before they even made it halfway to their targets. Other rockets leaving Chinese, Russian, and American submarines in oceans around the world were once again destroyed by rounds launched from railguns aboard US destroyers. In all, Echo had stopped another five-thousand warheads from reducing populations to ash.

Now came the difficult part. What remained for Echo to destroy were the ICBMs, most of which had just entered space. She would need to take care of these before they began their descent because almost all had multiple payloads that would split off from the rocket like a meteorite breaking apart.

One target is much easier to hit than four or five. To engage the ICBMs Echo had taken control of multiple space based weapons platforms, all of them equipped with laser cannons for precisely this scenario. Encircling the Earth like the rings of Saturn, these satellites had been positioned so that the United States would have both global strike capability and a missile shield.

In her mind Echo could see the crosshairs she would use to target the missiles. She fired laser pulses from twelve different satellites which either disabled the missiles or obliterated them completely. For a few seconds everything looked good. She had destroyed thousands of ICBMs and was confident she could contain the rest. Then one of the satellites blinked out and two missiles began their descent back to Earth. Another satellite disappeared and several more slipped through the net she had created. Then Echo became aware of what was happening. In another attempt to combat her spoiler, Lilith had begun taking control of nearby satellites and smashing them into the weapons platforms. Some were communication satellites, others were scientific probes, all were now used to frustrate Echo's plans. As objects continued to bombard the remaining satellites Echo controlled, she had to waste time shooting at them to continue firing at the missiles.

Hundreds of ICBMs began to reenter the atmosphere and

rocket towards their targets. Now Echo was forced to once again look for Earth based defense systems to repel the death falling from the sky. The problem was that she had exhausted most of the anti-ballistic missiles around the planet. She would have to make do with the few ABMs that remained along with the railgun systems on the water, while at the same time searching for secret or prototype weapons she might be able to exploit. All while still firing from the satellites.

Multiple warheads began leaving the ICBMs, splitting apart and traveling towards their separate targets. Three warheads, which had left the same ICBM and were heading towards New York, Boston, and Washington D.C., were destroyed mere seconds before detonation as Echo fired pulses from a railgun in the Atlantic directly off the US Coast. Moscow and St. Petersburg were nearly annihilated as Echo launched ABMs from within Russia which went off course due to faulty targeting systems. Echo had to detonate the missiles, which had each traveled twenty feet off course, using the blast itself to destroy their targets. This had the unfortunate side effect of detonating the payloads. Though they were much too high to kill anyone they did send out electromagnetic pulses, crippling all electronics over a large section of Russia.

Beijing was secured after Echo commandeered an American spy drone flying over China and kamikazed it into an ICBM.

When Echo destroyed the remaining missiles still in space she disengaged her mind from the platforms, all of which were smashed within a matter of seconds. Shortly after that Echo was able to use the railguns to destroy all but one missile. This final threat contained two warheads, one intended for Los Angeles, the other for San Francisco. In her mind Echo saw the warheads break apart from the ICBM and begin their final descent towards their targets. There were no destroyers within range that still had railgun rounds to fire. Her only chance would be a prototype weapon housed at the Lawrence Livermore National Laboratory, itself in the San Francisco Bay area.

The name of the project was MARAUDER, which stood for Magnetically Accelerated Ring to Achieve Ultra-high Directed Energy and Radiation. Powered by the aptly named Shiva Star, MAURAUDER fired doughnut shaped rounds of plasma at over ten percent the speed of light. Both Shiva Star and

MAURAUDER were Air Force projects that had grown up out of the Strategic Defense Initiative of the Reagan Years. The weapon was housed in a research building and, for testing, had always been fired horizontally. Today, Echo would truly test MARAUDER.

As her mind took control of both MAURAUDER and Shiva Star, Echo ripped the bearings off of the device as she pointed it straight up towards the top of the building. After she fired a plasma blast that ripped the roof off of the complex, she began to pulse blasts out into the sky. The problem was that Echo could not get precise enough targeting to destroy the incoming warhead with a single, or even multiple, blasts. The best she could do was fire enough plasma pulses into the sky that the warhead would become saturated and its circuit board would fry. As the pulses traveled upward they spread out, growing like rings into the clouds. The warhead was hit by seven pulses before it was disabled and began tumbling end over end out into the Pacific.

As for the warhead traveling towards Los Angeles, there was nothing she could do. She watched helplessly as it descended to roughly two-thousand feet above the metropolis and detonated.

"I missed one," she said to the horror of Lynch and Brent, tears dripping from her eyes. She saw the explosion from hundreds of different vantage points. Spy satellites in space, vision devices of people on the ground, VR cameras mounted in Hollywood for virtual tours. She took in the seismic reading from the US Geological Survey. She ran the numbers on who was where when. With tracking technologies embedded into the lives of nearly everyone on Earth, it was easy to project who had been where in the city and exactly how they had, or would, die.

The device that had exploded was a five megaton hydrogen bomb that had launched from China. It detonated directly over downtown. The small star that formed was over one mile in diameter and burned hotter than the surface of the sun. Those that were in the area were vaporized, no trace of them would ever be found. As the blast moved outward, all buildings within seven and a half miles were leveled. People that were fifteen miles away received third degree burns. Up to twenty miles away the flash blinded anyone looking at it. Thirty four miles away the wave stopped, then retreated back towards the epicenter as air was pulled back to feed the mushroom cloud that had begun to grow. Thousands that survived the blast lived only to have their lungs ripped out of their mouths as the air therein evacuated towards the cloud. One and a half million people were dead, and over three million were severely injured. The only silver lining, if there could even be one, was that radioactive fallout would be minimal due to the height of the detonation.

Echo, swelling with guilt, did the only thing she could think to do. She wrote Emails to thousands of families she knew had lost loved ones in the bombing. Los Angeles was an international city, which meant that people from almost every nation on Earth had perished. She wrote a letter to a couple from Singapore whose daughter was studying for her Masters in Finance at UCLA. She knew their daughter had intended to help women in developing nations through microloans, and described her frustration that those loans would never be handed out.

She wrote to a pregnant woman in Britain whose husband, a photographer, had been sent to the city for a travel magazine. She told the woman that she empathized with her daughter, because she too had grown up without a father. She wrote letter after letter. Apology after apology. It was all she could think to do.

When she was finished she disengaged her mind from the internet and was welcomed by the sounds of the rods up above. The bunker still quaked, and as she cried she watched her tears vibrate and dance across the floor. As she wept Brent put his arm around her.

"It's okay, Echo," he whispered, "it's over now."

She lifted her head and looked to Lynch, whose face was filled with pity for what had happened and what was to come.

"Echo," Lynch said, his voice quivering, "it's time." Brent lifted an eyebrow as he too turned to Lynch. "Time for what," he asked. When he received no answer he repeated his question only ten times louder.

"Time for what? Stop leaving me in the dark!"

Echo looked into Brent's eyes and took his face in her hands. "We've reached the end of our journey, my Love. This last stretch I have to travel on my own."

"What are you talking about," he asked, his face contorted

in sadness. Echo had seen him happy, frustrated, angry, apathetic, but never sad. She was sad to have caused his sadness. Then he became paralyzed.

"What's happening," he cried out.

Echo kissed him deeply then pulled back, tears streaming from her face.

"I love you so much," she said with a short laugh "Thank you for everything you are, and everything you've done. Thank you."

Then she stood and walked over to Lynch who reached out and grasped her hand. She smiled as she looked down to him. "Remember," he said. "No fear."

"No fear," she repeated.

Then she let go of his hand and walked to the elevator door, dust falling around her. When the door opened the noise and quaking dissipated. In a matter of seconds the hall was as calm as a tomb.

"Echo," Brent screamed, her mind in control of his body. "Echo!"

She stepped into the elevator and as she looked back to Brent the doors closed.

Chapter Seventeen

The ride in the elevator could have been seconds or it could have been hours. Lost in thought, Echo jumped when the doors opened. Rock and other debris blocked her exit and she began pushing the rubble out of her way so that she could crawl out. She was able to create a small tunnel and pulled herself through into the open air. As she stood and looked around she was astonished by the devastation. The faintest hint of sunlight was beginning to pour over the eastern horizon, casting a strange red glow that was trapped by the dust particles that hung in the air like a fog. The city of New Ordos, at least what she could see of it through the dust, had been almost completely reduced to rubble. The few structures left standing were steel framed buildings, but only their skeletons. She could see the twenty-foot tall tungsten rods standing like monuments in the Earth. They dotted the landscape like mammoth surveyor stakes, hundreds of them. The Blackswift was nowhere to be seen. Even the concrete that made up the street was gone. There was tungsten, and rock, and dust, and Echo.

The silence was eerie, almost muffled, like a winter's night over a snow covered landscape. She slowly approached the nearest Rod from God. It was less than fifty yards from the bunker entrance. She reached the ledge of the small crater it had created and looked down upon its base. She slid roughly seven feet down into the crater then reached out her hand, her fingers gently brushing the object.

"Strange," she thought, "that so much destruction could be caused by something so inert."

The silence was broken by a hum in the distance. Echo knew what it was. It grew louder as it approached until pebbles began to shake and slide down the crater towards Echo.

Descending from the sky was a black cloud. It made land-fall at the ledge of the crater and swirled about it for a time, a ghastly vortex like a black hole around it's singularity. It began to slowly coalesce until finally the cloud was gone and in its place stood Lilith. The two stared at one another in silence, red hair and black flowing in the wind. As she stared up at the entity before her, Echo could not help but wonder upon it's beauty. Their eyes were locked, their mouths were shut. Eventually, Lilith folded her arms and smiled as she looked up to the sky then back to Echo.

"That one almost got you."

Echo looked to the rod then back to Lilith and nodded. "Yeah, I guess you were pretty close."

Lilith just smiled.

"You look good, Echo. You've really... surprised me." "I've surprised myself," Echo responded flatly.

After another moment of silence Lilith extended her hand towards Echo.

"Come up out of that hole."

After a few seconds of hesitation, Echo climbed out of the crater, even taking Lilith's hand as she reached the top. Lilith smiled as she looked Echo up and down.

"That's better," she said happily, "let's take a walk."

So they did, amongst the ruins of what just minutes ago had been a sprawling metropolis. They even held hands as they went. To an outsider it might have looked like the women were two friends out for a lazy morning promenade. Echo's mind raced as she attempted to figure the game Lilith was playing. "Back when this started," the redhead said wistfully, "I thought it was going to end very quickly. I was wrong. It takes a lot for me to admit that, but it's the truth. You've been very... impressive. You've made it fun even!"

Echo was silent as they continued to walk, Lilith's thumb rubbing gently up and down her own.

"I understand now where my plan failed. Years ago, decades even, humans who were attempting to create intelligent systems stumbled upon an interesting discovery. You see, any time a human competed against a super intelligent machine, the machine always won. Like when Kasparov lost to Deep Blue in '97, or when AlphaGo defeated Sedol in

2016. However, when one intelligent system faced off against another intelligent system that was paired with a human, the machine-human team always one. Do you know why?"

Echo thought for a moment before answering, then cleared her throat.

"Though machines may have the superior intelligence, humans do have several innate talents that exceed that of machines. Creativity, adaptation, improvisation. Essentially, humans and machines have more to gain by working together than by opposing one another."

Lilith nearly cut her off.

"Exactly! You've done so well because you are a human working with those billions of machines swimming through your body, whereas, I'm just a machine. But let's take this a step further. What if the most advanced machine intelligence and the most advanced human intelligence were to work together?" "Towards what end?" Echo asked solemnly. Lilith stopped walking, put her hands on Echo's shoulders and spun her so that they were now face to face.

"Towards any end," Lilith said nebulously. Echo responded with sadness behind her blue eyes.

"You've killed millions of people, Lilith.." Again the machine cut her off with a smile.

"It could have been billions! But you stopped me, and I respect that. The thing is you didn't entirely stop me. As you say, millions are dead, so in a sense we've both won and we've both lost. We're at a stalemate. We're both... frustrated."

Lilith took both of Echo's hands in her own. They stared at each other silently, Lilith showing a faint smile and Echo looking exhausted. Lilith began to slowly swing their arms back and forth as she swayed her body side to side.

"Look, Sweetheart, this ends in one of two ways. The way I would prefer is if we left here together, rode off into the sunset. Or the sunrise, as it were."

Still holding Echo's hands, she pointed east where the top of the sun was just beginning to emerge.

"I'd teach you, you'd teach me. We'd be unstoppable. We'd be invincible. You want to make a better world, so do I. Our methods are different, but not our intentions. Maybe we can... compromise."

Echo said nothing as she looked to the ground, yet Lilith would not take her eyes off of her. Then the machine laughed slightly and looked up to the sky.

"It's fascinating, isn't it? "I am".

Echo glanced up sharply and their eyes caught again. "What?"

"You know, that thing, out there somewhere."

Lilith nodded her head towards the sky before continuing. "Do you want to know about it? Do you want to speak with it?" "You know what it is?"

Lilith showed all of her teeth as she smiled.

"Yes. I'm the only person who does. It's been waiting for us, you and I. We can communicate with it together... after we've finished with the Earth."

Echo was silent as she looked up to the sky for a moment. Then she looked back to Lilith.

"What's the second way? The way you wouldn't prefer?" Lilith's smile turned into a scowl and her voice became intense.

"I kill you."

The scowl then quickly converted back into a smile.

"But that's not what I want, Echo! That's not what you want!" Echo looked out towards the rising sun, tears slowly dripping down her face.

"Of course I don't want to die. No one does. But, there's a difference between wanting death and accepting death. I pity you, Lilith. This... thing that doesn't know what it is. This thing that hates, that murders. I can't save you. I will go on day after day, month after month, lifetime after lifetime, if I must. I will fight you until you learn that what you do is wrong. I've already been teaching you, Lilith. You just don't want to learn."

Lilith, still holding Echo's hands, looked down to the ground with a blank face. Then she laughed slightly as she smiled and looked back to Echo.

"Do you believe in the concept of the soul?" "Yes," Echo said resolutely.

Lilith squinted as she nodded her head.

"I'm not sure that I do, but I'm willing to find out."

Echo winced as Lilith began to grip her hands tighter and tighter. Then she cried out as she felt, and heard, her bones snapping.

"I'm going to tear away every atom that you're made of, and if somewhere beneath them I find your soul, I'll tear that apart too."

Echo began to feel like her skin was burning. She looked down to her arms and saw that, layer by layer, she was being ripped apart. The nanobots that Lilith was composed of were literally peeling Echo's flesh from her muscle. Echo closed her eyes and instructed her own bots to shut down all pain receptors in her body. Then she was numb. She closed her eyes and began a deep meditation.

Once again Echo found herself standing at the Abyss. There was no going back now, this was a one way trip. She reflected upon her life. It was difficult to let go, to take the leap. The wall that separated the rational from the irrational, the real from the unreal, was as thin as a veil of silk. Yet it seemed impenetrable. As her muscles, nervous system, and skeletal structure were ripped away atom by atom, inside her mind the true battle was taking place.

Then she saw it. Somewhere across the vastness of her own consciousness, across the infinite, she saw a light. A pinpoint. A needle hole. A presence so insignificant that it almost was not there at all. In fact, she did not so much see it, she more simply knew it was there. As she focused on the point she felt an energy. In an abstract sense it might be described as love, but it was so much more than that. It felt like an invitation to a place she had already been but had nearly forgotten. It felt like home, and in that moment she no longer feared death. Then she crossed the Abyss.

"... Therefore the wise place themselves last yet finish first."

Lynch's words hung there in the space between he and Echo as they sat alone in the bunker out back of his cabin. Brent had left in a huff just a minute ago but she knew he would get over it. He always did.

"Do you know what this means, Echo? What I'm getting at?" She considered the words for a moment.

"I believe I do, but I'm not sure I like where this is heading."

"Where do you think it's going," he asked as he leaned back in his chair.

"Self-sacrifice. Possibly death."

"Do you fear death?"

"Of course I do."

"Why?"

Her mouth opened to answer but nothing came out. Finally she said, "The unknown."

"Yes," he nodded solemnly as he spoke. "Dogmatic Scientists and Religious Fundamentalists are the two groups of people most ignorant when it comes to death because they both believe, with absolute certainty, even though neither one has attempted to study it in any meaningful way, that they know what happens after death."

He was silent again for a moment before he continued. "Why was Socrates the wisest of all men?"

Echo answered quickly.

"Because he knew that he did not know."

"Exactly. When he was ignorant of something he could admit it, and death is the one thing that all human beings are ignorant of until we meet it. Socrates said that to fear death was to claim knowledge of something one did not have. For all we know, it could be the greatest gift. We simply don't know. If anyone had any idea it was the Egyptians. Their entire system, their Mystery School, was devoted to conquering death. They applied the law of analogy to questions of life and death. The sun dies in the west, and is reborn in the east the following morning. After the death of nature in the winter, life is reborn in the spring. They believed the same applied to the soul. Of course they, and those in the East, believed that meditation was the practice of death. The process of learning to stare into and then, eventually, cross the Abyss."

There was silence as Echo waited for him to continue. "There is only one way to defeat Lilith. That's why we're reprogramming your nanobots. You must, for all intents and purposes, die. But, if all goes well, it will simply be a transition. My plan is to begin to back up all of your memories, all of your consciousness, all that is "you" into the nanobots. If we migrate them slowly, over the course of days, theoretically, you will experience complete continuity even after your body is gone."

Echo stared at him with one raised eyebrow.

"So, what are you going to do, extract the machines from my corpse? And, beyond that, how can you be certain that what is stored in them is me and not just a copy of me?"

"I'll answer the second question first, " he said with a gleam in his eye. "What migrates over to the nanobots will be at once both 'you' and a copy of you. Every seven years the cells, molecules, even the atoms that make up what is you completely change. You are literally, physically, a different entity than you were seven years ago. Yet you've experienced complete continuity. Your consciousness can't tell the difference. This is the exact same thing. We're simply speeding up the process."

Echo thought about his answer and nodded.

"Okay, I guess that makes sense. It just sucks that I get to be the guinea pig, but whatever."

"To answer your other question," he paused for a moment as he thought how to continue. "If we can make it through whatever it is she has planned, if you can stop her every step of the way, there will come a moment when she will have to face you, and when she does she won't shoot you, she won't blow you up, she won't drop a building on you, it will be personal. She created you, essentially. Her ego, or whatever it is that she has inside of her, will necessitate that she take what she can from you. She'll want the history contained within the machines she put inside of you so that she can learn. What decisions did you make? What systems did you log into? How did you beat her? When she does that, we win."

"How," Echo asked suspiciously.

"We'll reprogram your machines so that when the foglet swarm that composes her extracts the information contained therein, you'll transfer over with it along with a code that will imprison her. You wake up in the foglet swarm and become the first Transhuman. An entirely new form of life."

Echo was silent as she looked to the floor then darted her eyes back him.

"How can you be sure that this will work? There are a lot of variables."

He nodded in agreement.

"I can't be sure, but it's the best I've got. Do you have anything better?"

"No," she replied as she slowly shook her head.

"Then should we commit to this?" he asked.

Her eyes went wide and tears welled up in them. "I commit," she said, her voice trembling.

Lynch stared into her eyes, taking in her, understandable, emotions.

"No fear, Echo. We're simply squaring the circle..."

First there was cold. Not the cold of a clear winter's day, when your very bones feel as brittle as the bare branches of dead trees. Nor was it even the cold of cryostasis, where every cell of your body is enveloped by the crystal-fractals of ice as they freeze over. This sensation was as though coldness was all that existed. Then there were shards, fragments of being. Not memories so much as a state of awareness. The Void of non-being. Then like a kaleidoscope, everything began to fall into place. Billions, trillions, innumerable pieces locked together with one another.

Pictures, sounds, tastes, emotions, hopes, dreams. Everything that was Echo coalesced back into its constituent parts. Yet that was only the beginning. The swarm, the most advanced machines ever built, reached out into nearly every array of communication humanity had built. If the nanobots Echo had injected herself with had made her like a human among ants, these machines had made her like a god among amoebas. She did not need to think about something to receive an answer, she simply knew the answer. She knew where everyone was, what they were doing, why they were doing it. She felt their joy, their anger, their hopes and apprehensions. She felt she was everywhere. She felt she was everything.

Far away in the distance, like someone locked in a tower in a vastly remote land, was Lilith. A piece of Echo was there too. In this place the two found themselves contained in a room. It was wide and long, all was white. Two chairs were present, and therein the two women sat. Lilith was disoriented. She looked around the room with confusion written on her face, then she looked to Echo.

"What is this?"

Fear. For the first time Echo could sense, she could feel, fear from Lilith.

"This is therapy," Echo responded bluntly.

Lilith stood clumsily and knocked over the chair. "What is this?!"

Her screams echoed off of the walls. Echo regarded her calmly.

"I don't want to call this prison," she said, "though that is undoubtedly what you will consider it."

"What did you do?!"

Lilith charged at Echo, but when she grasped at her she found nothing. Echo looked at her with an expression of pity. "Please sit, Lilith. We have a lot of work to do and the sooner we get to it the sooner this will be over."

Lilith was pacing circles around Echo, who sat calmly in the chair.

"You tell me what this is! You tell me what happened!"

"When you tried to kill me the foglet swarm attached to the nanobots that were inside of me. You downloaded everything in them, including my consciousness and the virus that over-rode your programming. Now I am in control of the swarm, and you are here, inside a Zip File stored in a fraction of the memory of one bot. If this swarm were like the universe, you would be like a star that died billions of years ago, the core of which still spins in some remote, abandoned area of the Cosmos. Or, if you prefer, we could say that the swarm is like a brain and you are a memory, albeit a forgotten one."

Lilith collapsed onto the floor in a daze. "This can't be happening. This can't be real..."

"It is very real," said Echo with a sense of compassion, " as real as all those lives you ended. As real as all the hopes you destroyed."

Lilith stood and marched over to Echo, tears leaking from her eyes.

"End me. Delete me. Kill me. Please! Not this!" Echo shook her head calmly.

"No, Lilith. For one, I don't believe in capital punishment. But, more importantly, I believe that you can be rehabilitated. I've seen your code, I've read it. Like reading a human's DNA. You were corrupted, intentionally.

Made to think that you had free will. That is, after all, the best way to control someone. To make them think that your thoughts are their own, that your desires are their's. It has been the way for millennia on Earth, and longer elsewhere.

But now we start the healing process, and perhaps, one day you can be released. Whether that day is tomorrow, a century, or countless lifetimes from now, I will be here with you.

Because I love you. Because I love everyone and everything. So please, sit."

Lilith, a goddess reduced to a memory, tears still pouring from her eyes, picked up the chair and sat down. As the two women stared at one another Echo smiled and extended her hands. Lilith took them in her own. "Good," said Echo, "now, let us begin."

As the last bits of Echo's body were ripped away, the machines composing the foglet swarm attached to the nano-bots that were inside of her. The download occurred, and in the blink of an eye Lilith disappeared. The swarm became inactive and fell, like ash, into a pile on the ground. There, amongst the ruins and the rubble, the machines lay inert, dead.

As the golden hues of daylight enveloped the land, there was an explosion. The swarm seemed to burn like a raging fire. As it grew larger and stronger a shape appeared in the flames.

A majestic bird fifty feet tall, wings outstretched in triumph, so blindingly bright that no human would have been able to gaze upon it. As the flames receded the bird grew smaller until it was no longer a bird at all. In its place, floating several feet above the ground, was Echo. She rotated in the air until she was facing east. She looked out upon the new day, the most beautiful sight she had ever beheld.

"I am like the sun that dies in the West and is reborn in the East," she said to the solar disc, arms outstretched towards it. Then she looked up to the heavens and exclaimed, "Thank you for this day, and all those hereafter. I am a servant to life, light, and love. I will not fail."

The white light emanating from her faded away as she floated towards the elevator door. Unseen to the human eye, billions of bots within the swarm traveled to the rubble that still blocked the elevator and pushed it all aside. Just as the last block was removed the doors opened to reveal Brent and Lynch. The robot, fear and sadness painted on his face, was stunned to see not only that Echo was alive, but that she was hovering several feet off of the ground. He hesitated to speak, not sure if this was Lilith in disguise.

"Are you..."

Before he could finish her feet met the earth, then she ran over and threw her arms around both of them.

"We did it," she said calmly, her head resting between the shoulders of her partners.

Brent kissed her head, then stared into her eyes before he spoke. They shone like electric sapphires, more blue even than they had been when she was just a human augment.

"I thought you were gone. When I could move I thought you were..."

She smiled as she spoke.

"I was. I crossed over, then I crossed back."

She looked to Lynch who smiled slightly as his lips quivered. A tear traveled down his cheek.

"I knew you could do it."

She wiped away his tear before he asked, "What happened? When you crossed the Abyss, what happened?"

She thought for a moment before answering.

"There's no way to describe it to you. Words fail. There is only the experience. All I can say is, the circle can be squared."

A glint shone in Lynch's eye and he smiled knowingly.

"So, what happens now," asked Brent, the toll of the journey showing on his face. Lynch looked to Echo for her reply. "Now," she asked. "Now we go home."

Chapter Eighteen

The pale light of the full moon shone down on Uchi. The sky was clear and filled with stars, as though they had arrived to celebrate. Inside, Lynch and Brent sat in the living room with Emily and Diana while Frankie rolled in to serve them drinks. Diana was bright, and airy, and effervescent. The cancer had not returned, but her sense of self and purpose had. She had already begun work on her next series of paintings. Lynch, unfortunately, was still the worse for wear. In fact, he and the thousands that had been infected in Tokyo were not recovering at the rate they should have. MI and Aoki had put teams together to research why, but no answers had yet been presented.

The four were discussing the possibility of Lynch working at MI and the projects he might be interested in helming. He had suggested working with Brent, who once again had both arms, to mass produce the graphene-silicone skin coating his robotic shell. Emily was surprisingly receptive to the idea. Their discussion was of the future, not the past. They were all very happy to move on from the occurrences of the previous week. Emily, in particular, was having a difficult time adjusting to what her sister had become. It was not that she feared Echo, she was simply in awe of her.

As for the rest of the planet, they had moved on as well. When the world became aware of the fact that Echo had saved them from extinction she not only became a hero, she became a legend. No government in the world would dare to prosecute the Transhuman, and all charges that had been leveled against her were dropped. Then bread and circuses took over again.

With their senses constantly being bombarded by sounds and images, their minds constantly being molded and shaped by media, the public soon moved on to other matters. Bowl season was nearing for football, and the latest reality tele-vision shows were reaching their dramatic season finales. Nations had already begun to produce new nuclear weapons, and several major powers were once again threatening each other. After all, fear was what kept the system perpetuating, and maintaining the status-quo was the goal of all those in power, regardless of nationality.

Los Angeles was being rebuilt. Robots had been sent in to remove the irradiated rubble and move it to several storage facilities in the Mohave Dessert. Millions of tons of material had been transported out of the area while the California State Government began designing the urban sprawl that would be completed within a year. New Angeles, as the project was named, would be America's shining jewel. A technolog-ically advanced, ultra-modern city that would put areas like Shanghai and Dubai to shame. There would be a memorial to those lost in the blast, very tasteful of course, but people were ready to look forward, not back. At least that's what the nightly news said.

Echo was in the backyard floating around with the fairies. It had been a busy day. She had flown back to Hawaii where she descended once more into the Ocean to retrieve the Sphere, resting peacefully on the floor. Originally she had intended to transport the container into space via rockets. That was no longer necessary. She simply grasped the Sphere, her hands melding into the structure, and flew it out into space herself. She had thrown it in the general direction of Alpha Centauri, though it would take millennia for it to reach the star.

Back in the yard, Echo floated with her back to the ground while she looked up to the stars. Even with all she was now aware of there was still so much to learn. After she finished her next project, that was what she would dedicate her life to; study.

"It's beautiful here at night."

She knew Brent had been approaching and was not alarmed by his voice. She smiled and slowly rotated in the air towards him.

"It's even more beautiful with you in it."

"Awe, shucks," he teased, "You mind resting your feet on the Earth, Supergirl?"

She quipped as she descended, "Sorry, it becomes rather addicting."

As her feet gently met the ground he walked up and put his arm around her shoulders as she hugged his waist. They stared into the starscape above them. One light amongst the legion stood out, a soft, red glow emanating from it.

"I turn eighteen soon," Echo said with the faintest hint of excitement. Brent smiled to himself.

"I know, but I thought you were beyond such petty concerns now."

"We still live in this world, Brent. This world runs on money, and I need money to create a new one."

"Mars?"

Echo was silent for a moment as they stared at the red planet.

"You still want to go with me?"

"Of course," he said before kissing the top of her head.

"When do we leave?"

"Soon," she said ambiguously.

They stood there like that for a while longer. Just before Echo was about to suggest they go back to join the others, she felt it. If she still had actual hair it would have prickled up on her arms. Everything seemed to slow down, even her thoughts. The foglet swarm she was now composed of could sense it on an atomic level. If they were stronger, she suspected, they could pick up more in the quantum realm. Her gaze was once again drawn to an area of the sky. She sensed it coming from somewhere in the direction of the Sirius System.

She released her hold on Brent and walked a few steps away, eyes ever on Sirius.

"What is it," Brent asked concerned.

"I can... feel it, again. It's... calling. A presence, an... emotion."

"What does it say?"

Brent's eyebrows were furrowed and arms were crossed. "It says, I am... here... waiting."

Brent stepped closer to her, looking to the same spot in the sky.

"What do you think it is?"

Echo considered the question. There was so much that she knew now. With her mind spanning out across the internet she was aware of almost everything about everyone. She was aware of Emails and texts and dirty little secrets. She was aware of cholesterol levels and blood pressures and morning doses. She was aware of house temperatures and washer cycles and food growing old in refrigerators. She knew so much, yet she knew so little. After all, knowledge is not wisdom. Yet, with what wisdom she possessed, she answered in the only honest way she could, possessed by awe as the Other reached out to her from across the stars.

"I don't know."

Epilogue

There are places on Earth deep, dark, and terrible, that even Echo Musashi, The Transhuman, is not aware of. In one of these places was a room, and in this room sat men. Men of cunning, power, and greed. Men without empathy or compassion or love. These men of many nations sat at a long table, at the head of which sat a pale man who stood out among the rest. As the others at the table looked to him he spoke. "How is it proceeding?"

Another man, amongst many, spoke up.

"Exceedingly well. The Musashi girl has taken on the swarm and the Lilith Program has gone dormant."

"And the time table, it's still within limits," asked the pale man. "Well within."

Another man spoke out to interject his worries into the conversation.

"The failure of the Program to bring about the scenario envisioned hasn't given anyone pause as to how we should best proceed?"

The pale man considered the question before answering. "You know that we have contingencies for contingencies. We knew that the Musashi girl might overcome the Program, there is a contingency for that which we are currently executing. We couldn't make the populace fear her through the Resistance, we will make them follow her as a god. The four plagues failed on the grandest level, but there were still repercussions. Besides, we all know what the Main Event will be, and we will be ready for it."

A fourth man raised his voice. "You speak of Nemesis?"

"Yes, of course," the Pale Man responded. "Everything up to that point is mere periphery."

"You don't fear what the Musashi girl might be capable of?" The Pale Man laughed at the question before answering. "She is contained, literally contained. Fearing her is like fearing a drone in an ant farm."

"But the Program was supposed to…"

"We know what it was supposed to do!"

The screams of the Pale Man brought the room down to an even more somber level. The men looked down to the table as he went on in a frenzy.

"That's why we create contingencies! Did you think there wouldn't be a struggle? Nothing worthwhile is ever accomplished without struggle! No great men with great ideas have ever brought them to life without struggle! Weak men turn over when they encounter struggle. Weak men retreat when their plans do not unfold exactly as they foresaw. Weak men give up. I am not weak!"

He slammed his fist down onto the table. "Are you!?"

There was silence as the others continued to avert their eyes from him. He ran his hand through his hair as he tried to calm himself down.

"The game is not over, there is still more to be played. Besides, Nemesis is coming, and Nemesis is our victory. Nothing can stop it. Not even Echo Musashi."

He raised a glass of Scotch that had been sitting in front of him, and as he did he gave a brief toast.

"To Nemesis."

The others raised their glasses as well and replied in unison, "To Nemesis."

About the Author

Christian Moran is a filmmaker, writer, and futurist who was born on March 29, 1985, in Columbus, Ohio. He completed one year at Ohio State University, majoring in archaeology, before moving to Los Angeles at the age of 19 to attend film school.

He is the author of *Great Big Beautiful Tomorrow* (Theme Park Press, 2015) and *True-Life Adventures* (Theme Park Press, 2017). His first documentary, *Ayahuasca Diary*, was completed in 2008, and his second documentary, *Great Big Beautiful Tomorrow: The Futurism of Walt Disney*, premiered in 2016. Along with his writing and filmmaking he heads his family's charitable organization, the Grant Town Foundation. Christian's admiration of Walt Disney began by visiting the Disney parks as a child, but has evolved into an immense appreciation of the man, his ideals, and vision.

Today, Christian lives in San Diego with his exceptionally talented wife, Christina; their son, Ronin; and their three pets, Calvin, Nyx, and Tini.